Mercy
First And Last

A NOVEL

Katie Hanrahan

Newcastlewest Books

Newcastlewest Books

Copyright © 2016 by Katie Hanrahan

First Edition: September 2016

ISBN: 978-0-9967131-2-2

The characters and events in this book, though based on historical fact, are fictitious. Any similarity to real persons, living or dead, is coincidental and not intended by the author.

www. newcastlewestbooks.com

Mercy

First And Last

SHE is far from the land where her young hero sleeps,
And lovers around her are sighing;
But coldly she turns from their gaze and weeps,
For her heart in his grave is lying!

She sings the wild song of her dear native plains,
Every note which he loved awaking
Ah! little they think, who delight in her strains,
How the heart of the minstrel is breaking!

He had lived for his love, for his country he died,
They were all that to life had entwined him,
Nor soon shall the tears of his country be dried,
Nor long will his love stay behind him.

Oh! make her a grave where the sunbeams rest,
When they promise a glorious to-morrow;
They'll shine o'er her sleep like a smile from the West
From her own loved Island of Sorrow.

She Is Far From The Land
- Thomas Moore

ONE

We fought with unbridled ferocity, granting no quarter, as only sisters can. For the slightest acknowledgement from our father we launched attack after attack, yet Gertrude held the field with an ease that further infuriated me. She mocked my efforts to improve my mind as a way to gain Father's attention, snatching *Paradise Lost* from my hands when I wanted to pass the afternoon in reading instead of following her orders. I would have landed a harder blow if I had thrown the book at her head instead of using the knowledge inside as a weapon. I would not have lost the war so thoroughly.

Down the stairs she flew with the leather-bound treasure that I intended to memorize so that I could be part of the intellectual circle that flocked to The Priory, our home on the Rathfarnham Road. I lobbed verbal missiles at her back, irking her to no end and pushing her to run that much faster. "In mercy and justice both," I said, "through Heaven and Earth, so shall my glory excel."

"One day I shall be married and you will remain here, a spinster, your mind ruined by education," Gertrude said, She flew out of the door into the back garden where dead leaves skittered across the gravel path.

"But mercy first and last shall brightest shine," I continued.

"And Father shall have to maintain you," she said.

"After he has married you off to a tinker because no other would have such a sour old witch," I said.

"Even the tinkers would not take you."

Her comment stung all the more because I valued her opinion. We were inseparable, Gertrude and I, and the thought of being torn apart by husbands was impossible to imagine. No matter how angry I was with her, however, the fact remained that she had stolen an expensive book that had to be shelved in the library before Mr. Curran returned and discovered that it had been taken without his express permission. As if to reinforce the danger I faced, Gertrude held the book aloft as she circled around the rose bed and charged through the garden gate to the carriage walk.

"Richard's friends are drinking tea with us on Sunday," she said as she raced around the house. Our older brother was a student at Trinity College and often brought friends to our home, to listen to one of Mr. Curran's discourses on the state of Ireland. We thought some of the gentlemen were rather handsome. "Do not expect them to take any notice of your sour face. Stick your nose in a book, little bookworm. You would not be missed."

She slowed just enough to let me get close, a trick that gave me false hope of catching her before she sped up and dashed through the front door. Up the stairs I flew, hot on her heels, but not quick enough to reach her before she had thrown open the bedroom window and dangled Milton over the sill. I leapt for it but she pulled it back. "They will not pay you any heed, either," I said. "Father tells everyone that he has no money and we bring nothing to a marriage. You less so than the rest of us."

Eighteen months older, and with an advantage of height, she held me at arm's length while waving the book around like a battle flag, taunting me with renewed threats to let the tome fall to the ground. "Admit defeat. Abandon this foolish quest and come for a walk with me," Gertrude said.

We faced off across the bed, Gertrude feinting a move to the right that put some distance between us when I fell for her ruse. I used the bedpost to propel my turn around the footboard, but she had the advantage of me yet again. She jumped across the mattress, only to tangle her feet in the coverlet. The book fell to the floor with a thud.

Screaming filled my ears, so many voices screaming that I was not sure if one of them was mine. Gertrude's black shoe sat under the window in a puddle of white linen, a still life from a nightmare. How long did I stand in place, unable to move, staring at her shoe? I looked around to find her, telling myself that she had thrown it at me, but at the same time I knew she had not. How did I make my way downstairs? The memory was never formed, the shock too great. Mercy, first and last. If only our father had read *Paradise Lost* and absorbed its philosophy.

I was told that one of the tenants carried Gertrude into the house and placed her on the dining table, a scene I was said to have witnessed in a state of absolute hysteria. A great wailing erupted as soon as Dr. Emmet declared my sister dead, a cacophony of tears and prayers offered up by the women who filled the room. The maids keened in a way that terrified me, a sound from the depths of hell. By the time Mr. Curran arrived from Dublin, I had been drugged into a numb haze, kept from Gertrude's side by our sister Amelia. It must have been her, rather than our mother, who slapped me when I kept insisting that Dr. Emmet was mistaken and Gertrude was in a deep sleep.

My head was swimming when my father took me by the arm and wrenched me from Amelia's crushing embrace. "How did this happen?" Mr. Curran asked.

"She fell," I said.

For the first time in my life I saw my father cry and his sorrow shocked me. He threw himself across Gertrude's inert form, cradling her broken body with care. He sobbed and cursed God, then cursed my mother for failing to protect his precious little girl, his angel. It was an accident, Amelia said, and Mr. Curran turned on her with his brilliant rhetoric and cursed her for caring about nothing but her own pleasures.

Black eyes spit fire, as if Mr. Curran could burn me alive with his rage. "How could you allow this to happen? How could you stand by and let her die?"

He shook me but there was no shaking out a reply to a question that had no answer. If I had not chased after her, if I had put the book away when she asked me to go walking on such a splendid day. If I was a little faster and had reached her, grasped her skirt before she fell. I might have saved her. Gertrude would still be alive. I replayed the scene, over and over in my head, changing the outcome in my imagination and wishing I had done even one of the things I pictured too late.

"It should have been you," Mr. Curran said when I failed to answer. He had wanted a second son, and then I arrived, a fourth daughter. I was always a disappointment. "Almighty God, why did you take my Gertrude? Why Gertrude?"

Once released, I ran to the darkest corner of the drawing room so that I could obey his command that I get out of his sight. I prayed that I might switch places with Gertrude, but all my entreaties went unheard, the ears of the Lord closed to me. I was still hiding when Rev. Mr. Sandys strode into the room, his severe appearance heralding a new round of weeping. For the briefest of moments, I felt Gertrude next to me, but when I tried to take her hand there was nothing there.

"What sort of mother fails to supervise her children?" Mr. Curran ranted, turning his ire on the woman who could not seek shelter from his verbal storm. From my fortress behind a chair I listened to the tirade. Both Dr. Emmet and Rev. Sandys beseeched my father to accept Gertrude's death as a tragic accident that none could have prevented. God's will be done, the minister said, while the doctor spoke in platitudes that did little to calm the madman who stalked the drawing room.

There was talk of calling the undertaker and making the necessary arrangements. A fierce argument erupted, all reason and sense taking leave of Mr. Curran in the moment of his deepest grief. I trembled as people came and went, the pounding of shoe heels reverberating in my belly. Guilt weighed me down, kept me from crawling out and running off to seek sanctuary with anyone who would forgive me for killing my sister. The barrage of hot words grew hotter, the skills of an acclaimed orator put to use in arguing against a normal burial. How Dr. Emmet's son discovered me I could not say, but he joined me on the floor and formed a strong wall against the assault.

"It was an accident," I said to him.

"Of course it was. A very sad, very tragic accident." Robert Emmet was one of Richard's closest friends, a young man I held in some esteem because he was so intelligent and yet humble. Unlike my brother, he was consistently kind to me.

"For the love of God, Jack. You cannot bury that child in unconsecrated ground," Rev. Sandys bellowed.

Robert patted my hand. "Your father is a prominent man, and his enemies may imply that Gertrude killed herself if Mr. Curran is allowed to proceed with his plan," he said. "You must be strong and close your ears to those who seek political gain through invective."

"He will not listen," Richard said. My oldest brother had come from school after hearing of Gertrude's death. What a dreadful, horrible journey he must have shared with Mr. Curran on the road from Dublin. He fell into the chair, reinforcement for my barricade.

"The fault is not yours, Miss Sarah," Robert said. "Mr. Curran is beside himself."

"Lost his senses," Richard said. "How can he even think to bury Gertrude in the garden, like some favorite dog?"

Mrs. Curran had grown increasingly hysterical since Gertrude was nestled into a lead box, sealed up, to never be seen again. The discussion over internment only added to heightened emotions and Dr. Emmet demanded that we retire and try to rest. Robert helped me up and escorted me to the door, but I did not climb the stairs with my siblings. Instead I drifted to the library, where *Paradise Lost* rested in its proper spot, likely returned by the housemaid. Or perhaps it had always been there and I was imagining some horror. My forehead felt warm. Surely I was delirious with fever and ought to go to bed. I made my way to the bedroom and saw Amelia standing at the window.

Torches glowed at the edge of the garden, in the grove that Gertrude and I had claimed as our own playground. Shovels and picks cut into the sod under our favorite tree as a gang of men worked in the cool autumn air. "He means to put her right there," Amelia said.

"Not in the family vault in Cork?" I asked.

"Cork is too far away. He wants to keep her here, nearby, forever and ever."

Flames and shadows danced in a macabre gavotte. "Will Gertrude not go to Heaven?" I asked. Convicts and suicides were buried in such places, hidden away, their sins making them unfit to lie with good Christians in consecrated ground. My poor sister was only twelve years old. How could one so young have been so evil as to deserve the same fate?

"Of course she will," Amelia said. "She is an angel now. Poor innocent child."

Not a feverish dream, then, but unbelievable reality. Put to bed, I stretched out my arm to find Gertrude next to me, as she had always been. Empty space filled my hand. I tossed her pillow to the foot of the bed but she did not chase after it or swing it at my head. There was nothing but nothingness, and a silence that rang in my ears like the buzzing of bees. I shivered despite the suffocating blanket that my sister Eliza tucked around me, shook with the chill that descended on The Priory.

"Mercy first and last shall brightest shine," I whispered. Darkness descended on The Priory, an unremitting black darkness.

TWO

For hours, I stood at the nursery window and watched the grove, always hoping that Gertrude would appear, even though Eliza and Amelia both scolded me. As the months passed, however, I noticed that the pain diminished to a dull and steady ache, while the emptiness remained raw in my heart. The vacant chair at the dining table was a constant reminder, and one that Mr. Curran masked with a barrage of his storied sarcasm. Meals were the most unpleasant part of the day, when we were all made to gather at five o'clock precisely and endure an attempt at normalcy that ended with Mrs. Curran fleeing the room in tears while Amelia sat like an obelisk to be an example to the rest of us. We had to endure, her rigid posture said, and tolerate what could not be avoided. John, my younger brother, would hold my hand under the table, as if he was afraid that I would disappear like our sister. I envied the babies, James and Will, and the peaceful sanctuary of the nursery.

Within weeks of Gertrude's death, Mr. Curran returned to his former habits and our dining room was again the center of political discussion. Usually his guests were fellow barristers or members of Ireland's Parliament who came to continue some debate begun in the afternoon. I much preferred the Sunday sessions attended by Richard's schoolmates, who looked up to our father as a bold spokesmen for Catholic emancipation. One of the most devoted acolytes was Tommy Moore, a close friend of Richard who earned a small stipend as my music master. He was one of the first Catholics admitted to Trinity, and he gave all the credit to my father for championing the rights of an oppressed majority. He showed his appreciation by acting as the voice of reason when a drawing room debate grew heated, often calling on me to perform as a way to calm the mood. "An Irish air, Miss Sarah," he said on such an occasion. "In the native tongue, Mr. Curran, and the pronunciation is flawless, I believe."

Tommy sat at the pianoforte and Richard joined us to turn the music. We were a small island of calm that quickly attracted Amelia and Eliza, who added their voices to our impromptu concert.

"Our Gertrude had the loveliest voice," Mr. Curran said. Gloom emanated from the tips of his fingers and painted the walls. "Silenced forever. How can you sing so merrily, children, when your sister lies cold and alone?"

Richard snapped the sheet from right to left. "A tragedy compounded," he said under his breath. I lost my place and forgot the lyric, stumbling over the Irish words that I knew so well but five minutes earlier.

"Her fluency in the language was remarkable," Mr. Curran said. "Our tenants took such delight in conversing with her, as it showed our unity with them. Many of my colleagues are endlessly devising some method to erase the language, to eradicate Irish culture at the point of a sword. They fear plots being concocted under their very noses, but rather than learn the language, they prefer to cause more unrest by demanding that everyone be as ignorant as them."

"English is the language of authority, and its use is intended to keep the Irish subservient," Dr. Emmet said. "Particularly among the poor, who are denied education."

"Will I live to see the day when a Catholic will be equal to a Protestant?" Dr. Emmet's son Thomas asked. Like my father, he was in law, and traveled a circuit that kept him from home for weeks at a time. Unlike Mr. Curran, however, he espoused armed rebellion as the only sure means to achieve their shared goals. "How can we be expected to govern a people if the populace is divided into two disparate classes? What say you, Robert? You are uncommonly quiet this evening."

"Mr. Curran was speaking earlier of the French and the bloody turn their revolution has taken," Robert said. "It seems to me that their society is divided into multiple classes, and it was the lowest that brought down the monarchy. Do we not face the same risks? Can we learn from the mistakes of our neighbors before violence becomes the last best hope, or is rebellion the only means to free the Catholics?"

Seditious talk was the centerpiece of my education. Mr. Curran was exceedingly radical, a man who agitated against inequality. His position put him at odds with the conservative government that was still smarting over the loss of the American colonies, the Crown doubly determined not to lose another corner of the Empire. Showing a lack of vision, our rulers in London thought that a shared religion was the dangerous link between the French enemy and the Irish Catholics. In fact, it was their attempt to snuff out Catholicism with punitive laws that fueled a smoldering rebellion. As my father so wisely understood, the short-sighted government all but pushed us closer to France when it should have embraced the Irish as equals.

The United Irishmen were the most vocal in demanding greater freedom, and with Mr. Curran's well-known sympathies it was natural that they would turn to him when the government clamped down. Like my father, they believed in equality and so the group was composed of Catholics and Protestants alike, but so soon after the French king lost his head, the authorities were overly sensitive. It was in January of 1794, after the society had been suppressed, that my father stood at the bar of the King's Bench in Dublin and delivered an impassioned speech that would prove prophetic. He spoke to men whose minds were shut up tight against reason and logic, and so the defendants were all found guilty. What the authorities thought was an end to the unrest was, in reality, merely the beginning.

The war with France was in its early stages, and fear of a French alliance with the Irish Catholics was the root cause of the guilty verdict. Those who supported the ideals of the United Irishmen understood that France stood to gain a decided advantage if it mounted a successful invasion of Ireland. The native Irish whose rights were denied would naturally fight for the French in exchange for religious liberty, and the French Army would gain a ready supply of reinforcements. Coordinated attacks across the Irish Sea and the Channel would overwhelm British forces, and it would be the heads of Britain's peers rolling in the gutters of London.

"The bigotry of the English is undermining Irish loyalty," Richard said. "Go back in recent history, to my father's defense of a Catholic priest against a peer of the realm. Who thought that the truth could prevail?"

"Precisely," Mr. Curran said. "His Lordship presumed that his title alone granted him privileges that included coercing a clergyman to violate his oath to God, and he further presumed that his title granted him the power to beat that priest for disobedience."

"But can we wait, Jack, until the King is put aside and a liberal government comes in under the Prince Regent?" Leonard McNally asked. He was a dreadful toady, currying favor with my father at every opportunity, even though they worked together. Mr. McNally was, without question, Mr. Curran's dearest friend, and my least favorite.

The ladies left the men to their wine and words, retreating to Mrs. Curran's sitting room. She found these evenings to be restorative, she said, because her girls had grown beyond the need for a mother's constant attention and such pleasant moments were approaching an end. Her spirits did seem to lift when we sat with our needlework while Amelia read the newspapers aloud, discussing weightier topics than the local gossip that filled her day. My mother had grown restless since Gertrude's death, and steered our conversations towards travel to the places mentioned in the news reports. Rathfarnham was too small a town to contain her and the place had shrunk considerably since the previous October.

"Eliza, fetch my Bible," Mrs. Curran said. "You girls must spend more time in studying God's word. The Psalms, for example. You should commit them all to memory. The Reverend Mr. Sandys believes that a young lady of good breeding must know more than the *Book of Common Prayer* if she is to be a good mother."

"What Psalm counsels a lady to be less argumentative?" Eliza asked, tweaking Amelia with a nasty reminder of last winter's social season and the cause of a broken courtship. Our oldest sister was strong-willed and strong-minded, two qualities not in demand in a wife. She wished to be married to her art, to become a painter, but independence was firmly denied.

"And what commandment tells us to love one another," Mrs. Curran said. "To do unto others as they would do unto us."

"There is no prayer to grant any of us a dowry that would erase any and all shortcomings in our temperaments," Amelia said.

We were a large family, it was true, and so we were costly to keep. Mr. Curran made no secret of the fact that his daughters would come to their grooms with very little, unlike his own experience. The money that Mrs. Curran brought was enough to start him in his legal career and by all appearances he had thrived. He could have gone higher, he liked to say, if not for his enemy Lord Clare ensuring that John Philpot Curran would not be made Master in Chancery. Thirty thousand was lost, we were told, the same thirty thousand pounds that could have been our marriage portions. Even a girl as plain-featured as Amelia could snag a prominent gentleman with that kind of bait on her hook.

"In time a liberal government will come in," Mrs. Curran said. "All that is past due will be received. A peerage at the least, when Mr. Fox replaces Mr. Pitt. We must be patient, girls, and while we wait, Amelia, you must control your habit of expressing your opinions."

"Hope for reward? Is that why our father continues to support the opposition, even though they never win an argument?" I asked. How often did he decry the blindness of his colleagues who refused to see what was obvious to any man of sense? During his frequent spells of melancholy he would cry out for a single victory, just one, to show he was in the right.

"For thou hast lifted me up, and hast not made my foes to rejoice over me," Eliza read aloud from Psalm Thirty, the passage our mother selected to demonstrate the comfort of holy words at a time when faith might waver. I imagined Mr. Curran silently repeating those very words as he faced another stinging rebuke from a judge or a conservative MP. With England again entering into war with France, his reasoned points sounded more like treason than good governance, and it must have taken great faith in the Almighty to endure all that while waiting for the Whigs to ascend. Waiting for his fortune to turn, and ours with it.

"Weeping may endure for a night, but joy cometh in the morning," Mrs. Curran repeated after Eliza's reading. "Our joy will come this summer, as it always has. No matter the strident voices in Dublin, we shall make our regular journey to Newmarket and find happiness among our relations."

Our parents were the offspring of County Cork gentry, and they had risen above their provincial origins. After he was called to the bar, Mr. Curran began his legal practice in Newmarket and gained sufficient notoriety to be awarded a seat in Parliament. He never forgot what it was like to be mocked for his stutter as an impoverished student dependent on a scholarship. He stood on the side of the oppressed, and like so many other well-read gentlemen of that enlightened age, he believed strongly in equality among men no matter what their religion. He set himself a near-impossible task in trying to sway those who saw a demand for equality as a cry for armed insurrection. Little good it did him when he was later proved correct.

"Mr. Sandys has said he will be in Cork as well and plans to call on us," Mrs. Curran said. "I expect three girls will be alert and attentive to his sermons."

The Reverend Mr. Sandys was another of Mr. Curran's worshippers, a friend for many years and a fellow believer in the liberal cause. He was a frequent visitor before Gertrude's death, but he had become almost a fixture in our household after that terrible day. Being in the minority politically forced him to find company with others like him, and the center of that small universe was The Priory. All our guests were part of that coterie, until I knew no other way of looking at the world than that espoused by my father's friends and associates. At the age of twelve, I was becoming as radical as Mr. Curran.

"He drones on so," Eliza said. "My arms will be covered in bruises from Amelia pinching me to stay awake."

"Memorize some brief passage and then repeat it back to him," I said. Gertrude had suggested that to me the year before, and I choked on the words. I was excused to take a drink of water, and dawdled long enough to avoid my mother's displeasure at such a sign of disrespect for a man of God.

Our sleeping arrangements had changed after Gertrude's passing, but we pretended that Eliza started sleeping with me because Amelia was a grown woman of eighteen, out in society, and had earned the privilege of a bed to herself. My sisters continued their habit of whispering to each other in the dark, as if a matter of great importance could not wait until the following morning. They were discussing the potential for fun in

Newmarket, wondering who might give a ball or a card party. I grew bored with their chatter until the topic shifted to Amelia's plans for her future.

"If you do not marry, what will you do?" Eliza asked.

The sound of our father's mournful violin penetrated the floorboards. He was working on a speech, or puzzling out a response to a detractor. Playing music helped him focus his thoughts, but he was known to play at all hours of the night when everyone else was trying to sleep.

"Better a spinster than a wife fallen into misery," Amelia said. "Are there any guarantees that I will not share our mother's fate?"

"What about Mama?" I asked. Of all the girls, Amelia was the closest to our mother. They spent a great deal of time together, with Amelia engaged in the rituals of courtship.

"Go to sleep, Sarah," Amelia said. "This does not concern you."

"It does. If you become a spinster, then I will too," I said.

"She confessed all this to you?" Eliza asked, confirming a secret not shared with me.

"As a warning. There have been others, kept in Dublin. A man can live as he pleases, Eliza, and never face censure while we are left to deal with gossip."

"What are we to do, marry clergymen?" Eliza asked. "Find a man who cannot escape the watchful eye of his flock?"

"And dress like a modest little mouse for the rest of my life? No, thank you. Better a spinster than the minister's wife."

"A fine curate's wife you would make," I said. How I resented being kept out of their circle when I had lost my confidante. Loneliness tightened like a band around my middle, squeezing the very breath out of me. I gasped for air and clutched at my nightdress, in a panic that I was going to suffocate. Eliza slapped me soundly between my shoulder blades and I burst into tears.

THREE

The summer of 1794 began as every other summer of my life had begun. The house fell into turmoil with packing and loading and Mrs. Curran fluttering through the rooms in a frenzy of instructions and orders to the staff. She had not wanted to leave Newmarket when Mr. Curran sought advancement, she let slip once. Her manic eagerness to return was evidence of an unremitting heartache that grew from the pain of leaving behind everyone she loved. The Priory had been enlarged over the years to fit her growing family, but a spacious house with fine furnishings was not the cure for her ailment.

Trials for the United Irishmen filled the court's docket and Mr. Curran was unable to travel with us until all the cases had been heard. Events in France had hardened the government against the society, and their leaders were put on trial to silence all dissent. If British support for the Bourbon royalists in France had been effective the United Irishmen would have been seen as harmless, but the military success of the revolutionary army only stoked fear of invasion. The Crown was determined to crush any and all Irishmen who dared to speak their minds, calling it treason. My father was the defense counsel in highest demand, even if his clients were routinely found guilty. His soaring rhetoric served a greater purpose, with his verbal skewering of the prosecutor's logic intended to sway minds and influence public opinion. In a way, he was fighting a series of battles meant to wear down the opposition, so that the war might eventually be won. He never saw the reinforcements forming up on his flank.

We spent our days in long walks to take the air, joined by Rev. Sandys. His presence helped to calm Mrs. Curran, who was forever in a state that I blamed on her unquenchable grief. When she grew agitated, we would pause in our perambulation while the minister offered clerical wisdom and axioms of fortitude in the face of adversity until Mrs. Curran was sufficiently recovered. After one such spell, she called her daughters to her side to walk with her while the men raced ahead.

"Soon to leave your old mother behind," Mrs. Curran said. Her eyes were red from crying. "Making your own homes while I wonder how you came to be old enough to marry."

"While I would be happy to relieve Papa of the burden of my maintenance, I have no immediate plans to wed," Amelia said. She had spoiled breakfast with an unpleasant dissection of the gentlemen she had met at Newmarket, a most unsuitable gaggle of geese who tried her patience.

"The day will come. A mother must let go of her children. So hard to accept, but it is the way of the world," Mrs. Curran said.

Tears rolled down her cheeks and I wished that she would stop turning to Mr. Sandys for advice. His words were soothing as they fell from his lips but she did not derive any lasting comfort from them. Indeed, she tended to spout nonsense. Let go of her children? William was only five years of age, far too young to be turned loose on the world. "I would not accept a man who would not accept my family," I said.

"How ridiculous," Amelia said. "Once you are married, you are at a husband's command. A man will tell you what he must to win your heart, but when he has snared you he may prove false with the knowledge that there is nothing you can do about it."

"You have become so old, Amelia," Mrs. Curran said.

"A woman must take great care," Amelia said. "There is no reason to act in haste. That is all that I meant. Prudence and careful consideration rather than misplaced exuberance."

"Wise girls, all of you," Mrs. Curran said. She embraced us in an awkward tangle of colliding bonnets. "I need not worry about any of you, as the Reverend has told me so often. Truly, you are on your own paths towards womanhood and I am superfluous."

"As for this year's dancing lessons," Amelia said. She was upset at being made to attend classes like a child when she expected to have leisure time to pursue her passion for painting. Rather than listen to a repetition of previous conversations, I raced ahead to catch up with Richard. He thought that his position as scholar would spare him from the ordeal of reels and gavottes, and I took great pleasure in telling him he was quite mistaken.

"Miss Sarah, I was just talking about your performance last night," Mr. Sandys said. He offered his arm and I tucked my hand into the crook of his elbow, noticing that I had to reach a bit higher because he was taller than Mr. Curran. "You are blessed with a rare talent and I hope you will make every effort to cultivate your voice."

"Richard is an excellent pianist," I said. "He promised to play a duet with me this evening. Will you come, sir?"

"Then I must play badly so that Sarah might shine," Richard said.

"So you will play as you always do," I retorted.

"A pity she is a female, Mr. Sandys, or she might follow in our father's footsteps. Turning a sarcastic phrase with such ease," Richard said.

"The Curran blood, in that case, but one cannot dispute the source of her pretty face. The Creagh line is evident in her features," Mr. Sandys said. I favored my mother's family. Gertrude had been the very image of Grandmother Curran, whom our father worshipped.

"So fortunate, Sarah," Richard said. "No man wants an argumentative barrister for a wife."

Our route took us to the spot below the town where a stream entered the Dallua, but we did not pause for a rest. Mrs. Curran was eager to get back to Grandfather Creagh's house in case Mr. Curran had been able to leave Dublin a little sooner than he first thought. His arrival would result in our departure from the Creaghs and there was packing to be done so that we could decamp for Grandfather Curran's house. Will and James complained of fatigue, but even that would not keep Mrs. Curran from walking at a rapid pace. I helped Will climb onto Richard's shoulders and took James' hand, while Mr. Sandys and Mrs. Curran took up positions behind us. Before long, I had heard enough of Amelia's complaints about being made to take lessons with infants when she was old enough to be a mother herself. I dashed ahead to walk with Richard, who was educating John about the realities of life at school for a boy whose father was well known and not all that popular with the ruling elite.

My belly was in turmoil that night and I retired early to avoid sitting down to a meal I would not keep down. Alone in the bedroom we all shared, I sprawled on the floor with my head to a crack in the floorboards, to listen to the rumble of voices that drifted up from the library below. I could not make out the words, but I could tell that my mother was speaking to her parents, an argument I guessed. Sobs and something about mercy angered Grandfather, who broke in with a harsh utterance that he punctuated with a fist striking wood. Indistinct sounds did not hold my interest and I took advantage of the long hours of light to read in private. As darkness crept in through the window my eyes grew heavy. Amelia woke me with a nudge of her foot.

The full moon cast a glow on our muslin nightdresses, transforming us into ethereal beings floating just above the surface of the earth. "Mama is deeply distressed," Amelia said. "We must be extra good to her tomorrow. Absolutely no gainsaying a thing she says, is that clear?"

"Papa is expected," Eliza said. "His presence always distresses her."

"All the more reason for us to be kind," Amelia said. "We don't want her to worry herself into illness. That would be the end of any amusement outside of Grandfather's house. I will not stand by while you two do anything to spoil things for us."

"But she accepted some invitations already," I said. "It would be rude to say no three days later."

"Hush, Sarah," Eliza said. "Go to sleep. You are too young to concern yourself with dances or parties."

Beams of moonlight tickled my eyelids until they lifted. I got out of bed to catch a breath of fresh air, wedged in as I was between my overheated sisters. Very slowly, I lifted the sash without making a sound and then leaned on the sill to admire the ghostly gloom of Grandfather's park. From the road came the distant clatter of hooves and harness, but my view was blocked by a large birch tree. A latch clicked below me, followed by the crunch of gravel under a delicate foot. My mother entered the scene, walking as gingerly as if she were treading upon hot coals. She turned her head towards me but she was gazing at the house, fixing it in memory. I lifted my hand to wave, but something in the shadows of her face held my arm in place. All the tension that dwelled in her neck and shoulders was gone at that instant and she was beautiful, more beautiful than I had ever before seen. Serenity washed over her features, even as the tears poured down her cheeks. At that moment, the moment of her death, my mother's heart shattered. She left nothing behind but a trail of tears that ended just beyond the gate.

FOUR

The household was up earlier than normal and I raced down to the dining room to see if Grandfather Creagh had some exciting news to share. As the local doctor, he was the first to know of great events like births and deaths and scandals. His anecdotes about injuries would see us out the door on our way to a charity call, a bit of excitement in an otherwise dull town. The housemaid passed me on the stairs and sighed, called me a poor little lamb, and then hurried away.

Grandfather paced the entry hall, dressed to go out in coat and hat, his clean white stockings accentuating his spindly calves. He slapped his gloves against his hand, turned on his heel and marched to the door before wheeling around, jumping in fright when he encountered me standing there.

"Has Mama returned, sir?" I asked.

He flew at me, took me by the shoulders and held me in place so that I could not fly away. "Did you know of her plans?" he asked.

"Did I know of what plans, if you please, Grandfather?"

"Leaving. Her plan to quit our company."

"Is Papa ill? Did she have to go to Dublin? Is that why Papa is not yet here?"

Before he could explain, Grandmother joined us, her red-rimmed eyes brimming with tears. "Do not make inquiries, Dr. Creagh," she said. She held out a letter, written in Mrs. Curran's hand. Whatever she said was garbled by a renewed spate of sobbing.

In dressing gowns, disheveled and half-asleep, we all gathered in the drawing room where Grandmother stood at the window, not seeing the rivulets of rain that rolled down the panes. I clung to Amelia for comfort while John held tightly to my skirts, seeking reassurance. Eliza had an arm around Will and James, the trio taking up a post next to Grandmother while Richard stood at her side, ready to catch her if she fainted. The one person who was calm in the emotional storm was Amelia. Had my eldest sister done something disgraceful, an act so dreadful that our mother had to fetch our father at once?

"She is dead to you now," Grandmother said. Was it possible that her hair had become so white overnight? "Your father is not the sort of man to forgive the smallest slight. An insult such as this will be impossible to reverse."

"Be brave," Amelia whispered to me. "A desperate woman has done a desperate thing, that is all."

"Not even the love of her children could stop her," Grandfather said. His body sagged in defeat and he turned his back on us rather than display the crack in his once solid facade.

"I am aware of the difficulty of her," Grandmother paused to find the right word. "The domestic situation. Lacking felicity."

"In short, children, your mother has eloped," Grandfather said.

"Run off?" Richard asked. "With Reverend Mr. Sandys, am I correct? How did I not see it. The filthy cur. Despicable man. A false cleric, a hypocrite."

"Why did she not take us?" I asked.

"Because she cannot," Richard said. "We are the chattel of our father."

"Poor, dear Amelia," Grandmother said. "Your chances are ruined, I fear."

"Not so dire as all that," Grandfather said. "In time this will fade from memory. A few years from now this will be forgotten."

An ear-splitting silence descended on the house and on our lives. Although much of the time after the flight became a jumble of images in my mind, my father's arrival at the Creagh home remained clear. He was an important man, one whose reputation mattered a great deal to his future in an anticipated liberal government. His outrage rattled the window panes. "She has made me a laughing stock," Mr. Curran roared. The town was too small to contain the scandal and every resident for miles around was aware that Mrs. Curran had run off with another man. Friends and relations all came to offer their sympathies and he shared with them the great hurt that had been inflicted on a decent, honest and respectable man. "My enemies frolic over the grave of my aspirations. I will not allow it, I say. She will not succeed in this attempt to define me as a cuckold and deflate my ambitions."

We were shunted to Grandfather Curran's home where the atmosphere was one of an army camp on the verge of a pitched battle. Grandmother Curran tried to shelter me because I was a somewhat sensitive soul, like herself, but with uncles and cousins gathering in conclave it was impossible not to be splashed by the gallons of bile poured on my mother's head. What advice my father might have received from his relations I cannot say. In the end, he created an even greater scandal that did him more harm than a minor domestic unpleasantness. Looking neither right nor left, he took the first step towards his downfall.

FIVE

I sobbed and could not get out of bed, could not eat, could not sleep. That I was mourning the loss of my mother was a crime in Mr. Curran's eyes, and so I was exiled until my thoughts were more cheerful. My father sent me to Lismore, to stay with an old friend from his university days. Reverend Crawford was a schoolmaster in an isolated corner of Waterford, a community that could boast of little besides the animosity of the poor Catholic tenants he regarded as stupid and venal. His wife was all kindness, his son a dreadful tease, and his infant daughter a delight. In the months I lodged with the family, I was astonished to discover that a home could be a place of peace, where conversations could be pleasant and even humorous. To my great shock, Rev. Crawford heaped praise on my voice, while Mrs. Crawford boasted of my musical ability to the parishioners after Sunday services. Never before had I been encouraged or complimented. The experience was thoroughly disorienting. It did nothing to improve my dark mood.

My time in Lismore was a period of intense introspection in which I analyzed my many flaws and located the reasons why my mother had forsaken me. In the process I came to see that The Priory was a place of melancholy, ruled by a cruel tyrant, and the Crawford home was a far more desirable residence. The separation from my sisters, however, was more intolerable than life under Mr. Curran's disdain. I taught myself how to paper over my thoughts with a pleasant demeanor, so that the Crawfords believed I was recovered. As far as they could judge, I was a quiet and pensive child, a bit remote as if distracted, but I had demonstrated a keen wit and was occasionally seen to smile or laugh. The laugh was subdued as it was the best I could muster, but it served my purpose. They brought me back to Rathfarnham.

O ur lives were in turmoil but the future glowed brightly, despite the tragedy that had befallen us. Everything that Mr. Curran had been waiting for began to fall into place, with the appointment of his good friend as Lord Chancellor of Ireland. The cherished post of Solicitor General was to be Mr. Curran's, an elevation to high office that would lead to a peerage and the potential for the Curran daughters to find favorable matches. Luck, however, was not on our side. The Lord Chancellor's first act was to put forward a bill for Catholic emancipation. The King recalled him immediately, killing the liberal movement in a swift blow. The men who once populated our dining room were seen with less frequency, and by the summer, it was clear that the debating society my father had named the Knights of the Screw was much reduced in membership. From the heights we all descended, and a deep melancholy filled the rooms of The Priory.

The garden offered a refuge, although I had not previously had much interest in the tedium. My mother had been passionate about her roses, and I thought I might make amends for earlier failings by tending the flowers with the same care. Early one afternoon I was clipping a few last buds to lay on Gertrude's grave when Richard stormed out of the house with Amelia on his heels. He paced on the path like a caged animal. "He has lost his mind," he said. "Gone mad, as I shall go mad."

He stalked the borders, decrying his fate to the birds that startled and flew away. Our assumption that Mr. Curran had come to accept the sorry fact that he was a rejected husband was incorrect. Nearly a year after Mrs. Curran's absence, I learned that my father had only been stewing, plotting revenge.

"A man too proud to let a grievance slide," Amelia said.

She put a comforting hand on Richard's shoulder, acting the part of matriarch, but with a bitter edge to her caring. For Amelia, there was no escape from her current position, a result of both paternal neglect and scandal. The greater blame was laid at our father's feet, but she had cross words for Mrs. Curran as well. I swallowed down my tears and tried not to think of our mother at all. It was no easy task with Richard bringing her back to life.

"To sue Mr. Sandys for criminal conversation," Richard said. "It was our mother who talked herself into leaving. What am I to do, Amelia? He has called on me to testify. In court, under oath, to tell the truth. He does not know the truth. He is blind to the truth, and God help me if I open his eyes. He will disown me on the spot, and how am I to continue my studies without his support?"

"So he means to extract some financial revenge," Amelia said.

"What good is a single shilling after the world reads the testimony? And it will be broadcast far and wide, you can be sure of that," Richard said. "Damages. What a cruel joke."

"The Priory has been our refuge while we hide from society," Amelia said. "It will become our prison."

Our circle had always been small, in part because we lived over a mile from Dublin and had few neighbors. In my view, we stood to lose little, if anything. Mr. Curran, of course, moved in an entirely different sphere and could count on political necessity to maintain bonds. However, the radicals in Commons might very well shrink from him after his conduct was put on display in a courtroom. As it was, the Conservatives were on the rise in Dublin, and getting stronger with every victory that Bonaparte claimed for France. To avoid further loss of prestige, the Whigs might decide to cast John Philpot Curran adrift. There would be no living with our father if his way to the top was blocked.

"He has made a terrible mistake, and we are powerless to stop him. He will listen to no one," Amelia said.

"Forced to speak against my mother," Richard said. "It is unbearable. Ridiculous, to accuse Sandys of seduction. He is to be commended for rescuing her."

"You will soon be reading the law," Amelia said. "Here is an opportunity to practice word play. You have a certain skill, Richard. Be confident in your ability to parry a thrust."

"Which is, to say a great deal while saying nothing," he said. "Then I shall stand in the dock as a disinterested party, with no stake in the outcome. You are right. The damage was done when the lawsuit was filed. The verdict does not signify."

"Repeated infidelity was not the sole cause. Isolation, a lack of society, is what drove Mama to act rashly," Amelia said. "Laws must be changed, Richard, to emancipate all. Catholics and women alike. Why must a woman be trapped in an unhappy marriage?"

"You are reading Wollstonecraft, I see," Richard said.

"And why not? Is her philosophy not as logical as any crafted by a man?"

"I did not come here to argue. Give me your word that we can stand united," Richard said. "The newspapers will be full of this case. Keep as much as you can from the girls."

"A man with enemies would be wise to remain circumspect in his private life," Amelia said. "Things die down of their own accord if left in peace, but he would keep the fire stirred up and blazing."

The day of reckoning approached and tension crackled from room to room, rattling the crystal. Two empty chairs yawned uneasily in the dining room where we gathered at precisely five o'clock on the evening before the trial was due to open. After supper, Mr. Curran retreated to his library with Richard to ponder the possible questions and craft the desired answers. Sick with fear over what might happen, I strolled in the garden until it grew too dark to see.

Alone, I wept with pity for Richard. He would have to walk a fine line in court, risking our father's enmity while under a barrage of questions from a man determined to extract what Richard did not wish to reveal. Pity turned to envy. Our mother might be in the courtroom and Richard would get to see her, perhaps speak to her, while I would be home with nothing but fading memories. I dug my hands into the boxwood hedge and ripped the leaves from the branches, tore holes in the perfectly pruned symmetry that gave Mr. Curran such pleasure.

The following evening, Mr. Curran did not bring the Dublin newspapers with him as he normally did, so I had no way of knowing how the trial was going from any other perspective than Richard's, but he knew almost nothing. I presumed all was well when our father entertained some of his friends as he had before. In keeping with their old habits, they debated radical principles over a quantity of wine, the chatter lasting well into the night, while Amelia scrambled to find places for them to sleep. The sounds of raucous laughter rang through the house, Mr. Curran's voice rising over the rest in an expression of merriment that indicated a successful skewering of his nemesis, the Reverend Mr. Sandys.

Days later, we heard from Richard. The court had found in Mr. Curran's favor, that Rev. Sandys had been guilty of seducing Mrs. Curran. Even though one of Mr. Curran's closest friends sat in judgment, the penalty levied was insignificant, indicating an insignificant degree of damage to Mr. Curran or a compensating level of damage inflicted on Mrs. Curran. The award of a few guineas told the world that our mother was justified in her flight and Mr. Curran was not the victim of an evil seducer.

We prepared ourselves for fury and rage, but instead Mr. Curran sulked. His subdued grief was expressed in deep melancholy, and he gave himself over completely to Commons and the King's Bench. He managed a display of cheer when he entertained, although it was only a mask that he removed after his guests had gone home. I envied Richard, who was free to remain in Dublin with friends when he wanted, and I envied my younger brothers who were away at school and far from the bitter diatribes that formed our evening entertainment. In a single evening, however, it all changed. Mr. Curran returned from the day's court session with a guest in tow.

"Mrs. Fitzgerald, may I present my daughters," he said. I felt Eliza's hand on my arm, squeezing tight as if she had caught herself fainting.

The bloom of youth was rather faded on Mrs. Fitzgerald's cheek, faded like the fabric of her gown. Her scent was one of bergamot and lavender with a top note of desperation. For an awkward amount of time we stood motionless in the entry hall, taking stock of each other.

"Will you be joining us for dinner, Mrs. Fitzgerald?" Amelia asked. "We always dine at five when Father is home."

The steward hauled in a small trunk and marched straight up the stairs, mumbling prayers to Jesus, Mary, and holy Saint Joseph. "This way, my dear," Mr. Curran said. He put a hand on his guest's back to guide her and then sat her down in Mrs. Curran's chair at the table. The Curran sisters exchanged glances, brief and subtle, but full of understanding. The scandal was being compounded before our very eyes. Sauce for the goose, with our mother presumed to be living with Mr. Sandys as his wife, had become good for the gander.

SIX

A French invasion force was sighted off the coast near Bantry Bay in December of 1796, and British hearts were instantly hardened. The local militia, organized by the wealthy merchant Richard White, stood by to repel the enemy who threatened to free the Catholics and erase Protestant privilege. Bigots like Mr. White took precedence, their diatribes stirring up a maniacal fear of rebellion that drowned out sensible talk of religious freedom. Mr. Curran was applauded for his desperate attempt to change the law peacefully, but still his dire warnings of a people abused beyond endurance were shouted down. Under such conditions, it was no surprise that the Irish Parliament sitting for the 1797 session would not entertain any notions of Catholic emancipation as a way to outflank the French. As it turned out, that was the last sitting of Ireland's Commons.

Even as radicalism withered in Dublin Castle, it thrived in the fertile minds of the university students. Richard and his friends brought their debates to The Priory, where we often gathered in the drawing room to discuss strategies of rebellion. My brother John never failed to agree with me when I dissected the works of Locke and quoted from Thomas Paine, comparing the methods employed by the Americans and the French. Newspapers, broadsheets and pamphlets were devoured after dinner. Points and counterpoints flew, with Mr. Curran inserting his perspective to tear down or build up a particular idea. Despite his assertions that legislation was the avenue for peaceful revolution, we were unshakeable in our belief that only armed insurrection would bring the change that Ireland needed. Had he not resigned his seat that summer, proving the point? Our country had to declare its independence from England.

The gatherings took on a different flavor at the end of the year, when Mr. Curran took to remaining in Dublin with Mrs. Fitzgerald. We had the house to ourselves and acted as if we were the adults, freed from parental constraints, our gatherings modeled on the French salon rather than the more stuffy British style of entertaining. We joked about our very Continental approach, especially as it reflected so well our father's rather French morality. His illegitimate child was soon to be born and he acted as if the event had nothing to do with him. A prominent man could not move about without drawing attention, yet our father would sire a child and then pretend that the late Mr. Fitzgerald had come down from heaven to impregnate his wife. His colleagues would ignore the scandal, of course, but the Curran sisters would have to dance around the matter. There were those who would not allow a son to be allied to a family tainted by such scandal, and our chances at marriage could be harmed.

While Mr. Curran's absence provided enough cover to maintain appearances in Rathfarnham, he had other reasons to remain in town.. The court's docket was filled to overflowing with United Irishmen on trial for sedition or treason and Mr. Curran put his heart into their defense. If not for an unexpected visit from Richard and his friends in the spring of 1798, we might have passed the rest of the year in uninformed isolation.

"You are all subject to a visitation?" Amelia asked after the young gentlemen explained the reason for their long trek from Dublin on a Sunday morning. "The Lord Chancellor is going to interrogate the students?"

"The fault lies largely in me," Tommy Moore said. "I had a letter published in the United Irishmen's journal and foolishly drew attention to the college."

"Was that your work?" Robert asked. "It was a brilliant defense of Irish independence."

"Too brilliant for that wastrel who sits in Dublin Castle," Richard sneered. The Lord Chancellor was none other than Earl Clare, who had once challenged our father to a duel. Although both sides were said to have been satisfied, His Lordship's burning hatred for Mr. Curran was not extinguished. Without needing to explain the situation, we all understood that anyone affiliated with John Philpot Curran was going to be a suspect in the earl's witch hunt. The authorities were hell-bent on driving all resistance out of the school, and Richard was very much afraid that loose tongues would point in his direction, dooming his chance to become a barrister. His nerves were frayed and his stomach churned from worry.

Amelia thought it best if we provided some light entertainment to alleviate the minds of young men facing their first trial. I sang a somewhat rebellious song to show the support of the Curran ladies, with Eliza providing a spirited accompaniment. "If only I were marching at the head of ten thousand men," Robert said. His enthusiasm startled me so that I could not continue with the third verse.

"Are you ready for the inquisition?" Richard asked. "I have heard that Tom Lefroy is one of the government's spies."

"The senior, that fellow from Limerick?" Thomas asked. "His jealousy of Robert's debating skill knows no bounds, I see. But our good friend here is not alone in the pantheon of enemies. Although I believe Lefroy's animosity towards Richard arises from his hatred of John Philpot Curran and everything the august gentleman stands for. I am a Catholic, which is reason enough for him to wish me gone from a once pristinely Protestant school."

"I will not submit," Robert said. "We all know my father's position. He has not made a secret of his opposition to the government. Why should I let them expel me in dishonor? No, gentlemen, I shall resign my place before they can humiliate me."

"But what will you do?" Eliza asked. "Without an education, how can you not fall below your station?"

"There are other schools in this world. In France, for example," Robert said. "Or I could go to America and make a fresh start."

"Just as they transported us to America before, you will transport yourself," Tommy said.

"But to give in to their demands that I name my colleagues in seditious thought would be a greater victory for the Crown," Robert said.

He went on to detail the letter he had written, approved by Dr. Emmet, in which he refuted the Lord Chancellor's demands with strict logic. I was taken with Robert's passion and spirit, warmed by the fire that burned within him. With so much at stake for his future, he saw the bigger picture of Ireland's future and did not hesitate to sacrifice himself for the greater good of others. Until that afternoon, I had never given Robert Emmet much thought, a slightly built young man who was inclined towards medicine for his life's work. By leaving the college, he was leaving all that behind, and he was bidding farewell to the professions with remarkable courage. His bold action was most estimable.

After our guests departed, I mentioned my admiration to my sisters. "Commendable or foolish, I cannot tell," Amelia said.

"Either way, he will have to make his way in the trades," Eliza said.

"No woman of our set could consider a match with him," Amelia said. The look she gave me was intended as a clear warning. "And what a shame. The family is so well regarded."

Within weeks, Ireland tumbled into a disjointed uprising. The authorities were well aware of all the plans crafted by the United Irishmen, having infiltrated the secret society with paid spies and saboteurs who made sure that the rebellion in Dublin failed. To my horror, I learned that the captured rebels were never put on trial or given an opportunity to offer up a defense. Instead, they were executed in an orgy of blood and slaughter. For many nights I did not sleep, worrying about the fate of my brother and his friends, wondering if any of them were hiding from the authorities after following Lord Fitzgerald into battle. My sisters, however, did not share my belief that Richard was bold enough to act on his rhetoric.

At the beginning of June, Mr. Curran returned home with John, James, and Will, accompanied by his concubine and their bastard son. The fighting was still hot in parts of Ulster and Wexford, close enough to alarm my father who saw the need to seek shelter. That he was a suspect was evident when Town Major Sirr came to call, the head of the secret police planning to expose a gentleman known to support the United Irishmen, and therefore a co-conspirator. The two adversaries retreated to the library while we sat with a woman who was all but a stranger, trying to make conversation.

"You may have heard that Dr. Emmet's son Thomas was arrested before the uprising began," Mrs. Fitzgerald said. "Quite a blow to the family, and that after the youngest son threw away a promising future. Although his incarceration doubtless saved his life."

From the library we heard our father's booming voice, much accustomed to carrying over the noise of a courtroom. "Do you seek to intimidate me, sir? Assassinate me, you may. Intimidate me you may not," he said.

Were we enemies of the King? I held my sewing on my lap, unable to pretend that I had no fear. What would become of us if Mr. Curran's head were spiked on our front gate? My breath came short and fast, a gasping that I could not control no matter how much Amelia frowned at me. The edges of my vision grew dark as the clouds gathered. Music had always been my solace and I turned to the pianoforte for comfort. The notes were immune to uncertainty, the melodies consistent and reliable. John joined me, suggesting we play a duet. He was as nervous as I was, well aware of the mood in Dublin.

"Did you hear any reports of the conflict in Wexford before you left Dublin, Mrs. Fitzgerald?" Eliza asked.

"A great many rumors," she said. "As Mr. Curran is not concerned about them, neither shall we be."

"Unless Dublin rises," Amelia said. "The rebellion would succeed if every member of the United Irishmen played his part instead of hiding behind a ridiculous notion that Ireland can thrive while ruled by a foreign power."

"There will be no treason in this house," Mrs. Fitzgerald said. "As Mr. Curran commands, so we will obey."

I worked on a few exercises that Mr. Moore had left for me after our last lesson, but an image of my father languishing in prison intruded and tangled my fingers. How many evenings had he entertained some of the same esteemed gentlemen who had been arrested? Major Sirr hated every cause my father ardently supported, and would look on Mr. Curran's arrest as the greatest achievement of the investigation. The musical notes on the page before me danced and leaped as I tried once again to play, throwing John into confusion. He, too, had lost his place.

So sudden was Mr. Curran's appearance in the drawing room that I jumped up from fright. He stood in the doorway, a black cloud of gloom hovering. "My acquaintance with Dr. Emmet is ended. He will no longer be welcome here."

The decree was issued and he retreated to his library, to soothe his melancholy with music. Dr. Emmet was a fast friend of long standing, and in the course of a single evening, the ties were severed. I could not imagine my brother Richard abandoning Robert with such ease. Neither could I abandon him when he was more in need of friends than ever.

SEVEN

The failed rebellion of 1798 touched my life in an indirect way. I never witnessed a single drop of blood spilled, but I was scarred by events just the same. Esteem for John Philpot Curran soared to the highest heights and I could not walk to church in Rathfarnham without one of our neighbors stopping me. Our Catholic tenants exhibited a certain reverence, as if Mr. Curran was almost a saint for his constant support of their religious liberty. Everywhere I went, I heard the praises sung for a barrister who clung to his unshakeable belief in British justice and equality. Certainly my father's enemies scoffed at his rhetoric, but there was an admiration hidden behind their mocking. So, too, did I come to admire my father for his fevered attempt to defend the leaders of the insurrection. Who would not, when his arguments were printed in broadsides and quoted by notable gentlemen.

In short, I believed his words, as did the young men who flocked to the drawing room discourses presented by the illustrious Mr. Curran.

Within the seemingly serene confines of The Priory we passed sleepless nights as the rebels were outed and rounded up. Richard was threatened for a time, due to his association with Valentine Lawless. The son of Lord Cloncurry was a frequent visitor to The Priory, sharing the liberal views of Mr. Curran, and would pay for his opinions with confinement in the Tower for over a year without being convicted of anything. Affiliation with a liberal was cause for suspicion, and fear of spies was everywhere. For that reason, Mr. Curran and Mr. McNally anointed Richard as their counselor and confidante, to better safeguard the defense's strategy. It was imperative that the Crown not have any idea what tack would be taken, in the event that some technicality might be found or a paid government witness outed.

As for the guilt of the accused, there was no doubt. Their employment of Mr. Curran was less a question of legal defense than a matter of eloquence. They knew they would hang, but the sacrifice would not be in vain if a skilled orator like my father could somehow reach the ear of the King or his ministers. The arguments that Mr. Curran had made for years in Commons were given a fresh airing in a different setting. So tireless was his effort that he was exhausted by the brutal battle. After the trials ended, he departed for a month in England to recuperate at the home of the Earl of Moira, formerly Lord Rawdon, a British officer despised by the American rebels during their recent revolution. For the first time, I allowed myself to believe that the worst was over and we were safe.

In November, Mr. Curran returned to the battlefield when he defended Theobold Wolfe Tone, one of the leaders of the failed uprising. Despite threats to his life, my father held to his faith in the rule of law and fought to spare the life of another man who dared to act against the tyranny of a corrupt regime. His words failed to sway the jury or the judges, but we all knew that Mr. Tone's fate was sealed from the first.

On the day of the execution, Mr. Curran went back to the court to ask that his client be provided with proper surgical care after Mr. Tone cut his own throat rather than give the mob the satisfaction of watching him executed. As usual, his request for humane treatment was denied so that the Crown could show how very cruel it could be towards those who dared to stand up for their rights. The message was not received in all quarters. If anything, the rebels grew more hardened and more quiet.

Gloom hung over us like a cloud in early 1799, with Mr. Curran's absence turning us into orphans. Mrs. Fitzgerald gave birth to a second son, which merited little more than a brief mention in the letter that Mr. Curran sent to Richard. It was evident that our father was too distracted by the rumblings of revenge that reverberated from Westminster. As if the recent rebellion called for harsher, more punitive measures, our British overlords dissolved the Irish Parliament and introduced the Act of Union, putting an end to self-rule. Mr. Curran felt the cold wind blowing and made sure that Richard was called to the bar before political intrigue altered the landscape. What should have been a happy time was marred by uncertainty, when our father could not predict what an act of union might entail and what it would mean for his fortunes. Melancholy grew like a noxious weed in his soul and sadness flavored his correspondence.

Instead of establishing himself in the law, Richard found excuses to spend time with us in the country. On a particularly fine September day, he invited his sisters to go out walking, a signal that he had something to say to us privately. We could not say which of the servants were loyal to Mr. Curran and which were neutral, so we exercised caution indoors out of fear that a report might be made to our father. There had been cross words between Richard and Mr. Curran about sedition and lack of respect for the government, with Richard's opinions judged to be bordering on high treason. The last such incident sank Richard into a deep malaise, one that he was only just recovering from when we set out to take the air.

To my surprise, we encountered Robert Emmet on the road coming towards us. Our families were strangers as I understood Mr. Curran's command, but the way that he greeted Richard suggested an enduring friendship. "The initial battle was lost," Robert said. "The war continues."

"When do you leave for Scotland?" Richard asked.

Thomas Addis Emmet was serving his sentence in a place that was not easy for his family to reach, further punishment for a conspirator who organized rebel bands in the countryside. That Thomas was still connected to the United Irishmen stationed in France became apparent as the gentlemen spoke, discussing the resurrection of a rebellion that had gone underground. Robert was to be the courier between the rebels jailed in Scotland and their colleagues in Paris, ferrying intelligence that would be used to organize an invasion more vast than the pitiful little band of French soldiers that landed on the west coast in '98 and were captured before their boots were dry. The idea of a full-scale attack, with an army sweeping up through Cork, Waterford and Wexford, was magnificent to contemplate. The Catholics flocking to overthrow the King, the Lord Chancellor in chains bound for a French prison, it all sounded so glorious when Robert and Richard described the hopes of the United Irishmen.

"Then, too, I should like to travel to Europe to see what opportunities I might find," Robert said. He turned to me and said, "I intend to enter into the professions, rather than accept an unjust banishment. I am not made to be a tanner, Miss Sarah, although my father would willingly fund such an endeavor."

We continued on, with Robert dropping back so that he could walk at my side and recite a few poems he had composed, seeking my opinion. His zeal for his mission was as contagious as a fever and I found myself flushed with a shared excitement that was increased by the thrill of tasting the forbidden fruit. No Curran was to socialize with an Emmet, but here we all were, conversing openly, and on such a dangerous topic. I complimented him on his stirring verse that so beautifully expressed his love and concern for his native land, now held captive by an increasingly brutal power. He promised to correspond with Richard, who could receive mail without interference, unlike an unmarried woman whose every move was scrutinized. It would be up to Richard, then, to correspond with his sisters, a task that my brother accepted with mock gravity.

"To further an alliance of which I most heartily approve," Richard said. "Even though it will require that I spend every waking hour at a desk with paper and pen, ignoring my clients."

A dissection of the failed uprising brought us well beyond our planned distance, into a village that bore the scars of the recent fighting. Scorch marks hinted at a torching of thatched roofs, and two hovels were tumbled down to a pile of rock. An eerie silence hung like fog over what remained, as if the widows and orphans who survived were gone to ground like a hunted fox. I had the distinct sensation that we were being watched.

We bid farewell to Robert and turned for home, hastening our step when we spotted the Curran carriage approaching the gate. There would be no supper for us if we were not seated at the table at precisely five o'clock, and it made no difference if our father was not expected. We were to maintain his standards in his absence, and we did not want him to know that we did what we pleased when he was away. The chaos of the Curran children assembling provided sufficient cover for our less than timely arrival, while the tablecloth masked the state of our dusty clothes. There was no time to change or even wash our faces, a mark of disrespect perhaps but an unfortunate necessity.

I was summoned to the library that evening and I feared the worst, but Mr. Curran only wished to speak to me in regard to my debut, which had been neglected due to the press of his duties and the unsettled state of the country. "I have been corresponding with your mother," he said and the shock of it shook me to the core. So many questions, but I dare not ask one. To show the slightest interest in the woman who was dead to me was treachery, punishable by social death. "And have assured her that everything will be done to launch you properly into the market. That being said, it would not be wise to invite people here who would invariably dredge up some painful episodes from the past. Therefore, I have made arrangements for you to come out with the daughter of my old friend Mr. Lambart, of Wicklow."

"Will my sisters join me, sir?" I asked. For as much as Amelia denied it, she relished parties as much as Eliza, and I knew that Eliza was desperate for some fun.

"I cannot afford to clothe all of you," he said. "It is all I can do to feed everyone. Do you not have frocks enough? Do your sisters not have ball gowns that go unused? It is time that you learned to make do, to prepare you for the time when your husband is in straightened circumstances as I am now, and you must manage his household with economy."

"Yes, sir," I said. "When will I go?"

"You will leave after Christmas. The ball is scheduled for New Year's Day. Some tell me it is a propitious time, with the arrival of a new century. May you have better luck than either of your sisters. But exercise great care. Do not be swept up in emotions that are not lasting. Neither should you fall victim to tender words from a man who is seeking advancement through a connection to me."

Like my sisters, I was not so much concerned with finding a mate as in enjoying myself as much as possible while I could. The atmosphere at The Priory was stifling, a closed cage that had little to offer in the way of frivolity. Mr. Curran did not wish to spend the money needed to host dinners or card parties, not when such activities did not directly benefit him. He shared his board and cellar with those who wanted to listen to him expound on the weighty matters of the day, and if some budding barrister took an interest in one of the Curran ladies, that was as useful as an expensive ball to provide an introduction to a suitable husband. With such a limited roster of young gentlemen it was no wonder that Amelia had not found a man she could tolerate. She had an artist's soul and a passion for painting, two qualities that she would never find in those who came to worship at the Curran altar. Even Eliza was beginning to despair, and had urged me to develop a wide circle of friends who would extend invitations and so expand my marital horizons. Cast a wide net, she said, and be a fisher of men in every possible sea. Better to throw back the excess than haul in an empty net from a small puddle.

"Your brother should also benefit from any connection you might make," he continued. "With so many considerations, I trust you will not act with haste, but neither should you dawdle. When you are young, time stretches out long before you, but you soon come to find that time is behind you and you are too late."

"Yes, sir, I will weigh all matters," I said.

"Have you given any thought to what sort of gentleman might suit you? Or have you perhaps set your cap for someone already?"

What men had I met at The Priory except those who yearned to reap the wisdom of John Philpot Curran? They knew more about me than I did about them, except for Richard's friends, who were only just entering their professions and were far from ready to take a wife. As for the sort of man I might choose, I wanted my life's partner to be kind and thoughtful, a gentle soul who would treat me with respect. I wanted, I realized, a man like Robert Emmet.

"No, sir, indeed I have not decided at all," I said.

"Remember, a handsome face is not so attractive in a few months time if the pocket is empty," he said. "Do not be swayed by the facade, but examine the underlying structure. Be sure it is sound, and you greatly increase your chances for future happiness."

With my lanky black hair and dark eyes, I was no great beauty, and would not expect a handsome man to even notice me. There was no danger on that score. The danger was in the foundation on which the underlying structure of my suitor was built. I never considered the vulnerability of sand as opposed to a solid base of bedrock.

EIGHT

After spending Christmas at The Priory, I was put into a post chaise and sent off to the Lambart home in Wicklow where I was made welcome by a family tied with my own through politics, the thread that bound me to everyone I would meet. If even half of them had gone off to fight in 1798, the British would have been severely outnumbered.

Within minutes of my arrival I made a friend in Caroline Lambart, a somewhat giddy girl who was much given to reading romances. We compared our families and our homes and found them nearly equivalent, as was our determination to have a grand time while our candles burned brightest. It was appropriate, then, that the Lambart drawing room glowed with the light of dozens of candles on the first night of 1800 when we were launched upon the adult world.

The *merveilleuses* has passed from fashion and so, too, had Eliza's ball gown. I did what I could to reduce the volume of the skirt but my sewing had been done in haste. The lace trimmings were a bit worn as well, and I felt rather shabby, like someone's poor relation. My hair was the very image of the latest style from Paris, however, with a mass of curls that had been cooked into my hair with a hot iron. In the crowded ballroom, I hoped that my dress would go unnoticed if my head was *au courant*. Caroline was confident that the gentlemen had no interest in frocks, not when their gaze was sure to end in the vicinity of my bosom. We were coming out into society, she said, and coming out meant exposing skin previously covered. The girls we had been in the morning would be transformed into women when we stepped into the drawing room.

I had little time to consider my appearance, at any rate, because it took all my concentration to remember the litany of names as Mrs. Lambart made introductions in a sea of people. My throat closed up with nerves as I struggled to make conversation, an art that was foreign to me. While Caroline chattered on about the most inane of subjects, I stumbled over words and failed to put together enough sentences to seem something other than a simpleton. Where was a person like my father, someone who dominated the stage and managed to do all the talking? I stammered and wished with all my heart that I could wake up and find myself at The Priory, far from the demands I was failing to meet.

"And of course you must know Mr. Emmet," Mrs. Lambart said, leading me to the side of a friend who was as welcome to me at that moment as a rope thrown to a drowning girl.

"Have you seen your brother?" I asked.

"Not yet. I was going to leave sooner, but then Mr. Lambart issued an invitation and I had to see you again. I may not return," Robert said.

"What do you mean?" I asked, only to find Mr. Lambart at my side with another gentleman interested in an introduction.

"Miss Curran, may I present Lieutenant Sturgeon, who has been captivated by your remarkably fair complexion and dark-haired beauty," Mr. Lambart said. "Lieutenant, this is Mr. Emmet, who is as adept at mathematics and science as you are."

There followed the expected sort of inanity, in which Robert and Lt. Sturgeon discussed their mutual interest in chemical experiments and numerical certainty before shifting into a dissection of geometry as applied to cannon fire. The lieutenant was more than an officer in the Royal Artillery. He was a student of warfare, one who sought to use scientific principles to improve military tactics. I was glad to be relieved of the loathsome task of chattering, content to listen to the gentlemen talk about topics that had nothing to do with me.

I took advantage of the interlude to scan the room in search of handsome faces or glances cast my way, only to notice that some men were pointedly ignoring me. That I was not the prettiest girl in the room was a given, but neither was I ugly, except for the freckles sprinkled across my nose and cheeks. A few sidelong glances provided as much explanation as I needed. In an old gown and Eliza's slippers that I had stuffed with cotton wadding to make smaller, I looked like some bog-trotter. The humiliation was almost unendurable but there was no escape from the stifling drawing room and the sly, mocking grins.

The mob shifted and I tried to fade into the wallpaper but Lt. Sturgeon took my hand for the dance. He all but forced me to step through a reel, putting my dreadful clothing on display for all to see, but there was no avoiding his request without lapsing into utter rudeness. We stood across from each other, waiting for the music to begin, and he launched into what I assumed was a courtship ritual.

"My late uncle, the Marquis of Rockingham. was an admirer of your father, Miss Curran," he said. "They were aligned in Dublin Castle, particularly in regard to the emancipation issue. Like many in my family,

I might add. But we are not to discuss politics or religion, are we, but safe topics like the weather. I find it rather cold. Do you find it rather cold, Miss Curran?"

"It is January, sir," I said, and was mercifully saved from having to elaborate by the movement of the dancers.

A new partner for the next dance put me in company with a somewhat dull fellow whose name I forgot as soon as it was mentioned. Robert managed to extract me from further misery when he brought me a glass of punch and led me off to a far corner where we could talk in relative peace.

"You said you were not returning," I said.

"I will not be pushed down into the trades by my political enemies, who would ruin my life if they could," he said. His dark eyes flashed with fire and determination. "If I do not seek opportunity elsewhere, then I am admitting defeat. I have considered emigrating to America."

"Mr. Tone tried to make a new life there," I said, recalling an anecdote my father shared when he was defending Theobald Wolfe Tone on a charge of treason. "He thought that the Americans were as enmeshed in a social hierarchy based on wealth as we are caught up in a hierarchy based on blood. More's the pity, Robert. He would not have died if he had found a way to accept what is nothing more than human weakness. What is a man to do with his ambition but act on it and advance himself?"

"And what is so wrong with allowing a man to rise through his own effort, instead of binding him to his station because of an accident of birth? Why must we be cursed with the offspring of the mad king when there are countless men more qualified to rule?"

"But to leave your family," I said. "How will you stand it?"

"That I must leave others behind weakens my resolve," he said. "There is one bond that would hold me back, but I cannot know if it is truly a bond or merely a wish on my part."

"I would hope that you do not abandon your principles for the sake of something that may not exist," I said. My father's ardor towards Catholic equality had certainly cooled after Parliament was dissolved, and he was less vocal in his opposition since the Act of Union was first read. Fear of the consequences, which he had witnessed first-hand, was weakening him. The greatest consequence would be a loss of prestige which depended on the good graces of those in power. He was not inclined to sacrifice more than he already had.

"We cannot know what the future holds," he said. He lowered his voice to a whisper. "Perhaps liberty is waiting for the right moment to land. After meeting with Thomas I will travel to France. But I can say no more."

"No, do not, not here," I said. His passion could get him into great danger, despite the fact that many of the Lambart guests were liberal in their thinking. Given the state of war and the recent insurrection, his European sojourn could be considered an act of treason. There was no telling who might be a spy for Earl Clare.

The press of my duties intruded into our conversation. There were many other introductions to be made, followed by dances and brief conversations that exhausted me. A walk to Dublin would have been less tiring than the exertion of speaking to strangers who were as empty of topics as I was. Foolishly I let my dance card fill up and before long I was ready to drop from fatigue, my feet aching in the too-large slippers. I hoped to find Robert later when the refreshments were served, but he was not to be seen in the dining room. Instead, I clung to Caroline's side while she entertained a clutch of potential beaux. Gentlemen whose names I could not recall brought me tidbits in a way that reminded me of birds courting and I found myself laughing as they competed with one another to gain my favor. Fatigue fell away and I found that I did not want the evening to end. The attention was intoxicating.

I had promised Mr. Lambart a dance and he approached to take my hand, only to be taken aside by a woman who had been studying me for most of the night. After exchanging a few words, they approached together and I was introduced to Mrs. Robert Wilmot, a friend of Mr. Cooper Penrose of Cork, one of the wealthiest men in the county. She took both of my hands in hers and held them for a moment, her warm smile putting me at ease. "You are more fortunate than poor Amelia, who favors the Currans," she said. "I see your mother in you. Very much."

"Thank you," I said. My feelings about my mother were too tangled to unravel, and my sentiments must have been written on my face.

"You are as I thought you would be," she said, her eyes taking me in from head to toe. "The picture of parsimony ill-placed. Of that I shall not speak. I will only report that your debut has been a triumph, and that you are well on your way to making your own escape."

"There is some interest in me?"

"My dear child, a mother's love never dies. In time your hard heart will soften, now that you are out in society and exposed to the world." Mrs. Wilmot took my hands again. "For your sake, she remains in the shadows, enduring the pain that cannot be eased, leaving to others what she would have done if circumstances had been different. There, I have said what needs to be said and must turn you over to the gentlemen who clamor for a chance to touch your hand. We shall see more of each other, I am sure."

For the rest of the evening I was in a fog, dreaming of a reunion with my mother only to imagine the dressing down I would deliver. I wanted to see her again and then I never wanted to clap eyes on her. The agitation in my mind translated into an agitation in my stomach and I had to step outside for a breath of fresh air. The chill of January cleared my head, muddled as I was by too much punch and overly-rich food that was not regular fare at home. I returned to the ball for one last dance before Caroline and I retired, to spend a sleepless night discussing the hidden meaning of every phrase uttered by every gentleman who spoke to us. Who might be a serious beau, or who was only a fortune-hunter? Was it wise to entertain a soldier's courtship, in light of the uncertain state of war? Did it matter if a man was dull if he was wealthy? We must have kept the entire house awake with our giggling.

"Mr. Emmet is enthralled, you know," Caroline said.

"What nonsense. I have known him all my life. He used to drive his father when Dr. Emmet came to treat us."

"Mr. Emmet is in love with you."

"Our fathers have had a falling out," I said. Could it be true, or was Caroline creating romantic notions? She had a tendency towards excess emotion. "Indeed, if my father knew I had spoken to Robert he would be furious."

"We are true sisters, Sarah, with a secret to be kept in our hearts. Not a word to anyone, you may count on my discretion."

"He has no fortune," I said. "As for position, he lost that as well. Cast down by politics and the cruelty of Earl Clare, punishing the father by harming the son"

"There are no Tories here to spoil things," Caroline said. "Can you imagine one of them at table with your father? An argument would erupt without question. Perhaps blows. Or a demand for satisfaction. I do not think we need worry about such a catastrophe. Most of that sort would not consider you as suitable anyway. I mean, what with your mother and all that dirty laundry that was aired. Some women have the longest memories. We saw enough of that this evening, did we not?"

NINE

My first season flew by in a crush of activities, from grand balls to small card parties, from country seats to town homes. Richard took it upon himself to bring me to Dublin so that I might benefit from exposure to a big city with a larger pool of unmarried gentlemen, but I was weary of barristers who sought a leg up through connections to a powerful man. Despite my lack of interest, the chatter was fascinating.

Wherever we went, and whoever we spoke to, the conversation revolved around the hated Act of Union that was going to become law despite the strong protests of the liberals. The Crown had no shame in handing out peerages to any MP willing to vote in favor of the act, which fueled resentment. Gentlemen without sympathy for Lord Fitzgerald's uprising voiced strong opposition to the loss of Irish self-rule, coming as it would through bribery and dirty dealing. Mr. Curran was too principled to even consider such a despicable gift, but still he sank into deep gloom, knowing that others were reaping unjust rewards while he, the worthy one, went without. One day he would rise, I believed, carried on the crest of a revolutionary wave that was forming in Paris.

My last encounter with Robert, before he left for Scotland to see his brother, was artfully arranged by Richard. He suggested that we tour the city, despite the brisk cold that numbed our cheeks within minutes. In company with Amelia and Eliza, we called on John in his rooms at Trinity College, a dusty and disheveled nook that smelled of cabbage. From the school we made our way to the shops, where we ladies were to purchase enough fabric for two gowns each. Mr. Curran described it as an act of generosity, but I had reason to believe it was the sting of embarrassment that loosened the purse strings. I had overheard a few matrons comment on the rundown appearance of Mr. Curran's daughters at Lord Kilwarden's ball, the discussion taking place within Mr. Curran's hearing. Excited at the prospect of velvets and silks, I hurried my pace to reach the drapers before the best goods disappeared. More than once, Amelia had to ask me to slow my pace.

I turned a corner and there was Robert, loitering in front of a shop. We decided to stop for tea so that we could converse at leisure, and escape the vigilance of the general public, any one of whom could be an acquaintance of our father. If Mr. Curran got wind of our meeting, that would be the end of a new gown and probably the social season. Knowing that I might never see Robert again, I decided that it was a risk worth taking.

After the usual inquiries about family and health, Robert leaned forward. "If you do not wish to become a part of this, then you should leave now," he said.

"We are all united in whatever you do," Amelia said. Judging by the look of alarm that crossed Eliza's face, I was not so sure of the unity.

"This is more than recognizing an Emmet," Richard said.

"By remaining here, and providing cover for this meeting, you put yourselves into danger," Robert said. "What we are about to discuss can never be revealed. So do not be ashamed to walk away and leave us. Indeed, there is no shame in it."

My sisters exchanged glances while I lifted my cup and sipped with as much calm as I could muster. By inviting us to join this vague conspiracy, the gentlemen were putting us on an equal footing, entrusting us to keep their secrets. Ladies of our class would never be suspected, and would a woman not make a perfect messenger? "We must all do our part, no matter how small," I said. "To cower in fright would be a greater shame. Our father never cowered from those who threatened him when he defended the rebels. I would rather be assassinated than intimidated."

"Words, nothing but words," Richard said. "What of actions? Would he have been so bold if he had been called on to take action?"

"Words, yes, but there is truth in them," Amelia said.

"Very well," Eliza said. "If only to know what you intend to do, though we retain the right to argue against something foolish."

Robert took a small pamphlet from his coat pocket and pushed it across the table to Richard, who hid it away without a glance. "Ciphers will be necessary to communicate. There are two copies of a code that will be used, if necessary."

"You have heard the speeches in Commons," Richard said. "Do you believe that there is any chance that the Act of Union will not be made law in June?"

"There is always a chance," Eliza said. "If enough honest men stand up for their country and put Satan behind them."

"A peerage is too great a temptation," Amelia said.

"Let the rule of law play out," Robert said. "None will claim that we acted rashly. After the expected result comes to pass, we will be prepared to move."

Speaking in low tones, even though we were quite alone in the corner of the tea shop, Robert detailed his plan for the coming months. His brother was in prison, but still in limited contact with friends on the Continent. Robert would replace Thomas Emmet on the committee that was negotiating with France for aid, taking a page from the successful American rebellion. Once that aid was secured, it was a question of organizing an uprising that could be coordinated with Napoleon's invasion of England. I pinched my hand, sure that I was dreaming. Could it be that I, little Sarah Curran, would one day tell my children about the day that Ireland took its first steps toward liberty? The Curran family would gain their rightful place, the place that our father had been trying to reach since he was a poor student at Trinity, dreaming of a career in the law.

The rebellion was more of a concept than a strategy, but I had absolute confidence in Robert. He possessed a brilliant mind, especially for analysis. While Richard was high strung and more likely to act impetuously, Robert was one for careful plotting. Whatever role he might design for me, I stood ready to follow orders like a dutiful soldier. As a woman, I did not expect to be asked to do much. Indeed, there was little that I could do besides write letters. Even delivering notes was not easily done for one whose movements were dictated by social constraints. Yet I would not be wrong to demand that the rebellion also bring about change in the feminine sphere, if only as a reward to those of us who cast our lot with the partisans. With something to gain, I felt that I had nothing to lose.

Three women swore an oath that afternoon, an act that felt revolutionary in itself. The Curran sisters would never reveal what had passed across cups of tea in a quiet shop in Dublin, a solemn vow of silence. I did not realize how difficult a task I had set for myself until I was back in Rathfarnham, shortly after the Act of Union was declared law. Mr. Curran's guests were united in their outrage as they discussed events after supper, but divided by opinions as to the next course of action. Mr. McNally, who had joined my father in defending the United Irishmen, led me to believe that he was willing to take part in an uprising, and I found dangerous words sliding to the tip of my tongue. "If you wish to act on your anger," I managed to say, "then you do so at your peril."

"Would you weep over my body, Miss Sarah?" he asked, teasing me.

"At the loss of my father's dearest friend I would of course weep," I said.

"And if mourning a rebel was a crime?"

"She would plead tears of joy at the removal of such a dangerous brigand," Richard said. "And be celebrated throughout our falsely united kingdom."

"And so our mutual friend has left for Scotland," Mr. McNally said. "An Emmet family reunion. I understand that Dr. Emmet's health has suffered since his son's arrest, and then Robert's expulsion added to his burden."

"We do not speak of that family," Amelia said. I wanted to laugh at her remark, which was as much an obfuscation of the truth as any defense Mr. McNally might mount at the King's Bench. Years of practice trained her to appear obedient to Mr. Curran's dictates, but her plan to remain a spinster also meant she would forever be dependent on our father. Like a sailor, she had to toe the line when so commanded, or risk punishment. I had no desire to live my life in constant peril. Only marriage could save me, and married I would have to be.

When the drawing room grew too stuffy I retreated to the garden, to take stock of the roses that I continued to tend, if only to have a supply of fresh flowers to share with Gertrude. Richard joined me in a turn around the beds. "I have been ordered to London to forge new connections in the event that all our Irish interests are lost in the near future," he said.

"One cannot predict what will come to pass," I said. "I wonder if you will one day be charged with molding our future."

"Any new government would need new laws, and who better to write them than a man versed in the law?" He plucked a leaf and systematically shredded it. "I do not wish to maintain the current system of injustice, but until I am in a position to change it, I would be wise to follow the straight and narrow path that has been so well trod over the centuries."

"Your time in London will be part of a disguise, in other words?"

"I must confess that I am drawn to London for other reasons. A certain tender bond that tugs at my heart and pulls me back."

"Will there be an engagement soon?" I asked.

"Unless her husband divorces her, it would not be legally possible," he said.

I stopped in my tracks, too shocked to move on. To break up a home was immoral, and yet. Was it wrong to love a woman whose marriage was broken, her husband a drunkard or unbearably cruel? Chivalry had its place, but playing the role of rescuer, no matter how good the intention, could upend a man's career before he was launched. Richard was taking a dreadful chance on inciting yet another scandal. We did not need a fresh dose of notoriety, and I said as much.

"You have never been in love or you would not suggest I break it off," Richard said. "It is a mere dalliance, in any event. Something to pass the time."

"You should be attending to your work and not have leisure hours in need of passing," I said.

"Yes, study, so that I can follow in our father's footsteps," he said. The tone of his voice indicated a return to one of his frequent spells of deep melancholy, a temperament inherited from Mr. Curran.

"What news of our mutual friend?" I asked, to turn his mind to more pleasant thoughts.

From his pocket he retrieved a small note without an address, the top edge torn as if a single sheet had been used to write two letters. The script was unmistakably that of Robert Emmet, neat and compact, describing his arrival in Scotland and the reunion of the Emmet brothers. At the bottom was a sketch of a harp with broken strings, entangled with a willow bending under a powerful wind. He wanted my opinion on his design, which would be fashioned into a seal for use on official documents, to prevent the authorities from forging correspondence. He had been so enthusiastic when I took up the harp, and I saw his drawing as a sign of deep affection that he dare not express.

"So much is conveyed without words," I said. What might I say in reply that would not entrap me? Or did I want to be entangled like the storm-broken willow?

TEN

After two months in Scotland, Robert crossed the English Channel and made his way to Hamburg with a fellow revolutionary. I waited as he waited to hear from the French authorities, and when he was granted a passport to enter France, it took all my strength to hold my tongue. How I longed to say to those who mocked Dr. Emmet's love of the downtrodden, "His son was cast down by Earl Clare a few years ago and where is that young gentleman now? Soon to meet with Napoleon Bonaparte to discuss weighty matters of national importance." He moved in the highest echelons of society and was welcomed into the drawing rooms of nobility, a guest of the Marquise de Fortenay who had herself been a guest of the Emmet family after she fled the French Revolution. His descriptions of the people he met and the places he saw were as vivid as an artist's rendering, as if Jacques Louis David had sketched out the scenes for my amusement.

The wheels of diplomacy were slow to turn, as I discovered while waiting for imminent news that never came. It was not until April of 1801 that I was blessed with a much-needed distraction from the grinding worry about the unknown. Mr. Curran was prosecuting a case and felt that his daughters would benefit by mingling with the Penrose family. I was already acquainted with Mrs. Wilmot, a friend of Mr. Penrose, and I hoped to meet her daughter while in Cork. Greater than my own pleasure, however, was my happiness for Amelia. Mr. Penrose was a noted patron of the arts, and there was much that my sister could learn by viewing his collection. Then there were the Penrose daughters, close in age to Amelia and equally enamored with the fine arts. My eldest sister would have an opportunity, no matter how fleeting, to be in the company of women like herself, to find fresh inspiration for her paintings and fresh conversation that was not to had within the bounds of The Priory.

We arrived at Wood Hill, the Penrose estate on the outskirts of the city, and I was surprised to find a Quaker residing in such a lavish home. The walls were decorated with exquisite paintings, and the music room featured a trove of instruments that reflected a great love of song. "Two vices in which I have indulged," Mr. Penrose said. "And for which I was once read out of meeting. In my opinion, practicing one's faith is more important than adhering to the letter of the law like some Pharisee. My brethren did not agree, although we have managed to co-exist in the meetinghouse."

We picked our way around the army of workmen who were building a wing onto the house, where Mr. Penrose planned to install a collection of archaeological artifacts. The latest mania for ancient objects had been started by Napoleon Bonaparte after his conquest of Egypt, and our host confessed to the same affliction. "The only cure, I have found, is to submit," he said. "And so I maintain my robust good health into my old age."

Anne and Bessey Penrose were such kind, dear, sweet ladies, welcoming us with warmth and an easy manner. Indeed, I felt as if our presence was as much a delight for them as it was for us to be in their company. Over tea in the garden we shared common acquaintances and explored political opinions, which proved to be of the liberal persuasion. I had not seen Amelia so flush with life as she sat and sketched our little group of ladies. She let her charcoal fall, however, when it was explained in detail why Mr. Curran had been called to Cork.

Mr. Penrose had come to the aid of Mary Pike, a simple-minded girl whose father had left her a considerable fortune. When her mother fell ill, little Mary joined the Penrose household and became a favorite of Bessey. It was to be expected, then, that Bessey would accompany Mary to call on her mother in Cork after Mr. Penrose received a letter from Mrs. Pike's doctor that implied the poor old woman was soon to succumb. With theatrical pauses and a lowering of her voice, our narrator held us all spellbound as she described the fateful night when Mary was kidnapped at gunpoint by a local gentleman who had spent beyond his means and found a devious way to acquire capital. Eliza squeezed my hand ever tighter as Bessey detailed the hurried ride that they thought would bring them to Mrs. Pike's side, the two women in the coach praying to arrive in time. A group of masked marauders halted the coach, absconded with Mary, and left Bessey with the driver and a maid, the harnesses cut so that they had to walk all the way back to Wood Hill to summon help.

"Mr. Penrose organized a search, but it was only when a sympathetic maid brought Mary the pen and paper she demanded that she could write to her uncle for help," Mrs. Penrose said. "She wanted to go home, of course, and had no comprehension of what Sir Henry told her."

"As best as anyone could judge, he brought in a priest to marry them, and he tried to convince Mary that she was his wife but she would have none of it," Anne said. Our glances asked a question that no gentle lady would dare express. "From what Mary told us, we have every reason to believe she was alone in a locked room that night. Her letter reached us the next morning and she was rescued immediately."

"The Crown prosecuted Sir Henry, but such incompetence," Mrs. Penrose said. "He ran from his home before he could be arrested, but then he hid in plain sight in Cork. For two years, free, after committing a capital felony. The remedy in the law is hanging for such a crime."

"Neither did he pay any price for terrorizing me," Bessey said. "I might have been murdered by his accomplice, or attacked on the road as I tried to make my way home."

"But as all ended well, we were willing to look the other way," Mrs. Penrose said. "Sir Henry, however, had the audacity to write to Mary recently and claim that his conduct towards her had been honorable. What changed Mr. Penrose's heart irrevocably were the threats issued by Sir Henry, to besmirch Mary's honor and destroy her reputation if she persisted in prosecuting him."

"What was Mary but a helpless orphan, taken against her will? Yet by turning to the law, she risks destruction at the hand of the kidnapper. My father saw his duty as a Christian, and as a gentleman whose duty is to fight for the weakest among us," Anne said. "Evil prospers when good men do nothing, Mr. Curran has said. It was impossible, then, to not act."

After supper we retired to the music room, where the Penrose sisters displayed their talent at violin and cello before insisting that their guests honor them with favorite tunes. Mr. Penrose was bursting with excitement when I selected the harp, an instrument he purchased in the hope that someday he would entertain a guest who knew how to play it. I could not do justice to such a fine instrument, lacking the skill that I thought was required. As for my voice, I felt my throat grow dry as I imagined failing in front of my father, my poor light reflected on him. Beads of sweat sprouted on my lip and my hands grew slick. "I am but a poor player, sir," I said. "A novice, truly."

"You are too modest," Amelia said. "Do not disappoint Mr. Penrose, Sarah."

My fingers rested on the strings but were slow to respond when I tried to move them. Like a child at its first lesson I plodded along, my singing as lively as a cart horse clopping down a rutted road. My pronunciation of the Irish lyrics was muddled, and if anyone listening understood the language they would have known I was making a stew of the words. I struggled through two verses and the chorus before finding a convenient point to stop. The enthusiastic applause of the Penrose clan had me near tears, so ashamed was I at my poor performance.

"Please, Miss Sarah, you must teach me," Anne said. Her face reflected all sincerity. She genuinely wanted me to instruct her when I had demonstrated a complete lack of talent. "We live for music in this house, as you might have guessed, and if I could play even half as well as you, I should be quite content."

And so we passed our afternoons while Mr. Curran and Richard were at the Cork Assizes, awash in Irish airs and Mozart sonatas. Both Anne and Bessey were attentive students, and by the time Mr. Curran delivered his closing speech, we ladies had organized ourselves into a little orchestra that gave its first and only performance at Wood Hill on a soft April evening. Our audience was rather large that night, as Mr. Penrose threw open his home to a variety of guests who came from Cork to meet the acclaimed John Philpot Curran, the man whose rhetoric cast a spell over a jury, and cast Sir Henry Hayes into seven years transportation for abduction and attempted defilement. The evening was lively, bordering on raucous, and not at all what I expected from a Quaker household.

In contrast to the festive mood, Richard was sullen and brooding. He shared portions of Mr. Curran's speech in a flat tone, as if he were reading from a book in a disinterested and distracted manner. "Justice may weep, but she must strike where she ought not to spare," he said. "What would I have said? 'Do not let Sir Henry's position in society influence you, gentlemen of the jury.' Where is the power in that phrase to influence the panel to bend to my will? I will never be a respectable barrister, Sarah. I do not have the words. I do not have the mind for it. I will be a failure."

"You will find the words in time," I said. "You will find the words of a new constitution, and you will find the words of new statutes and laws. Be your own man. Find your own place."

"There is no place for me."

I suspected he had taken a little too much drink, which had become a habit with him after Robert Emmet left for the Continent. A good friend was needed to talk sense, not a younger sister who was enjoying a delightful evening in good company. "Did our own father not falter at first? It is no easy task, to speak with eloquence. Be patient. Who knows what tomorrow may bring?"

"Tomorrow may bring a treaty, I have heard," Richard said. "The grand coalition may soon be down to a single member, and will Bonaparte be so keen to fund our venture when he faces England alone?"

"If he plans to conquer England, I would think he would be more willing to add an ally," I said.

"Would we be an ally, or another conquest? Do we throw off one tyrant to acquire another?"

"Do you think the same men who support our cause would turn their coats?" I asked.

"In matters of the purse, Sarah, a man will turn his coat as often as needed to secure his income," Richard said. "Not all men, of course. Mr. Emmet would never waver."

I loved my brother and it broke my heart to think that he was suffering from self-doubt and a loss of confidence. There was no cheering him when he fell to the bottom, weighed down by an excess of strong spirits. "Is this any time to fret over matters that may or may not occur?" I asked. "Come now, tell me all about the trial. How did Sir Henry appear? Did he shake with fear? And when the verdict was read, what was his reaction? Transportation, Richard, seven years on the far side of the world. And for a man of influence. Were there tears, perhaps?"

He drifted out of the doldrums once he had satisfied my curiosity about the courtroom scene and described the mood of those who sat through the trial and continued to argue the case after the judgment was handed down. It was when he was describing the way Mr. Curran accepted the accolades of the crowd that he paused to recall something important he was supposed to convey.

"What was it? Ah, yes, we were walking towards the carriage when we spotted a group of soldiers loitering near a tavern and our father charged me to inform you that a military man had asked for permission to correspond with you last year, a request refused because, to quote the estimable Mr. Curran, a soldier makes a poor husband. Someone must have brought up the fighting in Alexandria, the heavy toll of dead and wounded. He would not see his daughter made a widow."

"The gentlemen I have met are all men of means, as best as I can judge," I said. "The truth is, an officer cannot help Father become a government minister, unless I caught the eye of the Duke of York himself."

"There is another more deserving of you," Richard said. "And on his account I am in a position to help you."

That night, I climbed into bed and found that I could not sleep. Neither could my sisters, who glowed with the happiness of young ladies admired and praised. For Amelia, the conversation was brilliant, the opportunity to speak her mind and make use of her intelligence so stimulating that her eyes would not close. Eliza was the object of interest from two local families, although both were Quaker and differences in religious faith posed difficulties for any future consideration. My circle of dear friends came to include Mrs. Wilmot's daughter Kate, and my connection to Wood

Hill was made fast with the love I felt for the Penrose sisters. We were inseparable for the remainder of my stay, often walking in the gardens and chatting about the difficulties faced by women in a world ruled by men who often did not notice us underfoot. Never did one of us suspect that Wood Hill would soon become a sanctuary for me.

ELEVEN

The honor of my presence was requested by Anne Penrose for a summer fortnight, but Mr. Curran declined. My father was complaining of expenses in 1801, with the cost of maintaining so many children an unwelcome burden. Political failures weighed heavily on his mind, and he debated between decamping for America or England, the utter defeat of his faction rendering him too melancholic to take action in either direction. So long had he nurtured a dream of a liberal government ascending, showering him with his much deserved rewards, but government was erased from Ireland in a single act. He was quite lost, without a seat in Parliament or political influence to provide an anchor.

The Curran sisters remained at The Priory, where our worn frocks would not be seen. We were cut off from society, except for the rare occasion when a neighbor invited us to a function where my sisters hoped to meet potential suitors but came home disappointed. Eliza was cross and short-tempered, but if Amelia felt the sting of being ignored, she did not show it. She was shaping herself to fit the mold of Anne Penrose, who was quite content with books and music and felt no need of a husband. Neither did Amelia wish to have children of her own, not when she took it upon herself to raise Will and James so that they would not be left to fend for themselves like wild animals. She would marry her art, she said. She would become a painter and there was no room for distractions in such a pursuit.

The isolation would have been more endurable if Richard had been with us, but he was trying to establish himself in the law and had no time for long walks in the country. He spent some time in London with Valentine Lawless after the gentleman was released from the Tower, managing some small legal matters that did not require soaring rhetoric to sway judges. The work was to his liking, it seemed, and my brother planned to accompany the future Lord Cloncurry to France until Mr. Curran stepped in. It was one thing for our father to associate with known traitors, but quite another for his son to be engaged by a suspected one. Richard's dalliance with a stage actress was likely a reaction to being thwarted, as evidenced by his boasting of malicious gossip that stung Mr. Curran's pride.

Little news came from Robert Emmet, but then again, there was no news to tell. He gave more hours over to long strolls in the gardens of the Tuileries than to meetings with French officials. The First Consul had other urgent matters to occupy his mind, with the crafting of treaties that upended the grand coalition. Who was Mr. Emmet, after all, but a very young representative of a very small country that did not signify in the greater schemes of Napoleon Bonaparte. My mind often wandered to some hazy future where I was the wife of an Irish hero, the mistress of a great house, receiving diplomats in a drawing room noted for its musical entertainments. I prayed for success, and soon.

Reports of the peace treaty disrupted my happy reveries. Richard came to Rathfarnham to share Robert's letters, a litany of disappointments. After months of drifting from one bureaucrat's office to the next, the Irish delegation had gained nothing. Financial backing for another uprising never materialized, lost in a fog of vague promises and shifting strategies. Robert did not trust the French, and believed that their help would come with too many strings attached, yet what choice did he have but to take what might be offered? Then the peace treaty was signed in March of 1802 and the state of war was ended. Whatever progress Robert might have made was undone with the stroke of a pen.

"The British government has decided to release some of the prisoners who were under arrest at the time of the insurrection," Richard said. "It looks as if Thomas Emmet will be forced to leave the kingdom, but at least he will be set free."

"What will he do?" Amelia asked. "Where is he to go?"

"To America, I suppose," Eliza said. "And didn't we come close enough to forced exile ourselves, when our father was in the throes of despondency? Thank goodness we were spared such an ordeal, to be torn from our roots and made to begin anew. To leave friends and family behind."

"All is now abandoned?" I asked.

"So it would seem," Richard said. "Robert may join his brother. He has no future here, that much is clear. You can be sure he has been followed since the minute he left England."

My every dream collapsed in an instant. Fighting back tears, I hurried off to visit the garden and speak to Gertrude. She was the only one I could tell, the only sister who would listen to my sorrows and not mock or criticize. Before I could tie my bonnet under my chin, Richard caught up to me. We were going for a walk, he said, a long walk, and it did not matter if my legs were weary or I had a headache. It was a demand, not a request.

We were a mile from home when my brother finally opened his mouth. "There is a great deal of turmoil among the leaders," he said. "Lawless has been accumulating weapons at his father's warehouses in Rouen. And possibly storing arms at Lyons House in Kildare, with or without Lord Cloncurry's knowledge I could not say."

"If there are weapons, he anticipates armed rebellion," I said. "Would the First Consul undermine a peace treaty and come to our aid?"

"There are those who see this peace as temporary. Something will be done to renew hostilities and we will then proceed as before. Others like to believe that Bonaparte has conquered all he wishes to conquer and will be content with a throne."

"Those would be the people who think he is selling land to the United States because he wishes to divest of foreign properties," I said. The Royal Navy had made it impossible for the French to manage their colonies in North America, which would have been a logical reason to sell the Louisiana Territory to the nearest neighbor. The exchange had been much debated in our drawing room, and Mr. Curran's guests generally agreed that the First Consul was only interested in the money that would land in his coffers. War was an expensive business, and the French had been at war long enough to deplete their holdings. The Treaty of Amiens was nothing more than the cease-fire Bonaparte needed to replenish his stores. But others saw the Louisiana Territory as an asset that was liquidated to pay for the next round of conquest. The French had over-run all of Europe. All that remained was England. And Ireland.

"Robert is torn," Richard said. "He can be stubborn, once he sets his mind to a task. He does not wish to abandon the rebellion. At the same time, he understands that he cannot wait forever to establish himself. America, at least, offers him some opportunity."

"What advice would you give him?"

"To think about it before making a decision," Richard said. "Sarah, he would leave for New York City at once if you would go with him."

"You cannot mean it," I said. I had suspected that Robert Emmet was smitten, but he could not freely express his sentiments unless I hinted at a mutual feeling, which would not be proper for me to do until he was in a position to offer marriage. Robert had probed, using my brother as his instrument, but I had to tread carefully. There was Mr. Curran to consider, Mr. Curran who had cut off contact with Dr. Emmet and was not likely to reconsider his decision with haste.

"Of course it would be more than foolish to do so," Richard said. "A man with little income and no prospects is not a man to be considered seriously. Dr. Emmet is supporting him abroad, you know. The family home is being sold. Money is in short supply."

Blood pulsed in my ears, drowning out all sound. Months earlier, Richard talked of promoting the match and I believed that I had some hope of marriage. He had changed his tune, it seemed, but with good reason. Until revolutionary matters were settled, then, and Robert restored socially, I would be wise to entertain other suitors. Yet when I examined the crop of eligible bachelors in the country, I found the poor, the old or the dull. I had no choice, as I saw it, but to wait for Robert, who had to wait for the directors of the United Irishmen to decide on the next course of action. At the age of twenty, I had a few years to gamble. Should events fall into place, I would make the most brilliant match of the season. The risks were well worth the reward.

We headed for home, with Richard sharing the news from Robert's most recent letter. Our mutual friend was a busy man indeed, parading through one drawing room after another. With the peace came swarms of the curious, and Robert spent many evenings in the company of fellow Irishmen who were traveling both for pleasure and business. He attended the theater, he diplomatically entreated a French minister for aid; he sat through musical soirees, he probed and pushed and all but begged for an answer that could not be given with any certainty. The words he longed to hear, the money he desperately needed, were always just beyond his grasp. His frustration was evident in his missive, while I hoped to disguise my own. To think that my future happiness depended on the whim of a self-styled emperor. I hated Bonaparte more than any general in the King's army ever could.

"At any rate, he will not quit France until he has some idea as to England's future intentions towards Ireland. There is talk of reconciliation, perhaps some accommodations to be made to the Catholics. Yielding to demands, so that the reason for further rebellion is removed."

"I do hope he will pass this way if he does decide to emigrate," I said. "Surely he would say good-bye to his friends and family before leaving. How sad, Richard. His parents are so old. He will likely never see them again."

"The authorities must suspect that he is on a mission for the United Irishmen," Richard said. "He runs the risk of being arrested if he does show his face. Although they might just keep him under observation if they are sure he is taking himself out of the game. Yes, I do hope he pays us a call. I shall miss him terribly."

Mr. Curran's gig was turning through the gate when we reached it, giving an appearance of dutiful children awaiting their father's arrival. His guests for the evening followed behind in chaises or on horseback, a bevy of important gentlemen come to dine and discuss politics far into the night. Richard and I waited for the others to enter before following them into the house. Mr. McNally, in turn, waited for me to walk ahead of him.

"Richard, so glad you are here," he said. "We are to have some fun at the expense of Town Major Sirr. But that is a discussion to be savored over brandy. First I must compliment your sister, who has grown to be a beauty. Cutting a swath through the drawing rooms of Dublin, Miss Sarah? Is any man safe from your beguilement?"

"We keep to the country," I said. No witty retort came to mind, as much as I wanted to banter with my father's closest colleague. Clever phrases did not pop into my head until hours after the conversation had concluded.

"A great legal mind does not lend itself to concerns of a young lady's heart," he said. "Your situation may be somewhat unusual, but not so rare as to be unknown. Others enter society without a mother to lead the way. May I call in Mrs. McNally to assist in this delicate endeavor? She would welcome your company while I am away, and like most women of her set, she would relish the opportunity to scheme and plot and make introductions."

I had no interest in further introductions that Mr. Curran would find lacking and send packing, but I could hardly say as much to Mr. McNally. With as much grace as I could muster, I lied with a smile and assured him that I would be most grateful for the opportunity to explore the opportunities available in the city. He continued the discussion when he took me down to supper, seating himself at my right hand. Mr. McNally droned on, giving me his best advice, which was the same advice every young lady received. Find a man with a good income, aim level and avoid the disappointment of shooting too high, consider the heart rather than the face, and seek the counsel of older women who knew a gentleman's family. "You have a musical gift that is worth more than whatever allowance your father can settle on you," he said. "A gentleman will accept your sweet voice as a dowry more valuable than money. You are blessed with a fine figure and expressive eyes. There is no reason to settle for a lesser man when you have so much to offer."

At breakfast the next morning, Richard quizzed me on my long talk with Mr. McNally, a man not normally given to expansive chats with young ladies. I believed that it was Mrs. McNally who had instigated the conversation, which had everything to do with courtship. Indeed, what barrister would chatter about such a topic unless a badgering wife demanded it? "He wants me to be a companion for his wife while he travels. Like so many of our acquaintances, he intends to see France," I said. "She is probably the sort of lady who enjoys the intrigue of arranging matches. I must admit I would not mind playing the game a bit. I do enjoy dancing."

"You know that our father will deny your request because it will involve expenses," Richard said. "The cost of a post chaise alone will be prohibitive, and he is too proud to suggest that Mr. McNally send a conveyance to fetch you. No, you are destined to remain here while Mr. Curran gallivants across France."

"But isn't that a very expensive proposition?"

"Father is a very generous man when it comes to himself. He has made arrangements, anticipating a generous compensation from the lawsuit he has taken on."

I burned with the anger of injustice. I had no money and no means to earn any. If Mr. Curran would not pay for my needs beyond the most basic, I was powerless to change my situation. I understood that people like Mr. Penrose were much wealthier, and could afford to bring an entire family on a grand tour. But my father was not a pauper, and it was cruel to deny me the funds I would use to improve my chances of making an excellent match that would serve us all in the long run. His unending penny-pinching was short-sighted, as I saw it. If he did not marry off his daughters, he would have to support them, and surely that would cost more than the price of a few gowns and transportation to Dublin.

At such times, when I was being practical, I would recognize that accepting a gentleman lacking financial means was foolhardy. I would acknowledge the possibility that Robert might never ask for my hand. What I felt for Robert might not be love, in which case it made perfect sense to browse the offerings in the marriage market. How could I be sure, if I did not allow myself to be courted by others so that I could weigh commonalities and differences in our personalities? Even if Robert was the perfect match for me, I still wanted to delight in the brief time that a young lady was allowed to be carefree, in search of amusements and concerned only with herself. My desires would go unmet if I was trapped behind the walls of The Priory, growing old with my sisters, forever at the mercy of Mr. Curran's parsimony.

"Surely he would not deny Mr. McNally, a dear and trusted friend of long standing," I said.

"He already has. Last night, when we were discussing the lawsuit against Major Sirr. To his credit, Mr. McNally fought bravely on your behalf. The man was quite obsessed with the matter, in fact. He has more interest in your future than your own father."

I did not wish to discuss the situation any longer, and managed to change the subject when Eliza and Amelia came to the table. We were all fascinated by the potential for either great glory or utter disaster in the pending suit, which would see Mr. Curran prosecute the Dublin Town Major for false imprisonment. Major Sirr was the very sort of jobber that Mr. Curran despised, a man puffed up with self-importance that was made combustible by a generous dose of blind loyalty to authority. The fact that Mr. Curran had won an acquittal for one of the 1798 rebels had created a bitter enmity between the barrister and the Town Major. It was that enmity that stole Major Sirr's reason and led him to illegally arrest the unfortunate gentleman on trumped up charges, to undo the earlier acquittal. Much abused, the gentleman had to fight to gain his freedom. In the process, he wanted to make Major Sirr pay dearly for abusing power.

The case was heard that May, and Mr. Curran triumphed. His victory would prove to be short-lived, like the peace between England and France. The Town Major was a vindictive man who bided his time, waiting for the right moment to strike so that he could have his revenge. That time was not long in coming.

TWELVE

Mr. McNally was a successful barrister because he was persistent. His assault on Mr. Curran was unrelenting, and I was fortunate to enjoy three weeks with a kind lady who wanted nothing more than to make a match for me. Regimentals aplenty colored Dublin that summer, a corps of officers with little to do besides flirt shamelessly and disregard the single female with no dowry to speak of. For my part, I had no interest in winning the heart of a man who would be turned away by my father for the sin of being a soldier. Free to be myself, not concerned with creating the most favorable impression to improve my chances, I found the entertainment that much more delightful. I returned to The Priory with a trove of anecdotes to amuse my sisters.

Eliza was on her sickbed when I arrived, her nose red and cheeks flushed. Amelia was at war with Mrs. Fitzgerald, who had learned of illness and thought it was her duty to provide the sort of maternal care that was missing. My sister stood her ground, having been the de facto mother for the past several years, and would not yield. Our cook was on the verge of giving notice, caught as she was between competing menus and contrary demands. Richard tried to steer clear of the heated verbal battles, extending his protection to our brothers. The boys spent a great deal of time out of doors, no matter how wet the weather or how great the risk of illness. The dining room was bedlam and I avoided the worst of the unpleasantness by retreating to the bedroom where I nursed Eliza, leaving her side only to take the air in the garden. The fight went on around us, to be re-ignited when Eliza was strong enough to spend an evening in the drawing room.

"Father arrived in Dieppe," Richard said, reading from the letter that came that morning. "Taken ill, he says. Likely the rough crossing."

The boys that Mr. Curran referred to as his nephews, my illegitimate half-brothers, were pounding on the keys of the pianoforte. John had enough of their rude behavior and swatted their hands away, which infuriated Mrs. Fitzgerald. She delivered a stirring harangue about respect for one's elders, while Amelia countered with her own observations regarding respect for one's betters. With a grumble of disgust, Richard quit the room after his demands for silence went ignored, vowing to write to Mr. Curran and demand written proof of authority as his own assertions were questioned. Not one to be cowed by threats, Mrs. Fitzgerald chased after him, promising to write her own letter that would lay out the truth.

I bent to my embroidery, piercing the fabric where the coast of Ireland met the Atlantic Ocean. The outline of the map had taken some time to draw accurately on the muslin, while the color scheme required days to sketch. My love of Ireland and my dream of a free nation would be expressed in careful stitches that I would present to Robert as a gift to mark our wedding day, perhaps, or the day that he stood in Dublin Castle and proclaimed our liberty. No longer would my sewing be inconsequential, a few bits of decoration that meant nothing. I would make a piece of art worthy of display, a relic to commemorate our new republic.

"This is unendurable," John thundered. In a few strides he reached the window, where he stood looking out at the garden, hands clasped behind his back. "I have had my fill, I tell you. Let him disown me. What do I care?"

"We have all had our fill," Eliza said. Her hope of marrying a gentleman with interests in the West Indies had come to naught after Mr. Curran refused to consent to the union. He believed that any business conducted in the Caribbean islands involved slavery, to which he was adamantly opposed. There did not seem to be a man in all Christendom who could meet our father's requirements.

The border along the Irish Sea came alive in a delicate back stitch. I paused to consider the color combinations I might use to delineate each county, nothing too colorful to detract from the flowers around the border, but not too bland either. The compass rose would be sewn with satin stitch using rose-hued silk, while the lettering would be best worked in black. I rifled the sewing basket, hunting for the green threads to see how many different shades I had to work with, and how to combine them to achieve the proper effect.

"You, at least, can make your own way," Amelia said. Despite her talent, she was prohibited from taking commissions for her art work. A daughter receiving compensation was not acceptable to Mr. Curran. "Free to go, while we are prisoners."

My sister wanted to be an artist, but she was denied equality with men lacking a quarter of her talent. The rebellion could change all that, with liberty for all, including the ladies. Just as we once looked to France as an example of ordinary citizens throwing off the yoke of tyranny, so too would the world look to Ireland as it freed its female citizens from the tyranny of unjust society. My sisters were intelligent. Why were they not allowed to read the law or enter a profession? Why could Amelia not be as well regarded as Joshua Reynolds?

"There is a world out there to be explored," John said. "And tomorrow, I am going to leave this place once and for all."

Before Mr. Curran left for France, our younger brother had put forward a plan that contradicted our father's decree that his second son read the law. Having watched Richard struggle to establish himself, John had no desire to join an already overpopulated profession. There were too many barristers in Ireland, and no need for another, but the argument fell flat. A career in the army was ruled out because Mr. Curran would not buy his son a commission.

"What will you do?" I asked.

"The senior Mr. Curran is not the only one with interests," John said. "I am running away to sea, where all ungrateful sons go to escape a domineering father. I should do well, don't you think? Trading such a father for a domineering captain will be easy."

"A common sailor? Really, John, you cannot be that desperate," Amelia said.

"No, not a common sailor. I enter the service as a midshipman. I have friends who have done me a good turn, thanks in large part to a captain who sees the end of the peace coming up fast. More than one commander is preparing to ship a full crew at the very moment hostilities resume. And I will be on one of those ships, making for the Mediterranean or the South Sea or anywhere but this cursed place."

"I wish you would stay," I said.

"Sooner or later I must go," he said. John took my hands and gave them an affectionate squeeze. "Perhaps I can find you a captain. Or an admiral. Wish me well, Sarah. It grieves me to see you sad."

John's departure was a moment of great sorrow, throwing Richard into a deep melancholy that held him in bed, nearly lifeless. He wrote at once to Mr. Curran, hoping that something could be done to keep John from risking his life for a King who had not earned the loyalty of a single Irishmen. Mr. Curran brushed it off, as if he was glad to be rid of a troublesome child or grateful that one of his sons was doing his duty to the Crown, proving that the Currans were not enemies of the state.

THIRTEEN

Paris was crowded with Irish visitors that summer, and I was not surprised to learn that Robert Emmet was part of their circle. Kate Wilmot wrote to me after a day in Robert's company, touring the Louvre and strolling in the Tivoli gardens. She was impressed by his personal magnetism, a strength of character that glowed in his eyes. The Penrose family had dinner with a mutual friend of the Emmet family and came away with a favorable opinion of the youngest child. I reported all that was said to Caroline Lambart, who continued to encourage my secret affection for a man who might soon be beyond my reach if our rulers went one way instead of another.

The Crown tipped its hand that autumn, while Mr. Curran was exploring France and finding it as miserable a place as he expected. Thomas Emmet was released from prison, along with several of those who were jailed prior to the opening of the rebellion in 1798, reflecting a partial admission that their cause had merit. My opinion was not shared by Richard, who assured me that I was looking at the world through eyes clouded with tender feelings. Other than that, he had little more to say, becoming increasingly withdrawn. With greater frequency, he was in Dublin for days at a time, claiming that the press of business kept him from The Priory, but never speaking of the business when he returned.

I had always been a restless sleeper, and the emptiness of the house without Richard or John worsened my condition. Wide awake, I turned from one side to the other looking for a comfortable position, only to grow weary of the activity. Mrs. Fitzgerald had gone back to Dublin, taking her sons with her, and the calm that settled on the house after they left echoed in my ears. Seeing no point in remaining in bed, I dressed and walked to Gertrude's grave, the burial ground shielded from view by the grove of yews that had grown thick and tall over the years. Dead leaves gathered against the stone slab that had pressed itself into the ground. "I shall bring a rake tomorrow," I said. A breeze rustled the leaves around my feet, startling me with the noise.

"Sarah."

I knew Robert's voice, knew his tone and timbre, the cadence. A dream, perhaps, but I was certain I was awake. A figment of my imagination, then, but I heard him again, heard him say my name softly. "Are you here? Truly here?" I asked.

He was unchanged since last I had seen him, not taller or older in his face, but there was a different light in his eyes. A fever burned within, and I recognized the intensity that Kate Wilmot had noted a few months before. We exchanged pleasantries, interspersed with awkward pauses. Our meeting was entirely accidental, but the fact remained that we were alone in the pre-dawn darkness. I should have gone inside at once, but we might never see each other again. Every word was precious, and carefully selected. I did not wish to convey any hint of emotional attachments unless I was certain, and I was not.

"Your parents, are they well? I have heard that your father is selling his home," I said.

"I returned from the Continent to find a frail, bent old man," Robert said. "They have suffered greatly, but their spirits remain unbroken."

"And Thomas? He is on his way to America?"

"His family has joined him in Paris. They live like tinkers, prepared to break camp at any moment. There was a rumor being spread for a time, that Bonaparte was going to evict the Irish. Unfounded, as we learned later, a lie spread by the British, but Thomas thought it prudent to make ready. He awaits further developments before deciding which direction he will take."

"Have you made any plans, for your own future?" An ill-mannered question, I knew, but I had to keep him talking, chattering away until the sun rose and shed its light on our illicit encounter.

"Such grand and glorious plans," he said with a grin. "Ten depots, Sarah, spread around the country, fully stocked with all manner of arms and ammunition. Almost all is in readiness for a mass rising, coordinated with a French invasion of England. Even Richard does not know the whole of it."

"I will say nothing. You can be sure of my silence," I said. He confided in me, and so placed his life in my hands. The responsibility was so heavy that I felt my knees buckle.

"Some business in the country brought me here. Richard has gone for the gig and we will return to the city. He wishes to tour the factory where I am manufacturing explosives. Yes, explosives. I have invented a rocket, but I have not yet tested it, although you will know when I do. A friend has offered me the use of his fields here in Rathfarnham, and I expect the noise will draw some attention. We are operating under the guise of a fireworks display, fear not. Dublin Castle will be none the wiser."

We turned in unison when we heard a clattering in the stable. The secret meeting was coming to a close.

"I will never forget that dreadful day when your sister fell," he said.

"Nor I. This spot is almost a refuge for me. I come here when I am troubled, and I think of Gertrude. Sometimes I talk to her."

Carriage wheels creaked and gravel crunched under horse hooves. "Until the next time," Robert said, and he slipped between the yew bushes, leaving me alone.

I made for the garden door in the back of the house so that I avoided seeing my brother, who would have asked far too many questions of a young lady up and dressed at such an early hour. Of course, my sisters were even more likely to ask me what I was about, so I turned around and headed for the shed. No one would question my reason for cleaning around Gertrude's grave. Not a week went by that I did not tend to the grounds, and while Amelia thought it was not a healthy pastime, neither did she try to stop me. I scratched away with a small rake until the house came alive with servants starting the day's chores.

A subdued air descended when Mr. Curran arrived from his sojourn that afternoon. He was joined by several guests, some of whom had also been abroad, and the gentlemen were most entertaining in the drawing room. They compared experiences and observations, with Mr. Curran bemoaning what had become of French culture under the malignant influence of a failed rebellion. Mr. McNally noted the change in his host's opinion, as Mr. Curran had once strongly supported a similar revolt for Ireland, under the expectation that the nation might become more like republican France. The republic, we all knew, had descended into chaos and a dictatorship that left most of Europe drowning in blood.

"We had opportunity to meet many of our fellow countrymen," Mr. McNally said to me in a low voice. "Some of whom regret the failure of 1798 and wish to try again. The Misses Penrose asked after you, by the way.

Apparently their father was painted by David, but only after much coaxing on Mrs. Penrose's part. You must ask for a full accounting when next you write. It will be a most amusing tale."

"He has a magnificent new gallery to fill," I said. Something in Mr. McNally's tone rankled, in the way that he seemed to be teasing my father about altering his views on independence. The French may have stumbled, but Mr. Curran was also an admirer of the American experiment with self-government, and they had not descended into anarchy.

"Coupled with the financial means to accomplish such a lofty goal," Mr. McNally said. "They are an influential family, and you are fortunate to be acquainted with them. As well as the Lambarts, I might add. Their daughter is quite in love with you, but she is far more flighty than you ever were, even as a child. Take care. Miss Lambart does not take a practical approach to marriage, which can prove detrimental to happiness. An open eye must be paired with a tender heart."

"Are you after arranging a match for Sarah?" Richard asked. He was a bit unsteady, the effect of too much brandy. "Before long, all the young gentlemen will be gone off soldiering and we shall have an army of spinsters left behind."

"John is to be commended," Mr. Curran said, and with that, I escaped from an uncomfortable discussion of future prospects when I saw but few prospects within my reach.

I returned to the grove every morning, hoping for another covert visit, but no one disturbed my solitude for a full week. The chill of November cut through my surtout and I was ready to give up when I was approached by a boy, barefoot despite the cold, dressed in peasant's rags. He addressed me in Irish, which was uncommon among those speaking to someone of my class. Either he had come from the back of beyond, or he knew that I was a fluent speaker. Without ceremony, he shoved a note into my hand and raced off across the park, making for parts unknown with great haste.

"My dear Miss Curran," I read with delight. I did not need to examine the signature to know who it came from.

Through a long-standing friendship with Richard, Robert hoped to return to Mr. Curran's drawing room as he had once been welcomed. Until that time, we could correspond using my brother as our agent, a suggestion that skirted the edges of good manners. I took this as a positive development, with the implication that Richard was again in favor of the match. Either my brother or Robert recognized the risks of inappropriate behavior, because Robert went on to assure me that he would not correspond if I found the notion offensive. At the same time he pleaded with me to ignore social convention until the rift could be healed and we could meet as we ought. I almost laughed at the sentiment and the concern for propriety. The man asking me to bend the rules was preparing for the ultimate in rule-breaking, an armed insurrection. Accepting a letter through my brother was hardly wrong in comparison.

Until Richard could convince Mr. Curran that Robert Emmet should be invited to The Priory as of old, my admirer had to hide in the shadows and I had to hide my joy at being adored by such a fine gentleman. Robert had nothing to offer me as a husband, with no income and no occupation, but it was delightful to know that someone overlooked my many faults and found something worth loving. I lost my head, even as I assured myself that our exchange of tender words was harmless. Instead of waiting for Mr. Curran to admit Robert into his circle, I entered into a secret correspondence while evading the watchful eyes of my sisters and our servants. Ah, the foolhardiness of youth. I thought I was the most clever girl in Ireland.

Rather than hide my activity, I penned letters to Robert in full view of anyone who happened to walk by the writing table in the drawing room. What protected me was my large volume of correspondence, the quantity of which caused Mr. Curran to frequently grumble about the expense of responding to my wordy friends. As a matter of course I wrote every day, and no one noticed if I was writing to Mr. Emmet or Miss Wilmot or Miss Lambart or anyone else who had struck up a friendship with me. Under the guise of a regular habit, I carried my sealed missives to the tray in the foyer, tucking one into a pocket as I walked through the rooms, without anyone realizing what I was doing.

Did they notice that I was happier than I had been for years? Did they not see the lightness of my step, the joy in my face after reading one of Robert's lovely poems? Something must have given me away. Why else would Amelia go snooping in the chest of drawers and search for the love notes I had so carefully tucked away in my stockings?

FOURTEEN

Dr. Emmet was a very old man, but it was still shocking to learn of his sudden death in December of 1802. The liberal element turned out to mourn his passing, and even Mr. Curran put aside his fear of association with the father of a known rebel sympathizer to attend services. We called on Mrs. Emmet, who had aged considerably since her son Thomas' arrest, and I took full advantage of the opportunity to sit next to Robert. Being near him was thrilling, to the point that I had to clutch my hands together on my lap to keep from touching his arm. We spoke quietly of his experiences in France, talking like two indifferent acquaintances making polite conversation. Richard stood at my side, an actor playing his role on society's stage. Robert and I were in poses common to any courting couple, almost alone together except for the supervision of a family member who maintained a discrete distance. I could not help but notice that Amelia kept an eye on us.

She pounced after we had retired for the evening, opening up the discussion while I took down my hair. "He cannot come into enough money to compensate for his station," Amelia said. "Did you think that our father would, by some abrupt change of heart, grant his blessing to such a union?"

"A tradesman," Eliza said. "A future tradesman, I should say. He has no means of support at this time."

"The future brings endless possibilities," I said.

"The future, as envisioned by men like Mr. Emmet or our brother, is less formed than the wispiest cloud," Amelia said. "There are no guarantees of success. There is no copper-fastened promise from France to land troops on Irish soil."

"All plans should be abandoned, is that it?" I asked.

"No. I am suggesting that you step aside to clear the path. We all agree that action must be taken or we are nothing but docile sheep," Eliza said. She stopped short, as if she was about to admit that we were all docile sheep, accepting the abuse of our master. John Philpot Curran ruled with absolute power in our home and we had no choice but to bend to his will. "Men must take the lead, and we then follow. We may encourage them to go in a certain direction, one that would be to our benefit, but we must not obstruct them. Yes, put your happiness in the hands of one whom you trust, but wait quietly. Do not be a distraction."

"A very pretty speech, but we cannot speak of men in general terms," Amelia said. "We are speaking of one man, a single individual, who is leading the vanguard. Is it wise for Sarah to follow her heart in this case, or is it wiser to take a different course?"

"Can I upend plans made months ago? Do I have the right to demand that Mr. Emmet choose between me or Ireland?" I asked. "Surely he has burdens enough to carry without another added by me. That would be cruel."

"You cannot ask him to make an impossible choice," Eliza said. "But you can proceed slowly. If the rebellion is successful, everything would change. Especially if Mr. Curran were offered the post of Attorney General, rather than the lower rank of Solicitor General."

"Which he has long coveted," Amelia said. "Be discreet, Sarah. That is my advice. You know that we will keep your secret. Do not reveal it to anyone else, no matter how trustworthy they appear. You have letters hidden. Burn them. Burn them now. Keep nothing. Sign nothing."

I yielded to my older sister, despite my desire to keep every scrap of paper that Robert had inked. His poems I transcribed in a journal, rendering them safe by making it appear that I had scribbled them myself. Anything with his handwriting had to be destroyed so that Mr. Curran would have no evidence that I was not conducting myself in a manner fitting the daughter of a gentleman. As December gave way to January, I had more reason to consign Robert's notes to the flames. He began to confide in me, revealing details of the planned insurrection and asking my opinions on strategy. Names, places and dates were shared, as I accepted a role in the rebellion. Knowledge was treason and so I was guilty of the crime, as guilty as Robert who was acting on the orders of those above him. There was no going back, but then again, I did not want to go back. Our venture was too important, too critical to the future of the Irish people. Cowardice had no place in my heart in 1803.

Still my life continued along an accepted course, as if I were two people. The rebel prepared for the revolution, while the young lady engaged in the normal activities of society in a most conventional manner. When one of our neighbors, Lady Shaw, invited the Curran sisters to a supper party, I eagerly accepted. We would talk of little besides suitors and good matches, the gossip that was typical of one of Her Ladyship's gatherings, and I fully expected that she would introduce me to someone she thought was ideal for me. The thrill of being courted was delightful, of course, but I was a practical girl who realized that Robert Emmet might not ever be in a position to take a wife. I had to be prepared, not knowing what the future might hold. Alternate courses had to be mapped out if I was to avoid permanent imprisonment in The Priory.

Lady Shaw's praise for William Fitzgerald was exuberant, as was her style, describing his background so that I would understand how perfect a mate he would be for me. Mr. Fitzgerald was my age, educated at Oxford, and connected through his family to other Irish politicians known to Mr. Curran. He was handsome, to be sure, and as wordy as my father.

His father was one of Mr. Curran's strong allies in the Irish Parliament, a supporter of Catholic emancipation. The elder Mr. Fitzgerald had fought vigorously against the Act of Union, and so had much in common with Mr. Curran. On those points, I determined that William was a man whose proposal would not be refused. Our families were of similar thought in politics, his parents did not seem troubled by my own family's past scandals, and I found my mind wandering away from Robert Emmet.

I had to consider my family and my sisters in particular when it came to my future union with another family. Mr. Curran was not born a gentleman, but I could help him overcome that deficiency by joining a politically influential circle. What smutty residue clung to him from his illicit affair with Mrs. Fitzgerald, or the criminal conversation suit, would be scrubbed away by a propitious marriage. In the back of my mind I tucked away another scenario that would yield an even better result. Should Dublin fall to the rebels, the father-in-law of Robert Emmet would be elevated to the position of Attorney General, the first lawyer of the land.

Immediate power and prestige had to be weighed against a gradual climb. Until I could choose my path, I had to keep all routes open.

While William chattered away, informing us all about the beauty of his family seat in Ennis, I puzzled over my role in the world. I was born to become a wife and mother, but it was no easy task for a girl like me, whose father was not wealthy enough to provide a sufficient enticement. Other young ladies of similar breeding could buy a better husband, and so I was already a lap behind in the chase. Neither was I poor, like our tenant farmers, who could marry for love because there was no hope of rising. They owned nothing and never would own anything, which made love the greatest gift a woman could bring, a treasure that the government could not tax. The more I thought about it, the more I realized that it rested on me to make the best possible match, to lift my siblings so that they could marry better than they might at present. My sacrifice would be required to improve their prospects.

No new territory was explored over supper. William asked about my family and how many siblings I had, and I asked the same about his. "A dull lot," he said. "I am the eldest, following in my father's footsteps like your brother. My younger brother will take holy orders, as is expected of any younger brother. Yours joined the navy. So much more interesting than reading the Bible, I would say. I hope you may meet my sisters soon. They share your love of music."

"How did you know I liked music?" I asked.

"You are an accomplished harpist, with the voice of a nightingale, and you have a head filled with Irish airs that you sing perfectly because you speak the native language. You have known sorrow in your life, but you can be made to smile with clever banter or a well-executed prank."

"Lady Shaw has, perhaps, exaggerated my accomplishments. My abilities are equal to those of any other lady of my acquaintance. Many are far more skilled."

"Can this be so? It is not what your former music master told me."

"You know Mr. Moore? He has been gone from Ireland for so long and I miss him terribly. I still practice the songs he taught me."

William signaled the steward to refill my wine glass. "We met in England, and had ample opportunity to discuss the events of 1798. That spirit lives on in some quarters, although our fathers, I am sure, would not approve of the methods utilized. I know my father does not. He forbade me from having anything to do with it, and I must, of course, yield, while I am dependent on his largesse."

My tongue searched for escape against gritted teeth. I longed to tell him something, anything, a few words about the pike factory in Dublin operated by a lumber merchant or the explosives factory near Thomas Street where Robert perfected his rockets. I longed to ask if he would join the fight once it began, if he would find the courage or if his father would recognize the justice of an uprising and send William off with a gun and a blessing. The wine would loosen my reserve and no matter how thirsty I was, I had to leave the glass untouched.

"After hearing all about you from Tom Moore, I had to meet you. Easily done, when you approach the right people and ask for an introduction. The wine is not to your liking? Not the best vintage, I agree, but we shall soon be filling our cellars with French wines once again."

"The peace will not last," I said.

"Mr. Curran is of that opinion, I have heard, since he returned from that blighted country. I should like to call on him to discuss the matter."

"I am sure he would welcome you to The Priory," I said. "He holds discourses on many such topics, and he encourages the young gentlemen to debate freely."

"Not much of a debater, I'm afraid, but I would like to listen. I am not a man whose mind is closed to argument or persuasion. Those of us who are called upon to govern should have an open mind, don't you think?"

All of Rathfarnham society took note of the way that William encouraged me to sing that evening. They could not help but notice the enraptured stare that he fixed on my face, making me so nervous that my voice broke on the high notes and spoiled the tune. My sisters were quite amused by William's enthusiastic applause. They teased me about it mercilessly as we rode home, and kept at it while I changed into a nightdress.

Nothing happened the following day. No message arrived, asking for an audience. Neither did William come to call on us. I felt as one with my sisters, who had been stung in the same way by gentlemen who appeared interested until they learned more about the Curran family. To add to our misery, marriageable men were in short supply, and we could count on jealousy to stir up old stories or cast aspersions on Mr. Curran's parsimony. It was evident, to an extent, in the lesser quality of our gowns and our lack of jewels. It was not the gentlemen taking note, of course. Our female rivals were the observant ones, and I feared that I had fallen victim to an old scheme.

The day was overcast and gloomy, a fitting backdrop for my mood. Even though I protested, I accompanied Richard when he went out for a walk to avoid Amelia's day at home. The ladies talked of little more than local gossip, with the same topic broached again and again with every new arrival. The recent party given by Lady Shaw would be critiqued and analyzed to a pulp, and I planned to stay in my room with a book rather than listen to tales of my competitors in the hunt for William Fitzgerald's attention. On that January day, Richard threatened to drag me out by my hair if I did not come willingly. He had something to show me, something I had to see.

A group of three gentlemen in workman's clothes stood in the middle of an empty field belonging to Mr. Ponsonby, another of Mr. Curran's many colleagues who resided in Rathfarnham. I almost did not recognize Robert in his coarse woolen coat, a battered cap on his head. He appeared thinner than he had in December, his color more sallow. His features shifted when he saw me, the crease between his brows disappearing as a broad grin spread across his face.

With the assistance of the men who were not introduced to us, we picked our way over the lumpy field and came to a halt at a small wooden ramp. "Gentlemen. And Lady," Robert said. He bowed with mock theatrics and we all laughed, although it was a nervous tittering. "This invention will alter the course of the uprising."

He took a peculiar object from under a canvas wrap. The closed metal cylinder was capped by a cone-shaped piece that ended in a spike, very much like a finial for an iron fence. The cylinder was attached to a short pole that Robert rested on the slanted board. We retreated to a position of safety while one of the assistants touched a punk stick to the wick that protruded from the bottom of the device. Like a firecracker it burned and hissed, until the spark ignited the material inside the tube. The rocket took off and traveled about forty yards, tearing up the ground as it flew. The cylinder came to rest at a distance, leaving a trail of destruction in its wake.

"Robert, you are a genius," Richard said.

"One more, for luck," Robert said, and repeated the launching. It was no less shocking the second time. The uncontrolled power of the device was terrifying in its lethal effectiveness. A square military formation could be decimated by the projectile, and the soldiers would be unable to defend themselves against horrific injuries.

We walked back in silence, awestruck by the display of an explosive that could replace countless guns, which were expensive and difficult to obtain. A rocket fired, the soldiers thrown into disarray, and the pike men would take the field at an advantage. The strategy reflected a military mind, the thinking of one who understood tactics. It did not seem possible that Robert had concocted such a plan on his own. He was acting under the guidance of others, and I thought of Valentine Lawless, manipulating us like pieces on a chess board from the safety of Paris.

FIFTEEN

A discourse on the sad state of Ireland was held on the last Tuesday of January, and commenced after a light supper attended by a few of that evening's participants. I was seated between William Fitzgerald and Robert Emmet, who was invited thanks to Richard's persuasion and an admission that the sins of the father, or brother, should not be visited upon the son. It was the most awkward, uncomfortable situation any lady could be put in, and I could not wait for the night to end.

While the men enjoyed brandy in the dining room, the ladies withdrew to the drawing room to prepare for a musical entertainment. I took up my harp while Eliza ran her hands over the keys of the pianoforte to loosen her fingers. Instead of tuning her violin, Amelia held it in her hand and tapped the bow against her leg, absent-minded.

"The reason for Mr. Fitzgerald's delay was due to a thorough investigation," she said. "Inquiries were made, to verify that he is not acting contrary to his father's wishes."

"Our Sarah might not be good enough for that boy?" Eliza asked.

"He is, after all, the eldest son," Amelia said. "The family seat is said to be quite splendid, and while the income is not immense, it would provide for a very comfortable existence. Our father thought that Sarah was not worthy of so high a gentleman and so he suspected that Mr. Fitzgerald was only toying with her affections for his own amusement. Implying, of course, that the senior Fitzgerald would call his son to heel when he learned of the potential entanglement. Young William is not the sort who stands up for himself against his father's dictates."

"Well done, Sarah, you may yet marry above your station," Eliza said. Her sarcasm was bitter, a noxious fog that filled the room. "I wonder, could this young gentleman be a distant relation of Father's mistress? Some distant cousin, perhaps?"

"Fitzgerald is a common enough name in this country," I said. "And if it were true, you can be sure that Father would have turned William away out of embarrassment alone."

"Five minutes in his company and I could have told you he would do nothing without first receiving parental consent," Amelia said. "That boy is incapable of making a single decision on his own. I am surprised he was able to finally pick which cheese he wanted this evening without having to send a special messenger to County Clare."

"He merely wishes to be agreeable," I said.

To amuse ourselves, and stifle an unpleasant conversation, we sorted through sheets of music to select a few songs that we might play. Our performance was just getting underway when we were joined by the gentlemen, who arranged themselves around Mr. Curran like acolytes surrounding Plato. "Miss Sarah, will you sing?" William asked, his exuberance raising Eliza's eyebrow.

I rested my harp on my shoulder and fingered the strings while Eliza and Amelia composed themselves into a living tableau, allowing me the honor of selecting the tune that would best display my talents. They might not have cared much for William, but they would not stand in the way of a good match. I played *Molly McAlpin*, one of the airs I had learned from Tom Moore, and lost myself in the mournful ballad. I sang *Eibhlin Aruin* for Richard, who was most fond of the tune. It was then Eliza's turn to shine with a performance of a Mozart sonata that amused our guests as they drank tea, with Amelia playing the role of hostess. The entertainment concluded, the discourse was begun, and I picked up my sewing while Irish affairs were given a thorough airing. Robert drifted away from the group and leaned over my shoulder to examine the embroidery.

"The four provinces have never been more beautifully rendered by any cartographer," Robert said. "Do you use a chain stitch, Miss Sarah? Our land is in chains, as your father has so cleverly put it."

"It is so very good to see you among us again," I said.

The empty phrases reflected my training in the art of keeping a man at arm's length. While it was true that Mr. Curran had made the first step in restoring Robert to a position of friendship, the first step did not span the full distance. I needed time, to see how events might play out, before I showed the smallest sign of any emotional attachment. Who could say but that William Fitzgerald might stir my heart if given the chance to win me over, and there was a match that Mr. Curran would bless at once. I could not deny that I very much enjoyed being the object of interest of two different men, and I saw no harm in allowing their pursuit to continue as long as possible. Too soon I would be married and the frivolity of courtship would fade into a sweet memory.

"I have missed these evenings, the stimulating conversation, the pleasant company," he said. "The family home will be sold, as you have heard, and I have decided to take a house in the area. The solitude of the country will serve me well, while the distance to Dublin is short enough to manage."

"We shall be neighbors," I said. "How delightful. If the split is thoroughly mended, I imagine you will often be a dinner guest. In time, perhaps, the old Knights of the Screw might be resurrected in some new form."

"But I cannot replace my brother Thomas," Robert said. "As I am not, nor can I be, a barrister. Would I be invited, do you think, if I were a lowly tanner?"

"In a newly modernized society, the occupation should not matter, in my opinion," I said. "We should strive for greater equality, as in France. Before equality fell victim to the guillotine."

My sewing fell into my lap, ignored, while we chatted about the changes that might be brought to a land that was freed of peers and life titles and all the privileges that fell to a man because of bloodlines. France was presented for dissection, with all her faults and flaws, still beautiful despite the ravages of war and decades of tumult. I was surprised at how swiftly the time flew that night.

Robert became a regular fixture at The Priory when Mr. Curran held his rhetorical soirees, while William Fitzgerald danced around the room in an effort to insert himself into my field of vision. The future politician was true to his word and did not join in the debate but listened attentively, sometimes asking for my opinion on a matter of trade or agricultural policy. It was William who was allowed to take me and my sisters for a drive in the country, while Robert disappeared for a fortnight. Mr. Curran brought Richard to London on business, to safeguard the family's connection to Mr. Fox and the liberals who were on the verge of ascending to power, and Amelia was left in charge of safeguarding my honor. She took great pleasure in any outing that William devised, reminding me of our poor mother and her despondency. The isolation of The Priory was too confining for a woman's spirit, and I realized that I had to escape as soon as possible.

The urge to become mistress of my own home became a near mania when the letters arrived from England. What was said to whom was never spelled out, and I could not believe that my father was so observant as to notice the attention that Robert lavished on me. The end result of Mr. Curran's flurry of correspondence was a stern warning from Amelia, acting on our father's explicit order. I was not to encourage Robert Emmet. I was not to communicate with Robert Emmet. All thoughts of Robert Emmet were to be erased from my mind. The space was to be filled with William Fitzgerald, if it had to be filled at all.

My life, indeed, my future happiness was not something to be decided by others. How could my father, who rarely said two words to me, have any idea what sort of husband would be best? He had failed miserably in that capacity himself, and was not in any position to judge suitability. Robert was a good friend to me, as he had always been, and I would not abandon a friend without just cause. Time, my old ally, would alter the situation. I had to play for time, for the invasion, for the rebellion, for the proclamation of Irish liberty. Before the year was over, I would know which way to turn, and it would be my decision to make.

Days later, Richard confessed his sin. Somehow, Mr. Curran discovered that Richard met with Robert Emmet while in London, which resulted in Richard accusing our father of spying. In the midst of a drunken outburst Richard blurted out the things that he and Robert discussed, including a marriage proposal that would be facilitated by Richard who was clearing the way to The Priory. My brother begged my forgiveness for revealing a secret and, what was worse, for turning traitor. No longer would Richard support any sort of entanglement, not when a courtship would bring added scrutiny that would endanger the planned insurrection. He reiterated the wisdom of encouraging William Fitzgerald, not only to avoid any action that would expose the rebels, but because William was a far better catch than Robert Emmet could ever be.

In matters of the heart, I confided in Caroline Lambart who would tell no one that I had not forgotten Robert when so ordered. Our correspondence was a running debate on the merits of a love match as opposed to one of financial gain, an issue that she, too, was grappling with. Marriage was so final, so unbreakable, that we both feared making mistakes that would leave us miserable for the rest of our days. Could either of us endure poverty for the sake of love, or would we lose that love under the pressure of drudgery? My mind was in turmoil until Caroline passed along a nugget of gossip that pertained to my future happiness. It was being said in drawing rooms throughout Dublin that William Fitzgerald was a man of loose morals, possibly a womanizer. Could I be content, she asked me, with a man incapable of fidelity? My poor mother had not been content. She had found it unendurable, to the point that she ran away. Of course, it was only rumor and it was possible that a rival was spreading a false tale to drive off the competition. After all, any gentleman of William's age was going to find unsavory female companionship until he had a wife to satisfy his natural urges. In the end, my friend encouraged me to juggle two hearts as best I could without losing one until I had chosen the one I wished to keep.

In March of 1803, William Fitzgerald left for Oxford, where he would be tutored in banking and finance while ingratiating himself with those capable of granting him a position.. He was slated to replace his father in Parliament, but Mr. Fitzgerald was not yet ready to retire, so William had to find some other means of support. A ministerial job, or some unimportant government post, would be paid for by the hard-pressed Irish citizens who were already taxed beyond endurance to finance the salaries of the privileged. At the same time, Mr. Curran saw the wisdom of better securing his interests and he took the same packet across the Irish Sea. I have no doubt that Robert knew exactly when my father left. He sent word as soon as the chaise pulled out onto the Rathfarnham road. I was to meet him at dawn at what would become our secret spot.

"I have taken a house in Butterfield Lane," he said. "To be near you."

"We cannot be seen together," I said, growing alarmed. All well and good for a man to act boldly, but for me such blatant disobedience could only be disastrous.

"Under cover of darkness I will come if you permit me," he said. "May I write to you? Please say yes. It cannot be wrong, not when our motives are pure and innocent. My maid will act as our messenger. You can trust Anne, trust her absolutely."

To communicate without parental consent was wrong, but so enticing. Robert's words would be mine alone, and Mr. Curran would not be the one to decide if I could read them or watch them burn to ash. We could be open and forthright, holding back only what we wished to hold back instead of checking our emotions because others demanded it. I saw no harm as long as no one discovered us. "How can you be so certain?" I asked. "Maids gossip."

"Anne's uncle has been hiding in the Wicklow Mountains since he made his escape in 1798. She is a rebel, Sarah, and accustomed to the secrecy demanded. And she is loyal to me. That loyalty extends to you, as if we are one." Robert paused, his face so close to mine that I felt his breath on my cheek. "I pray that one day we shall be one."

What a dull life I had led until that moment. What I had previously done, or not done, had been in accordance with Mr. Curran's whim, but it was time for some of the universal emancipation he so famously proclaimed as the right of all who stepped onto English soil. I would emancipate myself, rebel in a way, and lay claim to a fragment of liberty. I was more than capable of deciding what was suitable or appropriate. Writing a letter to Robert Emmet was no different than writing to any other friend. I enjoyed his missives, as I enjoyed those from others who shared their thoughts with me. Nothing cheered me like a message from a friend, and there was no sound reason to give up such a harmless indulgence. Trusting in Anne's discretion, I would not have to surrender the correspondent whose words delighted me more than others.

"If, from time to time, I might see you," Robert added. "I would be happy for nothing more than a glance from you as I pass your home, or if you should pass mine, would you look for me in a window? Do not even acknowledge me, just let me see your face as you walk by."

"You must have many burdens weighing on you," I said. "Will I not add another?"

"Quite the opposite. I cannot explain how you ease my every burden." The sounds of the morning grew louder, with a few solitary bird calls expanding into a chorus. From the outbuildings we could hear the servants going about their chores, prodded by the cook who wanted the eggs gathered with some speed. "Take great care, particularly with Mrs. Fitzgerald. She is looking out for herself alone, and would knock you down if she had to. She is not content with her lodgings in Dublin and intends to make her home here if she can."

It was advice I should have heeded, but I thought I knew my father's household far better than I did. I discovered my oversight after I had exchanged dozens of letters and, in the process, fallen madly in love with Robert Emmet.

SIXTEEN

The sketch that Amelia made was burned with so many other incriminating documents, but I cherished it for the short time that it existed. So lost was I in reading a letter from Robert that I did not notice her, charcoal in hand, making a study of me. She captured the emotion, and of course must have recognized it, but I was certain that I was a master of disguise. In my innocence I thought that my face would never betray me, as if I read the words of a lover with the same nonchalance as the words of an acquaintance.

"What news from Mr. Fitzgerald?" she asked.

"Who?" I was startled out of a reverie and had not heard the question.

Amelia held up the charcoal portrait and repeated her question. "It must be good news, judging by your moony gaze," she said.

"Oh, no, not much news at all," I said, folding the sheet. Whether I would have an opportunity to pore over the contents seemed unlikely. For safety's sake I burned Robert's letters so that no one could discover them, but I usually had an opportunity to copy a few phrases into my journal so that I could preserve a sentiment. "He hopes for a posting that will further his career but it depends on what his father determines to be the most useful."

Under the guise of obtaining ribbon for a bonnet I was trimming, I took advantage of the lovely Spring weather and walked to the shops in town, extending my journey further along to Butterfield Lane. No shadow appeared behind a window, and I could only guess that Robert had run up to Dublin to supervise the work at the arms depots. I slowed my pace to listen for sounds coming from behind the garden wall, hoping that Anne might follow after me so that we could meet away from the house. Never could I dare to knock on the front door, let alone enter the residence of an unmarried man who was a stranger in the town. Instead, we had to play a silly game so that a few words could be exchanged without drawing unwanted attention. All was quiet, as if the house were empty. The road, unfortunately, was not.

"I know why you come here," Richard said, taking me by the arm and hurrying me back to The Priory. "You have been told to stop, and I am warning you that I will speak to our father about your conduct. What has come over you, to endanger your reputation like a common milkmaid, chasing after a man?"

"Have you broken off your friendship as well? And I might ask why you are here," I said.

"Here on business that does not concern you," Richard said. "You have a gentleman of property and excellent prospects caught on your hook. Be satisfied and land your fish."

"Why must I settle? In a year's time, what is a good match now could be a mistake. Fortunes can change," I said.

"Here is what is about to change," Richard said. "Mrs. Fitzgerald has a spy in our home and she is about to report the kitchen gossip to our father, and your fortune, my dear sister, will be drastically changed. How will you explain yourself to him, or do you think you can deny all? Throw yourself upon his mercy, perhaps? There will be no mercy, I assure you."

"I can plead my case," I said. "He would understand that I am in love. And I do love Robert. I love him with all my heart, my soul, my being."

"Sarah, stop this nonsense. What you want cannot be. Write to Robert and break this off before you compromise yourself. I suspect that Mr. Fitzgerald is positioning himself to make a proposal, and if you have an ounce of sense in your head, you will tell Robert that you are going to give your hand to another. And be done with this flight of fancy."

"He will think me inconstant and I cannot part from him if he does not think highly of me," I said.

"What woman has not been accused of inconstancy? Consider this plot he is hatching. I see doom, Sarah. A repeat performance of 1798 with a new cast performing the same lines."

"How do you know? Do you have all the details that you can judge with such certainty?"

"What I know with certainty is this. You must break it off at once, do you understand? I will stand over your shoulder while you write the letter and I will see to it that Robert receives it. Do not force my hand. I would betray you if I had to."

"Do you speak for our father, or for yourself?" I asked. Richard cut me with a glance so cold that I shivered.

"One night you might pick up the Bible instead of a book of philosophy, and commit the Commandments to memory. As you appear to have forgotten at least one of them."

"Obey a tyrant?"

"If that tyrant is your father, yes."

"A tyrant who preaches liberty. A hypocrite."

"All that, and more. Because you must honor your father or violate God's law." Richard clasped his hands behind his back as he walked, his face reflecting some inner turmoil. "We both know what is coming before the year is out. By an unfortunate coincidence, our father left for London on the same packet as Robert. I fear that Major Sirr's spies have one or both gentlemen under observation at all times. Do you not agree that Sirr would connect two unrelated events and wrap up innocent people in his imaginary cabal?"

"Baseless innuendo," I said.

"Not baseless, Sarah, if a courtship is exposed. The implication follows, that a rebel was allowed into The Priory, made welcome, permitted to call on a daughter of the house. You do not have Father's consent, and you may be forced at some point to prove that fact in public, to expose yourself in a way that no woman wishes to be exposed. Break it off before Father returns from London."

While Richard played the pianoforte to mask his close observation of the writing table, I followed his order. The letter was long, two full pages that offered my apologies while assuring my beloved Robert that we would always be friends. I felt so powerless as I penned what I hoped were witty phrases that masked my misery. In closing, I dared to say that I was about to marry another, not for love but for the security a husband provided. In case Richard read my note, I twisted a sentence that expressed the grief I felt at hurting Robert, turning it in such a way that I doubted anyone would comprehend my meaning. Two tears rolled down my cheeks and I wiped them away with my sleeve to keep the drops from falling onto the paper and smearing the ink. Before sealing the packet, I acted as if I had to mull over my writing and wandered around the room, pausing at a basket of millinery trimmings on the tea table. While Richard was preoccupied with the music, I snipped a piece of ribbon and cut a small lock of my hair, which I attached to the ribbon with a pin.

The pages were filled with words and I had one more thing to ask. Taking a third sheet to serve as the cover, I wrote a few lines on the inside to strongly suggest that he destroy all the poems I sent to him, as well as my letters. If anyone were to discover my identity, all that Richard feared would come to pass if the rebellion should fail. I sealed it before my brother took a notion to read it, if only to feel that I retained a fragment of privacy.

"Tell him to burn this as well," I said. "I have told him every time to burn the letters, but he may try to keep this one because it is the last."

A response was not long in coming. I was pruning the roses when Anne slipped into the garden, doing her best to attract my attention while hiding in the shadows to avoid detection. Maids did not normally call on ladies, and I had no doubt that her message was critical to take such a risk in delivering it. She tucked the note into the boxwood and scurried away. I waited for what felt like hours before taking it, and only after scanning the grounds to be sure the gardener did not notice.

As requested, I waited for Robert at Gertrude's grave, rising well before dawn and taking the utmost care to not rouse anyone in the house. He was distressed, nearly frantic, and struggled to keep from pacing while he spoke in whispers that I almost could not hear, so low did he keep his voice. His grief touched me and I took his hand to offer comfort. The heat of his grasp melted me. I let go as if burned, but it was too late. My heart was his and I would not reclaim it.

"Your happiness is all that I wish for myself," he said. "My attachment to you has not diminished, but has increased with every passing hour. Can you tell me with honesty that you wish me to go? If it is your ardent wish, then I will leave this place. But if there is yet some hope for me, I beg of you, give me some sign."

What sign could I make that would express how I adored him, while at the same time I feared for my family's safety in a climate of insurrection. I had no right to endanger anyone other than myself, but I was not a solitary being free to come or go as I pleased. I did not want Robert to leave, but I could not ask him to stay. I was torn, and my tears expressed what I could not utter in words. He embraced me and I felt so safe in his arms, as if he had closed out the world and it was only us in the grove.

"Let us part, for now, and I will ask nothing more from you but a promise," he said. "Promise that you will wait for me, to see what the future may bring. We will be happy one day, Sarah, but you must promise me that when that day comes, I will find you here, waiting for me."

"Here, in this spot," I said. "We will meet here."

"I will be in Dublin a great deal," he said. "There is much to be done, from the writing of a proclamation to the manufacture of arms. Anne will continue to act as our messenger."

"And you will burn all my letters?" I asked. "I have tried to burn all of yours, but I always retain the last one until you send another in its place."

"It is too painful to discard them like excess paper," he said. "If it becomes necessary, I will destroy all documents in my possession. You need not fear discovery, my dearest Sarah."

"I must not be seen too often on Butterfield Lane," I said. "Nor can Anne be seen too often at The Priory. We must devise a way to exchange letters by leaving them in some secret location."

"I will put Anne to the task. She has a talent for espionage and secrecy."

A chink near the base of the entry gate wall became my private postal box, a small gap on the outside of the wall where I could tuck a letter without drawing attention. I checked it daily, but letters from Robert became increasingly rare. The French had resumed hostilities in May, and the invasion of England was expected in September, leaving him little time to complete preparations. The rebellion would begin in September as well, with a belief that the King would rush all available troops to protect the homeland and leave Ireland to her fate. With that, a provisional government would be proclaimed and the banished rebels would flock home. I would wait for events to unfold, and then my life would begin.

It was early in June when Robert arranged to meet me in the grove where I was often seen decorating Gertrude's grave. As was our custom, we used the cover of darkness to hide us from prying eyes, but I could still make out the drawn features of the man I loved to distraction. Too many cares had been piled on Robert's slight shoulders and he was stooped by the weight. His cheeks were sunken, suggesting he was not eating, and his eyes were clouded from lack of sleep. His entire face lit up when he saw me, as if a spark of life had ignited his spirit. He needed me, as much as other men needed food or drink.

"The day is fast approaching," he said. "Sarah, I have laid bare my heart and soul to you. I have dared to believe that you return my feelings, and present as evidence this very meeting, held in secrecy and skirting the limits of propriety. Will you marry me, Sarah? Will you give me your pledge now, at this sacred moment?"

Words failed me, but my lips did not. Without conscious thought I put myself into his arms and let him kiss me, a kiss that burned me to the core. Happiness bubbled up from my toes to my head, leaving me dizzy. I was engaged, secretly betrothed to the most intelligent, bold and brilliant man in all of Ireland. 'Mrs. Robert Emmet' had such a delightful sound, as harmonious as any music I had ever played. My friend Caroline Lambart would be as happy as I when she heard the news, my triumph to be celebrated without celebration.

My head was in the clouds for days as I tripped along through my usual routines, the recollection of Robert's lips on mine rippling through my body. We would have to move to Dublin, and I would have to become accustomed to the sort of mindless banter that passed for conversation in company. That we would entertain important people was expected, with a procession of foreign dignitaries parading through our drawing room. Perhaps we would host Napoleon Bonaparte some day, after he had deposed the hated King George III. Whatever reticence I might have had would have to be overcome, for Robert's sake. He could not be a highly-placed government official with a wife too shy to open her mouth.

Such fantasies filled my head from morning to night, and often invaded my dreams. I put greater effort in practicing the harp so that I could play with some skill. Our entertainments would include Irish music as I promoted the native culture to the world, separating my country from the empire that had tried to stifle us for centuries. When my time came to trod upon such an important stage, I would be ready to shine. I had but a few short months to prepare.

SEVENTEEN

Our visits to Newmarket had become infrequent, but in 1803 we made a point to call on Grandmother Curran. She was growing old and we did not want an opportunity to slip away into an everlasting regret. Even so, we were eager to get back home that summer. Our neighbor Mrs. Ponsonby had invited us to a country dance to be held at the beginning of July, and she promised to populate her drawing room with gentlemen of varied ages so that all three Curran sisters might discover a gem of Irish manhood previously unknown. While Eliza was filled with hope, I was filled with nothing more than a desire to see Robert Emmet again, and would have accepted an invitation to anything that brought me back to Rathfarnham.

While we had always made charity calls, I set out with remarkable frequency, ferrying food to the poor who lived in the vicinity of Butterfield

Lane. I tried not to search for Robert's face in a window as I passed his house, knowing that my curiosity would give me away, but I saw no harm in Robert seeing me. His notes, left in the gate wall by Anne, mentioned the pleasure it gave him to admire my beauty, the color in my cheeks telling him that I felt his eyes on me. The image inspired a poem that he wrote about blooming roses and Ireland blossoming, one that I carefully copied into my journal before burning the original.

On the day of the Ponsonby dance I rose early in the hope that Anne had left a message from my beloved Robert, but the chink in the wall was empty. I was startled by the sound of a carriage approaching from the west, a very fine carriage that turned into the gate and made for The Priory. A guest for breakfast was most unusual, especially when Mr. Curran was due to plead in court that day and did not like his thoughts to be disturbed. Only after the front door had opened and closed did I make my way to the garden so that I could slip into the house without adding another distraction, but curiosity got the better of me. The driver of the coach was in livery, and I was certain that I had spotted a family crest on the carriage door. Someone of great importance was speaking in Mr. Curran's library and I had to find out who he was. On the lightest of feet I walked through the house, shuffling across the floor so that my boot heels did not clatter. I held my breath as I leaned my head against the door.

I jumped when Richard pushed it open, nearly striking my ear. He did not laugh at catching me spying, instead he displayed a rather vacant look like a man in mental distress. "The Earl of Wycombe," he whispered. "Just come from Butterfield Lane. We may be undone by a lack of funds."

"Father is bankrupt?" I asked.

"The rebellion, Sarah," he said. "Those who so generously invited Robert to lead are not being generous when their generosity is most needed."

Richard left me in the entry hall, with no time to explain when he was in a hurry to send for refreshments. I knew that Robert had sunk every shilling he had inherited from his late father into the venture, and I suspected that he had other sources of revenue. The laborers working in the depots to manufacture the weapons of war had to feed their families, and the supplies to make those weapons had to be bought with money rather than promises. Was our father part of the group that held tight to the purse, and had the Earl of Wycombe come to beg? Or was it a legal matter, with His Lordship seeking a way to force his colleagues to make good on their promises? As much as I wanted to know, I would not learn anything that morning. I gained nothing more than a brief glance at the earl when the footman entered the library with a tray and Richard closed the door immediately.

All afternoon, as I tortured my hair with the curling iron and stabbed my head with countless pins to keep the tresses in place, I plotted out a note to Robert. He kept much from me, but then again, it was not my place to be fully informed of his work. What part did my father play? I could not know. What part did my brother play? Of that, I was aware of some small details, but again, I was not party to the full plot. For all I knew, our many neighbors were all supporters of Robert Emmet, just as they were all supporters of Mr. Curran's doctrines. We were an enclave of liberal politics in Rathfarnham, which must have been of great help to Robert when his activities could not be completely secret. His underlings reported to him every evening, a bustle of regular activity that would otherwise have been brought to the attention of the authorities. Did he really have the backing of nineteen counties, with men waiting for the signal to rise up? Did he have my father's blessing, and if so, did that blessing extend to our union?

One puzzlement was clarified when we arrived at Little Dargle, the country seat of Mr. Ponsonby. Richard handed me down from the carriage after my sisters had alighted and gone ahead. He held me back so that he could talk freely in the few moments available before we entered. "The Knight of Glin died two days ago, hence the meeting this morning. An ardent rebel silenced by death, and his covert funding dried up as well. A move to postpone was voted down. September is set in stone."

In less than three months, my life would begin. My father would love me for being the agent of his elevation, and would speak fondly of me to his friends. He would compliment me as he once complimented Gertrude, her abilities fading into the background as my star rose. Such heady thoughts lifted my chin as I climbed the stairs, my face glowing with anticipated pleasure when I caught sight of William Fitzgerald. He was in company with the Earl of Wycombe. The blood rushed from head to my toes and I almost stumbled.

I could not shake the feeling that the earl had seen me before, judging by the way he examined my features. He was quick to ask me for a dance, certain that my card would be filled if he did not make his request before I entered the drawing room. "What chance does an old man like me have when you are surrounded by young swains clamoring for a reel?" he asked. "Mr. Fitzgerald here is champing at the bit, are you not, William. One dance, and then I will release the lovely Miss Curran to your company."

He offered his arm and escorted me into the room. The music had not yet begun, and we moved towards the wall where clusters of dancers stood waiting for the orchestra to strike up the opening tune. "There is a dangerous game being played, Miss Curran, and you are engaged in one of your own, I believe. I know of your connection to Mr. Emmet, and I know your father is unaware. Tread carefully, my dear. This is no time for tender feelings but our mutual friend will not be dissuaded from his pursuit when he should have nothing on his mind but the coming battle." He smiled, as if we were exchanging pleasantries. "Are you in earnest?"

"I am, yes," I said.

"Madness," he said. "Advise our mutual friend to focus on matters of urgency. Assure him of your constancy if that will ease his sore heart, but remove yourself from his consideration until such time as he has leisure for romantic pursuits. You put him in danger by distracting him."

"Have you spoken to him?"

"Frequently. He must hear it from your sweet lips. Tell him your father forbids it."

"He is well aware that we are acting against my father's wishes," I said.

"If it were within my power, Miss Curran, I would send you to London and put you beyond his reach."

"I will speak to him, I promise," I said. The rebellion was made up of countless parts, and Robert had to keep them all working in unison. I could not insert myself into the machine and expect the mechanism to operate smoothly. We saw each other so little, what difference would it make if we were apart for the next three months?

"Mr. Ponsonby is marshaling the troops, I see. We are in agreement then?"

My steps were not as graceful as I would have wished, but my mind was elsewhere. Until that moment, I saw the uprising as some hazy image on the horizon, a goal that would not soon be reached. His Lordship brought it forward at lightning speed, into sharp focus. My thoughts turned to my brother John, serving the King's navy. What would become of him if Ireland, his homeland, was no longer British? To which nation would he pledge his allegiance, or would he be allowed to make the choice?

Even before I curtsied to the earl and thanked him for the honor he bestowed on me, William was at my side with a glass of punch. He was bubbling over with excitement about his upcoming excursion to London, and I choked on my drink when I recalled Lord Wycombe's words. He would send me to London, he had said, and I saw the subtle suggestion that I encourage William and forget about Robert. Fathers were to be obeyed, after all, and what else could I expect from His Lordship but a reminder of my duty. I had a duty to Robert, however, and Robert took precedence.

"Not even a journeyman, but an apprentice will I be," William said. "My knowledge in matters financial was but slightly improved by the month at Oxford. My father is quite right, I am not yet ready to sit in Parliament. My servitude commences in September."

"You are still quite young," I said. "Although I wish you were not going to London in September. There has often been talk of a French invasion, I know, but the rumors seem more credible this time."

"Thank you for your concern, Miss Curran, you are so kind to fear for my safety when I myself have no such fear. I trust to the King's army and the Royal Navy to protect us all while I gain the experience I need to manage the estate." He paused, to search for the safest words. I wanted to die on the spot. My phrase had more meaning than I intended and William was free to color it with his own palette. "Your thoughtfulness has touched me deeply."

"You are wise in that you know what you do not know and seek to improve. Your tenants will benefit, I am sure. That you would work towards such a goal is most commendable."

He stood close to me, our hands brushing as he shifted to allow another guest to pass behind him. "It is my strong impression that you understand me. My motives, my goals, my dreams, perhaps."

"I am influenced by my father," I said. "He, too, put his mind to improvement as a young man, and I admire my father very much. A man who strives, rather than one who seeks a life of leisure, is one worthy of admiration."

"Perhaps you are eager to leave his side," William said. "To form your own household."

"Indeed I am not," I said. "While I may, I seek a life of leisure. You must think me a hypocrite for criticizing those whose habits I emulate, but I do not wish to throw away the carefree days that are fleeting for a young lady."

"I cannot, for one minute, believe that you are a lady of leisure and indolence," William said. "You are so often out that I wonder if I must make an appointment to call on you."

Was it coincidence that William visited The Priory when I happened to be haunting Butterfield Lane, or was I gone from home too often for others not to notice? "The needs of the poor are great and it is our duty to alleviate distress where we can," I said. "My charity calls seem to increase with every passing week."

"My mother is also deeply concerned about the poor in our district, and I admire her greatly for her desire to help them where she can."

"Parliamentary reform would be of great help, I think. The waste due to corruption could be used to feed and clothe the unfortunate."

"Precisely. That is where I can make my mark, when my time comes. An end to the rotten boroughs, the sycophants and laggards who sponge off the public purse."

My sisters must have decided that I had been conversing with one gentleman long enough. Amelia and Eliza intruded, pulling me away under the pretext of needing my opinion on the color of Miss Owenson's dress. The music started up again and I danced with a freshly minted barrister whose admiration of Mr. Curran knew no bounds. As there were more women than men, I was able to avoid another dance without inconveniencing my hostess. It was refreshing to stand in a clutch of other ladies and chat about fashion, to escape from the fears that plagued me.

The uprising was forever in the back of mind, rousing me from sleep. At any minute, Ireland could explode in a shower of Robert's rockets. The French could send an army as part of an alliance and then imprison Robert while Napoleon Bonaparte added our little island to his vast empire. We could all be arrested, I sometimes imagined, and put on trial for being Protestants or insurgents or dangers to the despot who would free the

Catholics. Was it worth the cost? I lived in constant dread, waiting for a note from Robert and then waiting for a reply to my response, around and around in a circle. I often dreamed of Anne that June, bringing me a letter with a warm smile on her face, to tell me that my love was hale and hearty. Other nights the dream would turn into a nightmare and Anne would arrive at the front door with blood splattered on her apron before disappearing like a ghost. I laid down my emotional burden at Gertrude's grave, finding comfort in the embrace of the trees that surrounded the grove, the thick yews that witnessed my first kiss and safeguarded my secret engagement.

It was all as ephemeral as a cloud, like the notes of the harp dying after the strings ceased vibrating. Everything fell to pieces in July.

EIGHTEEN

Anne was clearly distressed when I saw her near the canal bridge, where she was waiting for me. Under the pretext of a peddler trying to make a sale she approached and asked if I would like to buy some lace. She pulled a bit of crochet work out of her apron pocket, along with a letter that was folded up tight enough to be hidden in the palm of a woman's hand. I went along with the performance, praising her handiwork and bargaining for different lengths, while Anne whispered the terrible news.

"An explosion at the munitions depot," she said. "Some say one killed. Some say one spy removed by his handlers after the sabotage was completed. All in disarray, Miss, and Master gone to Dublin."

"Has he been unmasked?" I asked. My hands were wet with nervous perspiration, soaking into the cotton thread and soiling the trim.

"Not as yet," Anne said. "When he can see you again he'll send word. 'Twill be silence until then I fear."

It was Richard who drew the attention, Richard who was pale as death and so nervous he seemed ready to take flight at the slightest noise. No one noticed me, equally distracted and unable to eat. No one except Amelia, who laughed at my pallor and accused me of pining for my love who was soon to cross the Irish Sea. The letter from William that arrived that morning was still sitting unread on the dressing table, and I almost told her as much, until I realized that I had great need of a ruse to mask the truth. Eliza saw fit to tease me as well, asking if I was perhaps pining for the house and grounds in Ennis, while Amelia corrected the word 'house' to 'gilded cage'. Ignoring the jibes, I watched Will and James laugh over schoolboy pranks they had played during the previous term. At the head of the table, Mr. Curran was pressing Richard to explain his incivility before ordering his son to the library for a conference. A screen could have descended, cutting the room in half, and we would not have noticed. Two separate worlds were at table, two planets with orbits that crossed but rarely.

Summer nights were long and I sat out in the garden working on my embroidery, taking advantage of the natural light so that Mr. Curran might save a few pence on candles. A long-gone image reformed when Amelia and Eliza joined me, with Amelia reading the newspapers aloud. Only our mother was missing, a woman dead while alive in England, or so Richard had told me, a wife to a man not her husband, her children erased from view. Did she miss us, or was Mr. Sandys alone sufficient? Or was she dead and Mr. Curran did not see the need to inform us? I wanted Robert so desperately at that moment, wanted him at my side to tell me that he loved me and would always care for me. We would be together always, I longed to hear it from his lips but I could not say if I would ever again hear his voice.

My youngest brothers were off skylarking on the estate, taking advantage of the thirty-five acres to escape the critical eye of John Philpot Curran. I could not help but wonder what Mrs. Fitzgerald was doing at that very moment, alone with her sons in Dublin, living outside of polite society. Who called on her, if anyone, or did her circle of friends consist of other mistresses of important men who saw no harm in a man's infidelity while expecting purity in their wives. She must have been lonely on those nights when Mr. Curran was home, and as I counted up those nights, I noticed that my father slept at The Priory with some increased frequency since the day my relationship with Robert was uncovered.

The steady crunch of shoe heels on gravel was an annoying distraction. Richard was a soldier on the march, up and down the garden paths, deep in thought. He sometimes paused and looked at me, as if I had the answer to the question in his head, but instead of asking it he turned on his heel and walked on. The faint sound of Mr. Curran's violin drifted out of the open windows and Amelia sighed with annoyance. Her repeated effort to study painting in Dublin had been rebuffed yet again, and her frustration left her short-tempered.

"Richard, what is come over you?" she asked.

"Nothing that concerns you," he said. "Come walk with me to the canal. I feel like a prisoner in this garden."

"It is rather late for young ladies to be out on the road," she said. Richard shot her a pained look that pleaded for consideration. "Unless we return before dark."

We set off for town, the dust of the road raising a cloud behind our feet. I found myself taking the lead, as if I could direct our route towards Butterfield Lane, to see if the shadow of a young man crossed the window of a certain house. Richard stopped to look out over the pasture of The Hermitage, as if the cows were the most fascinating creatures he had ever seen.

"It is remarkable how the best laid plans can be upended in a single day," he said. "What seemed so certain last week is called into question."

"The explosion?" I asked.

My brother turned on me like a wildcat, fury in his dark eyes. "What do you know of it? Who told you?"

"Whatever are you talking about?" Amelia asked.

"The munitions factory on Patrick Street in Dublin was damaged on Saturday, and therefore exposed," Richard said. "The arms depot that Robert Emmet created. That rocket he demonstrated months ago was just one of many that have been constructed, to be used in an uprising."

"Good heavens, Richard, this is so much more than you led me to believe when we met Robert in Dublin," Eliza said. "How deeply involved are you?"

"A small role," he said. "I will ask you all to swear on your immortal souls that if it becomes necessary, you will burn some papers that I carry on my person. If the authorities come to the house, I will give one of you a packet that you are to take to the fire without delay. Swear to me."

"You know we would protect you against any foe," Amelia said.

"I put it to you that a contingent of soldiers has pounded on the door. I hand you the packet, and I go to see what they want. You hear the sounds of a scuffle, a fight perhaps, or the report of a gun. You run to see what has happened. And what of the documents? Do you leave them on the fire, where they may not be fully consumed?"

"We would remain at our post, stirring the embers to be sure that all was consumed," Eliza said. "I will swear."

"And if they kill you where you stand, you expect us to act as if nothing is happening at our own front door?" Amelia asked.

"Yes," Richard said.

"This is madness," Amelia said.

"To rise up against the government is madness on its face," I said. "To take a risk is madness, but is it not also madness to accept a beating without turning on your attacker?"

I had said too much in the heat of the moment, letting emotion rule. A horseman clattered by, making for Dublin at some haste, and I wondered if it was a messenger in search of Robert, to tell him the rebellion was on. Or the rebellion was off. Or the rebellion was delayed. And how would Robert know if the report was the truth, or a lie inserted by a secret agent? Had Anne not told me that the explosion could have been an act of sabotage rather than a simple accident? The rather nebulous concern that Richard expressed to us became solid to me at that moment and I shuddered.

"On the appointed day I will signal a messenger who will then notify the brigade in Wexford that we march," Richard said. "The less that you know, the safer you will be. I will leave the house, and you will not know why I have gone."

"What day?" I asked.

"The day selected by the committee," Richard said. "It was to have been in September but we cannot wait for the French any longer. The discovery of the depot has changed all plans."

Tension, fear and anticipation held my eyes open at night and stirred my legs during the day. How many times did I take the embroidered map of Ireland from its muslin cover and examine it for the slightest flaw, to ensure that I presented a perfect example of a womanly art to the man I loved? Days went by and I began to think that the explosion had toppled the entire operation, with Major Sirr picking off the foot soldiers and bribing them to expose the ringleaders. The house on Butterfield Lane looked empty and no one stirred. No notes were tucked into the gate wall, nor did Anne appear anywhere in Rathfarnham.

Tuesday dawned and the Curran men rode off to Dublin to defend a gentleman accused of attempted murder. Wednesday was the same, followed by Thursday and then Friday, but no one moved in the house on Butterfield Lane. On Saturday Richard fell into one of his melancholy states and could not get out of bed, dosing himself liberally with whiskey to numb the pain he claimed had settled into his bones. He was still in bed at two o'clock when a message arrived from Dublin. He gave it to me to read.

"Light the fuse," I read. The missive was not handwritten, but printed, so that no distinctive style of writing could give the messenger away.

"It is impossible," Richard said. "Hopeless. We do not stand a chance."

"The signal," I said. "You must do your duty, Richard."

"To send good men to their death? I cannot. I cannot."

"Where is the rocket? I will light it. For the love of God, you must send your men."

Richard turned his back to me, and when I persisted, he draped an arm across his face so that I could not see the tears that flowed. His shoulders quaked with sobs, but I could not understand why he wept when he had one simple task to accomplish. The men from the countryside would arrive in numbers, all those downtrodden Catholics who could no longer endure the bigotry and injustice of their rulers. They would not arrive if no one informed them that it was time to come, and without the pike men, what chance did Robert have? I grew frantic, beating at my brother with my fists to pound the answer out of him. He would not yield.

Growing desperate, I ran to the stable and searched through the straw, dug my hands into sacks of oats and rifled through every crate I could open. There was nothing, no metal cylinder, no fuse, no rocket to shoot off so that the volunteers waiting in the countryside beyond Rathfarnham would see the cascading sparks. I cried with frustration and took to the garden, hunting in the hedges and probing the flower pots, but the rocket was gone. Perhaps it had never been there, or perhaps Richard had thrown it into the canal when he feared the plot was uncovered. Until it grew too dark to see I scoured the fields and hedges, finding nothing. I came home in tears, covered in dirt, a madwoman.

How could I explain to my sisters the reason for my hysteria? Words did not serve, inadequate to the task of expressing fear such as I had never before felt, along with guilt for those moments when I hated my brother with a burning passion. Eliza helped me undress and Amelia dabbed my temples with rosewater to cool the fire in my brain. I drank brandy and water until I stopped trembling, but lapsed into deep sobs that stole my breath away. I was suffocating, as if the hangman's noose was around my neck.

Through the open window I thought I heard the sound of soldiers marching, the troops called out to suppress an insurrection that was missing a contingent from Wexford. How many had joined the fight? Did Robert stand already within Dublin Castle, proclaiming a new government and holding the Lord Lieutenant hostage to force the Crown to yield? "It has come," I babbled. "It has come and we have failed."

"God help us, she has lost her senses," Eliza said, the tears falling.

My sisters held me through the night as I alternated between profound gloom and hopeful elation. At the slightest noise I jumped up and ran to the window, searching the dark distance for evidence of a battle. The flash of rockets never lit up the sky. No boom of explosives disturbed us. It was no different than any other Saturday night of July, the air sultry, the roads quiet. The sun rose on Sunday morning and we were all safe in our beds, no soldiers beating down the doors to arrest us. I dared to believe that Robert had listened to cooler heads and postponed the rising, to hold to the original plan that coordinated a rebellion with the French invasion.

Despite a throbbing headache I rose and dressed. This was the time to seek God's help, to attend services and pray for Robert's safety. Mr. Ponsonby and Mr. Foote stopped us outside the door of the church to ask if Mr. Curran was aware of some incredible news. The details of the previous night, sketchy and incomplete, told me that my love was beyond God's reach. The rebellion had been a failure, a lightning quick failure. Mr. Curran's friend Lord Kilwarden was dead, and the gaggle of ruffians who accosted him were scattered. Robert Emmet, leader of the mob, had disappeared into the night.

NINETEEN

My desire to hurry to Butterfield Lane was so strong that I tripped over my feet in the churchyard, leading my sisters to think that I was fainting. Mr. Foote sent for his carriage to take me home, and I sat with my back to the horses so that I could monitor the road behind me. My heart beat so rapidly in my chest that I feared it would burst, while the pain radiated through my core. I felt ill, almost feverish, and had to be helped up to my room where I was put back in bed. Richard came in to see me, looking as wan as he had the night before.

"A message arrived after you were gone to church," he said. "With any luck, Robert is well on his way to the Wicklow Mountains."

"What will become of him?" I asked. "Where can he go?"

"Flee to America if Lord Wycombe can manage it. My God, this was a foolhardy enterprise that should have been delayed. The men from Kildare came in and went home when they refused to accept Robert's leadership. Volunteers in Wexford believed the rising was postponed and they never came in." Richard sat on the edge of the bed, his head in his hands. He was an image of defeat, utter and disastrous defeat. "Why did he not stop when he realized he did not have the numbers he needed?"

"He saw that his cause was just," I said. "Emancipation of the Catholics, an end to the tithes that they are forced to pay to benefit the Protestant church while impoverishing their own. An end to injustice is a goal too noble to be put aside for another day that could bring just as many surprises."

"He could have used a dozen men with your level of conviction," Richard said.

"I would have fought at his side if he had called me," I said, but I regretted the words as soon as they left my mouth. My brother had been called, and had turned a deaf ear. The implied accusation cut him deeply and he broke down. When he returned to the Four Courts on Monday, he was a changed man, his shoulders slumped as if he were sinking slowly into the earth.

All of Rathfarnham was alive with talk of the uprising, with Robert Emmet's involvement suspected by those who knew him and his family as dedicated republicans. The Emmets were highly respected in our community and no one spoke ill of the young gentleman, who was described as overly romantic and too exuberant for his own good, a man far too young to be fomenting insurrection. I heard nothing but sympathy for his fate from the many callers who stopped at The Priory on Amelia's day at home, so much esteem that I thought it safe to use a charity call to disguise the true reason for my presence on Butterfield Lane. I found Anne sweeping the front stoop and shared a brief glance. She sang softly in Irish, but the lyrics were invented to pass along a message.

Richard remained in Dublin with Mr. Curran that evening, preparing a defense for any of the rebels who would be in need of counsel. With only my sisters at home, my brothers being away on a fishing holiday with the Crawford family in Lismore, it was easy to slip down to the grove in the early morning hours without being noticed. I shook with excitement and worry in equal measures, and when Robert appeared I threw myself into his arms and sobbed with relief that he was alive, mixed with sorrow that he had to leave. We did not need words to express all that we felt as we kissed for the last time. I pulled his face close to mine, to commit every feature to memory, and regretted that I had not confided in Amelia. She might have drawn a sketch for me to keep always, to hold Robert's memory forever in my heart. All I had was the power of recollection that I knew was faulty. I could not quite recall my mother's face any longer, and would my memory of Robert fade as well? The notion brought on a new round of sobbing that he muffled against his chest.

"The Dublin men failed us," he said. "Those I counted on the most proved to be cowards, but all is not lost. What we fought for, Sarah, the principles of justice, can never be suppressed. There were no Catholics in the leadership and their cause is not harmed by what I did. I take comfort in that."

"Richard," I said, but thought better of it. There was no need to tell Robert that one of his trusted allies had been too frightened to do his duty. By not acting, Richard proved his belief that the rebellion would fail by ensuring that it failed. What was done, was done, and I would bid Robert farewell without tarnishing the name of his dear friend.

"He is prepared to destroy what must be destroyed. Well rehearsed, and prepared for different scenarios so that he cannot fail," Robert said.

"What are we to do now?" I asked.

"I cannot remain here, that much is clear. Sarah, I asked you to marry me and you accepted. Now I must ask you to run away with me."

Decent women did not run off with gentlemen, even if the goal was a respectable marriage. The scandal would strike my family at a time when

Mr. Curran would be most endangered, with his enemies already standing by to attack him. My father had defended rebels a few short years ago, and there were those who would see his hand in Robert's activities. If I fled, like some wanted criminal, I would do little more than lend credence to the rumors and suppositions that were sure to fly. My sisters would never recover from a new blow to the Curran name. But I loved Robert. Loved him to distraction, to the point of madness. To the point of recklessness.

When I did not answer, he understood that I could not reply at once. This was a matter that required long consideration. It was a dreadful step to take, to remove ourselves from society, to never be received in the homes of friends. Realization dawned and I dared to give in to the madness. We would have to make our escape to America, where we had no friends who knew of our wickedness. No friends, no family, no occupation, no means with which to live. The plan was ill-conceived, impossible in fact. I wanted so much to go with him, to put my life in his hands and trust to his abilities. What would stop him from reading the law in America, and claiming his rightful place? Money, of course, money to pay the costs of a wife and the children that would follow. I was so confused, so torn, that I could not speak.

"I thought to hide in Wicklow but I could not remain there without you," he said. "Friends will help me escape, but I will not go unless you are with me, to share the rest of our lives as we had hoped. Please, Sarah, say you will. I cannot remain here any longer, the sun is rising. Write to me. Anne will look for your letter and bring it to me. Do not hesitate. I do not know how much time I have before I am found."

Before the week was over, I heard reports of homes being searched. It was clear that Robert was the chief suspect, and those who had any association with the Emmet family were subject to a visit from Major Sirr and his troop of brigands. The rebels who had been caught on Thomas Street had refused to talk, but their silence was a reflection of strategic planning. They did not know Robert Emmet, had never met him, and did not know that he stood at their head until they were called out on Saturday. Those who were aware of the facts had kept themselves at a remove, like Lawless in Paris or Lord Wycombe hiding behind his position, and they would never be brought in because they were above suspicion. Where did Mr. Curran fit in? I lived in dread of a knock at the door, the red-coated scoundrels rifling our possessions.

For loyalty and fearlessness I could not commend anyone more highly than our messenger Anne Devlin. She risked her safety by moving between Wicklow and Rathfarnham so that Robert could communicate with me as I debated the course I would take. His letter was filled with pleading, an expression of such profound adoration that I was ready to accompany Anne to the hiding place and leave my former life behind. Robert described his companions in light-hearted terms to ease my worries, but I did not laugh at the notion of Anne's uncle Michael Dwyer playing the role of nagging wife demanding that her recalcitrant husband take passage to America. He had ten men with him, all who stood ready to renew the fight if Robert would lead them, but the time for rebellion had passed.

Despite all the precautions he had taken, it was inevitable that someone would reveal the name of Robert Emmet, and that someone who knew he was living under an assumed name would expose his false identity. The population of soldiers increased in our neighborhood and I suspected that they were acting on information that, thanks be to God, was old. Steeling myself against the pain I would experience, I took the last letter from Robert and put it on the fire in the kitchen, waiting until the cook was preparing dinner so that the heat was at its highest and the paper consumed completely. My tears would have put out a raging blaze, so much did I cry as I watched the precious words melt away into ash. The cook grew alarmed at my behavior, which I made no effort to disguise. Amelia shook my arm to wake me from the trance I was in.

"What are you doing?" she asked. "What papers do you burn? Is this addressed to My Beloved Sarah? Who wrote this? Answer me, Sarah."

The weight of my secret was too heavy to bear alone and it spilled out. My clandestine meetings, the engagement, the chance to find happiness by committing a sin that would soon be forgotten when I was gone. The blatant disobedience to our father drew a slap that startled me back to my senses. She wrenched the last few letters from my hands and threw them into the flames, poking and prodding until no evidence remained.

"You have lost your reason," she said. "Gone mad, I tell you, ready for Bedlam and if it were up to me I would put you there. To even consider eloping, why, I am shocked. How could you entertain the suggestion, let alone consider it as a suitable action?"

"You have never been in love," I said. "You do not know how miserable I am, how I cannot sleep with worrying about him."

"Are you still in communication? If you love him as you say you do, you will insist that he leave this country at once."

"I will not say good-bye forever," I said. A new idea formed in my mind, created out of a ready supply of hope. "If he has prospects abroad, why could we not anticipate a union at some later date?"

"If you wish to trade in daydreams, then spin the prettiest yarn you like. Pretend that society would not shun you for leaving your father's house, alone and unmarried, to arrive at some unknown port with nothing more than a promise to wed. Who will ensure that Mr. Emmet is still sincere? You could be ruined and there would be no one to turn to, no friends or relations."

"I have no doubt as to his sincerity, nor do I doubt his constancy."

"The future cannot be predicted with any accuracy," Amelia said. "He may be in Kilmainham even now, or on a pirate's brig bound for Calais."

"I know he is not. He will not leave me until I have answered him."

"Then answer him with all haste. The fool. To think he can hide. Have you heard of the new law that Parliament enacted? We must post the names of every resident of our house on the door, and I suppose the soldiers will muster us on the carriage path and count heads to verify the list. It is not safe anywhere in Ireland, and you must make that clear to Mr. Emmet. If you truly love him you will send him on his way."

From Richard's bedroom window I could watch the soldiers at the canal bridge, where they set up a checkpoint. My suspicions were confirmed, that they had determined Robert's former location on Butterfield Lane, when I saw Major Sirr ride towards the house with a small contingent of soldiers behind him. They did not return before I had to dress for supper, but I thought that I heard a large party pass by several hours later. I could not eat, my stomach in turmoil as I prayed that Robert had not left anything behind that would identify me. I had disobeyed my father, and I would pay dearly for the infraction if it was discovered.

When I did not hear from Robert, I told myself that he had fled, taking the advice of all those around him. Neither did I see Anne again, and I assumed that she too had taken to the Wicklow Mountains. The conversation at supper proved me wrong. Terrifyingly wrong.

Mr. Curran was preparing defenses for some of those caught up in the hysteria, innocent men who might have been involved but could prove otherwise. He brought Mr. McNally home for supper so that they could work into the night, to construct an opening speech that would direct the judge to throw the case out on lack of merit. We had heard nothing but rumor since Saturday and welcomed some news from Dublin that was likely to be more factual than fantasy.

That Robert Emmet was the ringleader was without question, based on the information that was extracted from those who were tortured into submission, or paid to turn traitor. Several arms depots had been found, containing a quantity of pikes and cartridges, along with copies of a proclamation that spelled out the grievances and goals of the rebels. Unlike the uprising in 1798, the participants in Emmet's rebellion were drawn from the lower classes, the disgruntled and disenfranchised.

"Here is where I would warn you to be on your guard," Mr. McNally said. "Sirr raided a home nearby where it is believed Emmet was hiding. That he was able to live there for months, perhaps, without being turned in suggests a level of cooperation in this town that has Sirr convinced that several persons in this vicinity were shielding him, and may be shielding him yet."

"Do you not think he is long gone by this time?" Mr. Curran asked. "A week gone by with no sign of him. He is an intelligent young man, clever enough to make his way to Cork, say, and book passage on the first ship heading west."

"His maid was brought in for questioning, and that after Sirr tortured the poor woman. Put a rope around her neck and hanged her until she was half dead, demanding answers. Up and down, five times I heard, hanging her until her eyes popped out of her head and then letting her breath again. She never admitted that she knew a Robert Emmet, even after abuse that would break a strong man."

"If she knew nothing, how could they extract information she did not possess, no matter what cruelty they inflicted?" Eliza asked.

"She is the niece of a notorious rebel who has been hiding in the Wicklow mountains since 1798, and she was seen coming from there earlier this week," Mr. McNally said. "Let us hope that she brought Mr. Emmet the means to depart."

"I would rather see him in exile than hanged," Mr. Curran said. "His father is to blame. Too staunch of a republican, too admiring of France and their rebellion."

"Yes, exile over death," Richard said. "He is a good man, better than most who sit in Parliament and feast on the wealth of this country, leaving the people to starve."

The words washed over me, as if everyone were speaking a foreign tongue. All I could think of was Anne, dear Anne who threw her lot in with the rebels and would pay a steep price. She might hang as a traitor, or languish in prison, forgotten, until she died. My hand touched my throat as I imagined a rope around my neck, pulled tight, my feet dangling off the ground, choking. I was not strong. I would shout out names, implicate anyone, turn in Richard and my father and Lord Wycombe and Lord Cloncurry's son. Sweat beaded on my lip and rolled down my back, a trickle of dread that soaked the chemise clinging to my skin. I had to contact Robert to reinforce my demand that he burn anything with my name on it, any scrap of paper with my handwriting or initials, and then flee.

I was seized by terror, a profound sensation that stole my breath away like the noose around Anne's neck. Mr. McNally was all apologies, thinking that his tale of horror had been too much for a lady's sensibilities. He helped me up and took me into the garden for some fresh air, leaving his pudding untouched so that he could make amends for his lack of sensitivity. "I forgot that he was often welcomed here, and naturally would have become a good friend to you and your sisters. Mr. Emmet was, perhaps, a particular friend of yours? So I was led to believe by your father, who was concerned at one time that you were forming an unsuitable attachment."

"Would that we could control who we love, sir, and we might all be disinterested parties," I said. "I am most distressed by these recent events."

"A young lady without a mother's vigilance can be prone to such a lack of control," he said. "Am I correct in my opinion, that you harbor strong feelings for Mr. Emmet? We speak in complete confidence, Miss Sarah."

A great weight lifted off my shoulders as I admitted my love for a renegade, a wanted man who had committed high treason. My father's associate did not criticize me for being silly, but agreed that Robert was a very decent individual, blessed with intelligence and cursed, perhaps, by passion. There was every reason to think that a match between us would have been welcomed if politics had not taken an ugly turn. But there it was, the wedge that drove our families apart. "Many of us who know him pray that he has escaped, even if we publicly proclaim a desire that he be brought to justice," Mr. McNally said.

"I have no idea if he has gone or not," I said. "There has not been a message from him for days. Do you think he did as I asked, and quit the country?"

"We can but put our trust in Divine Providence," Mr. McNally said. "If he should contact you again, if he remains nearby, will you tell him that I stand ready to help him complete his escape? I would gladly pay for his passage if he would have the sense to accept my gift. I realize he cannot come to see me, but I would go wherever he was to bring him money, clothes, or whatever he might need. I watched you grow up, you know, and hoped that you could find happiness after the afflictions visited upon this family. It would make you happy to know he was safe, would it not?"

"I cannot tell you how happy I would be, to know that he was out of danger. If he went abroad, he could make a new life, and perhaps, do you think, Mr. McNally, that my father might consider a match?"

"You would have my support, and the power of my persuasion in your arsenal. A pity he did not leave when his mother asked him to go. He would be free now to return in triumph, to claim his bride. If wishes were horses, eh? You appear recovered. Shall we return before your father starts to worry?"

"What will become of the maid?" I asked.

"A trial, eventually, or a period of incarceration until the investigations are complete and all the players rounded up. I suppose she will suffer for the embarrassment that Mr. Emmet caused. No one in Dublin Castle expected a thing, and you can well imagine that His Majesty is more than a little concerned about the lack of intelligence. That's where Emmet showed his brilliance, in the tight web of secrecy. He was undone by desertions, in Mr. Grattan's opinion. He told me just yesterday, and I might add he is despondent over the failure, that the people are incapable of redress, and unworthy of it. Neither does he believe that the French have any intention of invading. The First Consul is quite cleverly threatening an attack at every instance, and forcing England to prepare for an attack. The expense could bankrupt the country if it continues."

"It is a game and we are the pawns, to be sacrificed when needed," I said.

"The game of chess is a game of war, with strategy and anticipation of an opponent's move. You will remember to put Mr. Emmet in touch with me, if he should surface? Let us work together to send him away."

TWENTY

Strange faces appeared on the streets of Rathfarnham, the faces of those I suspected were searching for rebels. Soldiers loitered at the crossroads, intimidating us all with the blinding sheen of their buttons and bayonets. I was sure that I spotted Major Sirr lurking in the shadows when I left Holly Park after drinking tea with the Misses Foote, but in those days my eyes played tricks on me. Fear of arrest, of being discovered, wore away my patience and I grew snappish, barking at Richard over nothing. He was equally peevish, wearing a cloak of black gloom that encased him like a shroud. If Mr. Curran noticed the toxic miasma that permeated his home, he never mentioned it. He was too busy defending a second crop of rebels and saw the opportunity to reiterate his oft-repeated arguments in favor of change at the highest levels of government. The rebellion had proved him right, but moral victories did not improve the plight of Ireland's Catholics.

My letters to John were filled with the events he would not know from reading news dispatches. I dare not confess too much to my brother, not when he was on a British naval ship where secrets could never be kept. He had known Robert, and I wanted him to remember our old friend as a patriot whose love for his homeland had brought him to ruin. Whatever the press might think of those who dared to stand up after being beaten down, I could not let that image linger in John's mind.

Days went by and I worried myself into dyspepsia. I was convinced that when next I heard from Robert, the letter would arrive from France or America, but it was a young man who brought me a missive and it came from Rathfarnham. Robert had found sanctuary with Mrs. Palmer, his father's old housekeeper, and he would remain there until we left together. As stubborn as ever, he had chosen his fate. Life without me as his partner was not a life he wished to live. The room spun as I read his words again and again, my brain in a fever. To be wanted was something I had long sought, but to be wanted with such powerful conviction was more than I could bear. The messenger waited for my reply but I could not compose a coherent sentence. How could I convince the man I loved that our love was deadly? Robert had drawn up such elaborate plans for a rebellion, could he not conceive of another plan that would bring us together in the future, in some other country?

More than marriage was tormenting his thoughts, and it broke my heart to read of his anguish. He had been expecting help from every corner but his allies deserted him. All the money that might have been used to establish himself in exile had been spent, without benefit to anyone. In some ways, he felt he had been duped, that his brother Thomas had been used by the highly placed who looked only for gain at no cost to themselves. Robert needed the consolation of a friend, but it would be madness to arrange a meeting when Rathfarnham was occupied by soldiers and yeoman. I could try to reiterate the wisdom of his leaving without me, but written words did not have the power to debate or sway opinion. I had to see him again, but I could not demand it. Only if he could slip away from his lodging with safety would we make our farewells. For now, I would stress, not forever. My heart was his. He would leave with no doubts as to my fidelity.

Surely it was a brain fever that drove me to follow the messenger at a distance, to watch where he went and see if he arrived there. Three soldiers were operating a checkpoint at the canal bridge, where a large group of men were made to turn out their pockets. My note to Robert moved from coat pocket to boot, a couple of stomps and it was down to the heel. The messenger continued on, turned out his pockets and demonstrated that he did not even have so much as a halfpenny in his possession. The crowd swelled with impatient farmers eager to reach Dublin for Market Day, and I lost sight of the man who had risked his freedom for the sake of a love letter.

To my annoyance, the world of The Priory carried on unchanged while my world was in tumult. Political discourse continued in the drawing room, filling my head with so much hot air that I thought my skull would explode. Less than a mile away a gentleman was hiding, someone who had taken action while others sat around and debated in comfort. That anyone could analyze the Parliamentary approach to the Catholic question was incredible, but Mr. Curran droned on as if he held the key to unlock closed minds. My musical abilities failed me often when I was called on to entertain our guests before their long-winded monologues began. I came under fire after the ladies retired, when Amelia and Eliza both took me to task for losing control of my emotions. This was a time for stoicism, for a blank face and an empty mind.

William Fitzgerald wrote to me from Clare, where his family remained for their safety. His plan to call on me in August, on his way to London, was uncertain due to the uncertain times. The mood in the west of Ireland was rather dark, in his opinion, and he was concerned that the ringleaders remained at large. His kind consideration for my well-being was touching,

145

but as I skimmed over the page covered in his bold script, I was overcome by guilt. As far as William was concerned, our acquaintance was becoming more intimate, and I should have ended our correspondence when I accepted Robert's proposal. How was I to break it off when no one knew of my engagement, and how was I to let William go when I could not tell him why?

Sleep was more elusive than ever and I walked in the garden to tire myself out, around and around the paths at all hours until I found my way to Gertrude's resting place. How many nights did I find relief on the cool stone slab, waking as the sun rose, still dressed in the same clothes I had worn the evening before. Amelia wanted to send me to Grandmother Curran's home in Cork, for the peace and quiet of the country, but I refused to leave. The suggestion gave me an idea that I thought to share with Robert. He could disguise himself and come along with me to Newmarket, where we could be married under false names, and then board a packet from Cobh headed for America. I badgered Richard to drive me to Dublin so I could go past the house in Harold's Cross, but saw no sign of my love. We arrived at the book seller whose shop I was so determined to call at, but I made no purchases. It was while I perused a book about the American wilderness that I realized how foolish my plan was. There was no respectable way to proceed. We were boxed in, like prisoners in a cage, confined by society that would punish my family when Robert and I were free of its clutches.

From the depths of despair to the heights of elation, my mood swung at the beginning of August when Robert appeared in the grove at the appointed time. The contours of his face had sharpened, with every care and worry deeply etched into his cheeks. A light still burned in his eyes and I felt hope again, a belief in a future together. We said little during that brief interlude, when he was so very conscious of daylight and the need to pick his way across farm fields to avoid detection. It was only after he had gone that I pondered his few words. He would not leave Ireland without me, to that he had made up his mind and there was no changing it. Neither would he listen to me, for if he had, he would not have returned to Mrs. Palmer's house but made his way back to the Wicklow Mountains, where he would find loyal friends to hide him until we could puzzle out some means of escape. What husband did as his wife dictated, I thought. Another man, an older man, was more likely to succeed into talking sense into the head of Robert Emmet.

There was no better person for the task than my father, whose power of persuasion was legendary. It was equally certain he could not be approached. While he would assist Robert out of respect for the Emmet family, he would never countenance the remainder of our scheme. It was highly likely that I would either be rushed into marriage with anyone available, or locked in the house for the rest of my days as punishment. A new dilemma presented itself. Could I dare to parlay with Mr. Curran, to accept William Fitzgerald in exchange for Robert's life? I was fond of William, although I was not in love with him. There was no passion there, no longing to see him when we were apart, nor fire when we were together. I could tolerate such a match if I could know that Robert was alive. My love would dwell forever in my heart, hidden from view, warming me from within.

Should Robert learn of my strategy he would refuse to go, and where would I be then? Trapped, tied forever to William while Robert ran for the rest of his life, always hiding, a stranger wherever he went. He might go to Wicklow, and what torment would it be for both of us to be near yet far, separated forever? At least he would be alive, and surely that was compensation enough for the agonies I would endure. While I debated with myself, I sent him another letter, spelling out the love I had for him and urging him yet again to flee. As always, I encouraged him to look to the future when fate might smile on us. Out of fear of sounding strident and unfeminine, I added some humorous anecdotes to lighten the tone, to make it appear that I was a pillar of strength if he needed a shoulder to lean on. To do otherwise, to tell him exactly how I suffered for his sake, would have been merciless and cruel.

Robert's reply broke my heart. He was determined to have his way, assuring me that he was perfectly safe with Mrs. Palmer, who would never give him away. In the event of catastrophe, he could make a ready escape by leaping from a back window and hiding in a nearby cornfield until he could slip away under cover of darkness. Valentine Lawless was ready to offer sanctuary if Robert could make it across to France, and Lord Wycombe needed nothing more than a signal to book passage to any destination desired. My beloved awaited only my answer, that I would join him. Robert could not comprehend the impossibility of his request, and the fact that I could not say yes.

The tide of war can turn when an ally joins the fight. On my side, battling for my cause, stood The Great Incorruptible, a man above reproach and immune to the temptations of bribery. By outside appearances, Mr. McNally was a short man, built like a barrel set atop short spindly legs, but his reputation gave him the power of men twice his size. He had always been like an uncle to me, so close to Mr. Curran that I did not hesitate to put my trust in him. Leonard McNally offered a helping hand and I grasped it willingly, never questioning his motives.

TWENTY-ONE

The continued presence of soldiers and yeoman in Rathfarnham told me that Robert remained at large. His correspondence with me, delivered by different messengers to avoid suspicious activity, reflected his strong confidence in the continued silence of his cohorts. Those captured refused to talk, preferring to die with honor than betray a fellow rebel. I was familiar enough with Major Sirr, after his many run-ins with Mr. Curran, to realize that he was not the sort to give up, and I could not envision a day when the manhunt would stop. Almost a month after the failed rebellion, I was more determined than ever to make Robert see reason and make his escape.

Since first approaching me with an offer of assistance, Mr. McNally contacted me with regularity. His inquiry was always the same, though hidden in some little gift like a book of poetry or sheets of music. How could he contact Robert before it was too late, the authorities were closing in and had good intelligence, or so he had heard from the Attorney General. The notes were arriving daily at the end of August, when I was tempted to call on Mrs. Palmer and so visit Robert. My longing to be with him, to touch his hand just one more time, filled my mind so that I could think of nothing else. Unable to eat or sleep, I was worn down, and the pressure from Mr. McNally finally broke me.

He spent the night at The Priory after a long night of strategizing with Mr. Curran, Richard, and their two clerks. The barristers had an impossible task before them, to defend rebels who had refused to flee to Wicklow after Robert decreed that the cause was lost. It was not the failed insurrection, but the murder of Lord Kilwarden and his nephew during the melee, that formed the heart of the trials. Somehow the link between the harmless march to Dublin Castle and the tragic demise of a respected peer had to be severed with nothing but the force of words. The two actions had to be uncoupled if the rebels would be judged on the facts, rather than heated emotion and a call for revenge.

As usual, I could not sleep and went down to the garden well before breakfast, to share my worries with Gertrude. Mr. McNally must have been watching for me, so quickly did he join me before I could reach the grove. "If you would save his life you will tell me where he is," he said. "Your silence is a tacit approval of the Castle's prosecution. Do you wish him to be caught?"

"Of course not," I said. Like a dam bursting, I broke into sobs, unable to catch my breath. More than anything I wanted Robert to live, even if it meant giving up any happiness I might ever find in this world.

"Tell me where I can find him. I will go to him at once, you know I would not hesitate," he said. He took me by the shoulders and gave me a gentle shake. His eyes held mine as he said, "Where is he?"

One more visit, one more letter, one more chance, and I might convince Robert, but there had already been so many other visits and letters and chances. Before me stood what truly was our last chance, the barrister who had defended the rebels of 1798 with profound conviction. "Please, make him understand that I say good-bye until that blessed day when we can be together again," I said.

"Where is he?"

"In Harold's Cross, he is in Harold's Cross. He is staying with Mrs. Palmer, do you recall Dr. Emmet's housekeeper? I beg of you, save him from himself. I cannot live without him, Mr. McNally, but I can endure if I must."

"Mrs. Palmer's, in Harold's Cross. Should I ask for Mr. Emmet?"

"Oh, no, you must ask for Mr. Hewitt. Would you like me to go with you, to prepare Robert? He knows you, of course, but if I can make him understand that you are acting on our behalf, and not removing him from Ireland at my father's request."

"If we were seen together, it could arouse suspicion. I would not be surprised to learn that Major Sirr has operatives watching our every move, and both of us arriving at a home connected to the Emmet family would present too great a danger. Leave it all to me."

"Rap at the door, three quick, pause, and then one with greater force."

"Three, then one. You may rely on me."

I poured out my heart to my dear friend Caroline, to share the heartbreak that became my constant companion after Mr. McNally departed later that morning. How I needed her advice and her consolation to help me deal with my loss, and decide which way I should turn. There was William Fitzgerald to consider, a potential match that I did not wish to accept as I was determined to wait for Robert, but would I wait forever? Was I foolish to hold out hope? Could my family possibly recover from another elopement if Robert remained steadfast in his determination? Hours after Mr. McNally had gone on his way, I had second thoughts, followed by reconsideration minutes later. My happiness would cause my father harm, and if my sisters had any hope of marriage I would end it with a single, selfish act. Better to be a spinster than cast the Curran name into the mud.

My sorrow was bottomless, a deep well that I fell into and could not climb out of. I wandered the garden at night, and then I could not rise out of bed in the morning. Food was intolerable, my stomach constantly churning as I waited for news. No word came from Mr. McNally so I did not know if he had found success, or been rebuffed. Or if Robert had moved on to another safe house. Nothing was certain, and the uncertainty ate away at me until my frocks hung loose off my shoulders. Amelia sent for the doctor, who could find nothing wrong with me beyond the usual sort of nervous disorders that were typical of unmarried young ladies of highly strung temperaments.

I stopped joining my sisters on their rounds of calls, finding the chatter of our friends too painful to endure. Rumors were flying around like flocks of wild birds, swirling and then landing before taking to the air in a new formation, to land in other receptive ears. Some were certain that Robert Emmet had been captured, while others were equally certain that he had made his escape to France in an open boat. Debates erupted to argue the merits of each possibility, every word like a twist of the dagger in my heart, draining me of my life's blood. I was exhausted but could not rest, finding peace in the empty house after James and Will returned to school. Then I would sit in the library with an almanac about the United States, to prepare for the day I prayed would come. Milton's *Paradise Lost* hovered over my head, menacing in its memory.

The first week of September came and went. Mr. Curran remained in Dublin, the court docket packed full with trials for high treason. We heard of his attempts to mount a defense from Richard, who reported on the proceedings that were mere formalities. Those who had been caught on Thomas Street with pikes in their hands were guilty as a matter of course, and Major Sirr had a stable of paid informants willing to testify to whatever they were told they had seen or heard to lend an air of legitimacy to the charade. The juries were equally packed, returning the desired verdict despite the lack of corroborating evidence. Good men went to the gallows without revealing the names of their fellow conspirators. Such examples of valor and bravery were inspiring.

On the ninth of September, a Friday, I passed yet another fitful night, wandering through the quiet house, watching the hands on the clock in the drawing room shift from three-twenty to four-forty-five while wondering what Robert was doing. Sleeping peacefully in his brother's Parisian lodging, or sleeping rough in the wilds of the Wicklow hills? I made my way back to bed, only to open the bedroom window so that I could feel the cool breeze on my face. The same wind could have ruffled his hair in France, brushed his lips and carried his love across the Channel to me. I sat on the sill and leaned against the casement, recalling the times we had met in the grove below, where I shared my hopes and dreams with Robert and Gertrude. Before long the tension in my shoulders eased and I climbed back into bed, hoping for a few minutes of sleep before the house came alive.

My dream was unpleasant, filled with the sound of a fist pounding on the door amid the cacophony of a man shouting. The images faded as I lapsed into that confusing place where reveries mixed with reality and I could not be certain that I was awake or still sleeping. Eliza shook me, rattled my brain with the violence of her demand that I get up at once. "Major Sirr is here to arrest you. God have mercy on us, Sarah, he has come to take you in."

My reaction was one of puzzlement and disbelief. My sister scrubbed at my face with a cold, wet flannel saturated with the rose-scented soap that I favored, and the harsh treatment brought me around. My senses exploded in an instant, an overwhelming wave that felt like fireworks in my skull. The bedroom door was thrown open and Major Sirr charged in.

Terror and humiliation created a poisonous mix and I could only scream to set it free. Scream and scream and scream while he spoke words I could not hear. A warrant, known conspirator of Robert Emmet, incriminating letters found on his person, and I screamed as he pulled open the trunk at the foot of my bed and rifled the contents. Bundles of paper, letters from friends and former beaux, disappeared into a leather satchel.

"I told him to go," I shouted, for I had told Robert to go and I had no doubt that Robert had been caught. As well as I knew my own name I knew my beloved was caught. "I told him to go. I did. I told him to go."

My sister came to my defense, raising her voice to the most dangerous man in Ireland. She ordered him out of my room until I was dressed, it was uncalled for to enter a lady's bedroom and accost her while she was attired in nothing more than a robe de chambre, half naked. He shot back with his only weapon, his belief that we would destroy evidence if not kept under observation, and dear Eliza countered with such indignation that I found the courage to do what I had to do.

In some corner of my mind, reason found a toehold. Who knew about Richard's involvement but me? I was a danger to him because I was not strong like Anne who had refused to talk even as Major Sirr performed one mock execution after another. All it would take to loosen my tongue was the presence of the noose. What of the other names in my possession, would I not reveal those identities to show that Robert was merely an agent of others? I would speak, indeed I would declare to all and sundry because I was weak, a coward. Yet death was not as frightening as Mr. Curran, whose wrath would be more terrifying than the grave. My disobedience was about to be discovered and there was but one route left to me to escape all that I could not face.

"I told him to go," I said. "Gertrude heard me. Gertrude heard me."

"Fetch Gertrude," the Major ordered.

"Gertrude is dead. Sarah, Sarah, our sister is gone these ten years," Eliza said. She held me to her heart and lashed out at my tormentor. "She has lost her mind. What have you done, sir? How could you abuse my poor sister who is already suffering? Get out. Get out. Are you not satisfied?"

"Gertrude heard us," I said, and I jumped up to obey the Major's command. I would go to Gertrude, and in a few strides I was across the room, my foot on the sill so that I could go to Gertrude, to fly to the ground as she had, never to rise, never to be dragged off to Kilmainham or Newgate, never to explain to my father why I could not stop loving Robert Emmet when our love was forbidden.

How I fought them when they held me back, fought like a wild animal. "I told him to go," I said, taking comfort in the repetition that was like a prayer. The psalms were prayers that were poems and I had committed Robert's poems to memory because I could not keep a scrap of paper written by his hand. "No rising column marks this spot where many a victim lies, but oh the blood. Oh, the blood. I cannot remember it. Eliza, I cannot remember it."

The Major was a large man, stronger than I to be sure, and he used his strength to put me back in bed and then had Eliza help him wrap the sheets around me so that I was cocooned. Still I struggled against the linen bonds, desperate to recite one of Robert's poems so that I could be satisfied that his words would not die. Major Sirr barked out orders and his minions obeyed, bringing me a brandy and water while another set off to locate a physician. He asked for paper and pen so that he could write to his superiors to Dublin Castle to inform them of events that he had never anticipated. He leaned over me, but I could not hear him, too engrossed was I in the whiskers that were trapped in the cleft of his chin. Had his barber been afraid to shave the spot for fear that a cut could lead to arrest for attempted murder?

His lips moved, he asked questions, but he was speaking a foreign language I could not comprehend. An intense ache engulfed my chest and radiated along my arms. I cried out in agony, aware that Robert had not escaped and would never send for me. He was as good as dead, with no help of salvation. My beloved, my love, my life, my everything was gone in an instant. When I struggled against the sheets Eliza held me down. I heard the window being shut and the order given to a yeoman to keep me from it.

A voice shouted from the dining room and Major Sirr excused himself to attend to his underling. Eliza curled up next to me and held me in her arms as our mother might have. "Richard and Amelia have burned everything. We are safe," she whispered in my ear.

We cried together, a sorority of the broken-hearted. "Robert," I said. "I told you to go. Gertrude heard me. I told you."

Eliza stroked my head as she shushed me but I could not be soothed. My beautiful Robert would be hanged for a traitor, and all because I would not go away with him. I as much as killed him, as I had killed Gertrude. "I should have gone," I said. "I should have gone."

How much time elapsed? It felt like years but might have been minutes when Mr. O'Grady let himself into my room, with Major Sirr on his heels. The Attorney General had often been a guest at The Priory, another of the great legal minds who enjoyed the company of John Philpot Curran. He had once complimented my talent when I played the harp, and asked me to play the last time he had dined with us, even though Mr. Curran was eager to get on to the evening's discussion of political matters. There is always time for a pretty song sung by a pretty girl, Mr. O'Grady had said.

"Mr. Curran is not at home, for the love of God, and you barge into his daughter's room like a common ruffian," he said. "My instructions, sir, were specific, that Mr. Curran was to bring her to his town house for questioning in private, in a discreet manner, yet here you are with a contingent of yeoman drawing unwanted attention to this home."

"She has gone mad, Mr. O'Grady," Eliza said. "You cannot move her. She must stay here."

"Given the circumstances, I quite agree," Major Sirr said. "We have searched the lady's apartment and found several letters. There is nothing more to be done here."

"Love letters from a gentleman who has no connection to Mr. Emmet whatsoever," Eliza said. "Would you seek to hold Mr. William Fitzgerald up to public censure by revealing that which should remain private between him and my sister? Is that what our government has come to, criminalizing love?"

"I told him to go," I said. "Gertrude heard us. I told him. I told him."

A storm roared in with the arrival of John Philpot Curran, a man overcome with blind rage. Modesty was cast aside as I flew out of bed, to throw myself at his feet and beg for mercy. The buggy whip whistled through the air before resounding with a loud crack against my skin. There was no escaping my father's rage, his grip on my arm as unbreakable as iron. Again and again he struck me. "Disobedient, ungrateful bitch," he said. "How dare you humiliate me. My chance to be elevated to the bench, destroyed by your conduct. Worthless parasite, you suck the life's blood out of me and then you seek to destroy me. All that I have worked for brought down by your stupidity. I loathe you. The very sight of you nauseates me."

I cowered like a dog at his feet, the sound of my blood pulsing in my ears rendering me deaf to the remainder of his diatribe. A sweet memory popped into my head, a time when Gertrude and I sang underwater like mermaids. Our voices were muffled, and in the same way the voices around me were distorted. Major Sirr and Mr. O'Grady spoke in angry tones, their faces flushed, but I could not make out their words. Eliza, in retreat at the far side of the room, sobbed and may have spoken, but what could she say that would alter anything? Robert was going to hang and if Mr. Curran would do me the favor of beating me to death, I would be content.

Too soon the punishment ended and I remained alive, to my great sorrow. "I told him to go," I mumbled. "I told him to go."

It was Mr. O'Grady who lifted me into bed and asked if the doctor had been called. "Despicable conduct," he said under his breath. "No drop of sympathy for his own child when her heart is breaking."

"I will submit to any inquiry you demand," Mr. Curran said. "I demand an interview with the Privy Council, to clear my name. Go on, arrest her if you have cause. That girl is nothing to me. Disobedient, no better than a common whore, sullying my name."

I was left with Eliza, left to wonder if she had just woken me from a nightmare. My body ached and I decided that I had fallen ill, seriously ill, an exotic fever from the tropics perhaps. I would write to Robert and tell him to leave for France at once, that I would follow as soon as my health permitted, but he was not to wait. He must not wait.

Before I could ask Eliza for paper and pen, Richard dashed into the room. "Oh my God, Sarah, what has he done to you?" he asked.

Breakbone fever, I believed that was the ailment I had read about somewhere. If only I could recall where, I could direct my brother to the information he required. "If not for Mr. O'Grady's intervention he would have beaten her to death," Eliza said.

A slight scent of roses tickled my nose and I discovered that Amelia was at my side with a washbowl and a cool flannel. She dabbed at my hands, which I was surprised to see were covered with bruises and crossed with thick welts. "Thank goodness for the blessing of time," Amelia said. "We were able to burn everything. One of the soldiers raked the ashes and took a few scraps but they will learn nothing."

"The Town Major will learn that Sarah has been courted by William Fitzgerald because that is the only correspondence he could find," Eliza said. "And much good it will do him."

"All I could determine from what I overheard is that Robert wrote to Sarah from prison and the letter was confiscated," Richard said. "Mr. O'Grady intends to suppress it, along with letters from Sarah that Robert was carrying. He will not subject her to notoriety, thank God."

"But our father would not hesitate to do so if it furthered his aims," Amelia said.

"Worried about rising to the bench," Richard said. "Does he think a display of paternal punishment will further him? To beat a girl for being in love? The courts want merciful judges, not an army of vindictive brutes."

"Robert?" I asked. My mind was so muddled, I could not think clearly.

There was no answer. The keening of the mourners resounded and I stopped listening. I stopped seeing. I stopped feeling. I was numb.

TWENTY-TWO

The footman carried me out to the garden where I was propped up in a chair and covered with blankets to ward off the chill. For a week I was an invalid, my battered body kept hidden from view. Neighbors came to call but I was too ill to see anyone, Amelia told them, too sick to receive callers who wanted only to uncover all that happened at The Priory on the tenth of September when Major Sirr and a contingent of yeomen raided the house. News of Robert's arrest spread through Rathfarnham, and despite Mr. O'Grady's attempt to protect me, it was not long before everyone knew that I had been secretly engaged. A forest of letters sprouted on the writing table in the drawing room as my friends wrote to extend their deepest sympathies. Caroline Lambart invited me to call on her family in the country, to heal my wounds at a distance from the scene of my tragedy.

Without thinking, I accepted, if only to get away from the guilt I carried like a millstone.

The Earl of Hardwicke, in his capacity as Lord Lieutenant, listened to Mr. Curran and immediately determined that the barrister had no knowledge of his daughter's conduct. My father's enemies longed to paint him into the rebel camp, but they could not use me as their brush. All that I had done, in the eyes of Ireland's rulers, was to fall in love with an unsuitable gentleman. As was so common in those days, they ascribed my strong opinions on political matters to be due to the influence of Mary Wollstonecraft, whose philosophy regarding female liberation and the cultivated mind were seen as dangerous. The two letters that Robert did not burn were taken as examples of just how dangerous such free-thinking was. If my father bristled at the sympathy shown me by the members of the Privy Council, he gave no indication.

Having discovered the truth about Robert's attachment to me, my father refused to represent him at trial. My poor wretched darling was left with little choice but to put his fate in the hands of Mr. McNally. The date of the trial was set for Monday, the nineteenth of September. Robert would not mount a defense. He had struck a deal with Mr. O'Grady, to keep my name out of the trial. The price he paid was far too high, more costly than I was worth. I put myself in the dock and found that I was guilty. Sentence was passed, and I planned to accept justice with honor.

Saturday was market day, when our tenants went into Dublin to sell their produce. Our steward left early in the morning, to complete a list of chores that took him into the city. I was able to enter the cellar without being noticed. There amid the scraps of wood, the spare window panes and old gardening tools, was a bottle of arsenic that was used to poison rodents who thought to make a home among the wine bottles. It would not be missed until later in the autumn, when cold weather drove the mice indoors. By then, it would not matter that I had taken it.

That afternoon, Amelia handed me a packet that Mr. Curran had sent from Dublin, along with specific instructions. Mr. O'Grady had returned the love letters from William as they had nothing to do with the case and did not need to be retained by the Crown. I was to send them back to William, along with a letter that detailed my abominable conduct and my shameful behavior. I was also to instruct Mr. Fitzgerald to cease all contact with me. My head was to be emptied of Robert Emmet at once, and I was to remain at home until Mr. Curran determined my punishment for soiling his name.

When I tried to write, the words did not align themselves into coherent sentences. I crossed out long sections and sliced out fragments so as not to waste the paper, but in the end I had nothing but a sheet soaked with ink and riddled with holes. 'Forgive me' was all that remained. I sealed it and bundled it with the letters, wrapping the package in plain paper. A tidy conclusion to a last chapter, I thought, and placed the memory of William Fitzgerald on the library table.

I rose on Sunday and Amelia was delighted that my recovery was progressing. At first she did not think it wise that I attend services, but I would not be denied. We had to pray for Robert, ask God to provide a miracle. Some said the French were already in Ireland with an invasion in the offing, the same invasion that was supposed to coincide with an uprising. If it pleased the Lord, I would ask that our would-be allies could swoop into Dublin and save Robert from the scaffold. My sister relented, although I was made to cover my face with a veil so that the marks of the beating were not visible to reveal our secret shame.

I prayed for my own soul that day, prayed all day and into the night. I wandered through the rooms of The Priory, begging for some other outcome than the one I did not wish to accept. The clock struck three and then four and then five. In my imagination I sat at Robert's side in his cold and lonely cell. I could feel the warmth of his hand in mine, the soft brushing of his lips on my wrist. My fingertips explored the sharp lines of his face, the nose long and narrow, his cheeks sunken from the hardships of his quest. I brushed his straight black hair from his forehead, those unruly locks that would not stay in place. "We will be together soon," I said. "Do not be afraid."

"Afraid of what?" Eliza asked.

Without my noticing, the sun had come up while I was sitting on the stairs. My sister skirted around me, took in my disheveled appearance, and suggested that I wash my face and change into something more suitable for daytime. The deepest melancholy would not change what was beyond our control, she said, and I did a greater service to Robert's memory by showing strength rather than succumbing to weakness. She sat next to me and wrapped her arm around my waist. I rested my head on her shoulder, grateful for the shelter of her presence.

Several of Robert's schoolmates from Trinity planned to attend the trial, Richard among them. He agreed to send word, if he could, and so we began an endless day of waiting. None of us could eat and the dinner was left on the table to grow cold. Amelia ordered tea when the candles in the drawing room were lit, but the smell turned my stomach and I declined her attempt to coax me into taking some nourishment. Had I really not touched a morsel since the day I learned of Robert's arrest? What did it signify, in any case. I would soon be beyond the need for earthly food.

It was near midnight when Richard came home, his cheeks streaked with tears. After an ordeal of twelve hours without respite, the expected verdict was reached. At the end, Robert made an impassioned speech that was heard despite Lord Norbury's repeated efforts to interrupt and silence the condemned prisoner. He spoke for an hour and Richard could not recall every passage, but he was deeply moved by the conclusion. "He made one request upon his death. He asked the world for the charity of its silence. 'Let no man write my epitaph,' he said. My God, the strength with which he spoke, and he was nearly fainting with exhaustion. 'Let my tomb remain uninscribed until other men and other times could do justice to my character, when my country takes her place among the nations of the earth.' We are about to lose one of the greatest men of our generation. Senseless slaughter. This government is an abomination. I want no part of its unjust laws and its unjust courts."

Richard composed himself, somewhat ashamed to have fallen to pieces when he was a grown man and not a child. "He does not yet know that his mother has died. Yes, Mrs. Emmet, it was all too much for her and God called her home two days ago. I pray he does not find out until she greets him upon his arrival in heaven."

"What time?" I asked. "And where?"

"Around three in the afternoon. He will spend his last night on earth in Kilmainham. The scaffold was erected on Thomas Street, on the spot where Lord Kilwarden was killed by that mob thirsting for blood. It has seen much use these past weeks," Richard said.

"Will you call on him before he...?" Eliza asked.

"No comfort of a friend is to be permitted," Richard said. "But the government cannot prevent us from standing as witnesses. All his old friends will be there."

The apostles slept while Jesus prayed in the garden at Gethsemane. I stood vigil through the rest of the night, my prayer book pressed against my heart as I offered to exchange my life for one more worthy. Did I not prove my sincerity by remaining awake with the one who would be sacrificed? I hoped it was compensation enough for my many faults, the price of a cleared conscience.

The sun rose on a dark day, the sky threatening. I dressed carefully, choosing the green wool frock that I had worn when Robert and I met for the last time. While I pinned up my hair I gave some thought to the close of the day. The embroidered map of Ireland that I once thought would grace our home would serve a different purpose. From the trunk that I had not opened since Major Sirr tore through it like the beast that he was, I retrieved my handiwork and spread it out on my pillow. Later, I would place my head there, to never lift it again. At breakfast I took some tea, spooning in sugar and stirring until it dissolved in an experiment that yielded useful results. Fully prepared, I watched the clock in the drawing room tick down the hours. At noon, when my sisters sat down to dinner, I made my excuses and slipped out the front door.

Did propriety signify any longer, or could I boldly walk to Dublin alone? I paused at the gate, and caught myself looking at the spot where Anne used to leave Robert's messages. We all could have run off to the Wicklow hills and been spared. My fault, my most grievous fault, for worrying about the opinions of others whose opinions I did not truly value. All of that was in the past, of course, and I had to look forward to what remained of my future. A trio of soldiers rode by and touched their hats with respect. Soldiers to keep order, in the event that the French made a magical appearance when I knew that the French were as inconstant as I had been.

A carriage approached and made to turn into the gate. From within I heard the occupants pound on the roof and recognized the voice of Mrs. Lambart. My dear friend Caroline almost fell out of the door in her hurry to embrace me. "Unexpected, I know, but I had no time to contact you. Mr. Lambart suggested that we wait outside the prison to be sure to see Mr. Emmet. Not knowing the route, it is the wisest plan."

"Dear, dear friend," I said. One last look at my beloved, what I wanted so desperately, was to be granted by the most Divine Providence.

On the surface I appeared calm, my innermost feelings evident only when Caroline took my hands and found that I was trembling. "We thought to call on Mrs. Emmet's daughter to extend our sympathies on her loss, and you can imagine our distress on learning that Robert was going to the gallows," Mrs. Lambart said. "What that family has endured at the hands of the Crown. At least Thomas Addis survives, to carry on the name."

My tongue was like a block of wood in my mouth, dry and unmoving, while my companions carried on a conversation that I could not follow.

165

The turn of the carriage wheels was like the clock counting down the hours until three, the last few minutes of Robert's life. I closed my eyes so I could put myself next to him once again, to transport us magically to the grove where Gertrude watched over us. Would she remember Robert? Soon enough I would be with her, to refresh her memory. We would all be together as a family, in paradise for all eternity. Instead of wishing time to slow, I wanted it to race, to shorten the time that Robert and I had to be apart.

A crowd was already gathering when we reached the prison. Thanks to the bullying tactics of the Lambart's driver we were situated at the cross of three roads, so that whichever way the procession went I was sure to see Robert. "Courage, Sarah, be strong for his sake," Caroline said. There was no strength to be found in that carriage. We were all sobbing over the tragic loss of a brilliant young man. My heart was going to the gallows with Robert Emmet, to be crushed under the executioner's boot heel.

I scanned the throng, foolishly hoping to see some desperate sort who might spring into action and abscond with the prisoner. All I saw was an army of curiosity seekers intermixed with the defeated who were resigned to their miserable existence in the British yoke. A pair of gentlemen came out of the prison gate and I held my breath, thinking that the time had come. I watched them walk away, walk towards the Lambart carriage, and I saw Mr. McNally in deep conversation with a man whose face I recognized but whose name I could not recall. Our eyes met and he immediately turned his head. He kept walking and avoided my gaze.

Moments of brilliant clarity should announce themselves with bright flashes like signal flares, but this one was as silent as the turning of a page. I knew, but could not say how I knew, but I knew with absolute certainty. Mr. McNally had exposed Robert. The person who revealed Robert's hiding place was me. I had trusted when I should have trusted no one. Not only had I consigned Robert to his death by refusing to elope, but I had handed him over to his enemies.

"Robert," I said, but I could say no more. I stuffed my handkerchief in my mouth to keep from screaming, bit on my fist to stop the roar that arose in my gut.

A contingent of soldiers formed up and took the lead, followed by the closed carriage where Robert sat with two clergymen, Would he feel my presence? Leaning as close to the open window as I dared, I waved my handkerchief, just a slight flutter in the hope that the movement would catch his eye. He seemed to be taking in the scene, his gaze shifting from side to side. I am here, my love, I wanted to shout, but a numbness was settling into my bones and I could not move. Then he saw me, just a glance before the prison carriage turned east towards the city. Not a smile, but an expression of pleasure and gratitude appeared on his face. I collapsed into Caroline's arms, overcome with the agony of a farewell I had created through my own stupidity and carelessness.

We waited for the crowd to disperse, but we would not have followed behind in any case. Never would we have gone to the place of execution to watch such horror, with the scaffold mounted on high to afford the best view. There were plenty of bigots who would relish the sight of Robert's head being cut from his body after he had been hanged. They would cheer as the executioner held that head aloft and declared "This is the head of the traitor Robert Emmet." I was grateful that men like my brother Richard would be there as well, to provide a wellspring of courage should Robert waver as he mounted the steps to greet the noose. I would have no such audience later, but I had no need. The courage I might have needed came to me from the glance I shared with Leonard McNally.

The return trip to Rathfarnham was passed in an ocean of tears, wave after wave of sorrow that would never ease. "When we arrive at The Priory, you will pack a trunk and come with us to Wicklow," Mrs. Lambart said.

"My dear child, you are in no condition to be alone, without a mother to care for you."

"You must, Sarah," Caroline said. "The quiet of the country and the fresh air will help to restore you in time."

"Yes, time," Mrs. Lambart said. "Forgive me for saying such a thing now, but I can promise you that time will be a great healer. You will mourn now, but be assured that this too shall pass."

In my mind, I felt the steps under my feet as I imagined my last walk to my room. Caroline and her mother could drink tea with my sisters while I prepared my own beverage. Having guests to entertain would give me the window of privacy that I needed, and I hugged Caroline out of gratitude for her presence at this critical time. They would say that I died of a broken heart, torn to pieces by grief, and then I would rest in the silence bestowed on me by the world's charity. Like Robert, I would have no epitaph.

The front door of The Priory stood open, framing Amelia and Mr. Curran. His stride reflected his anger as he crossed the carriage path, forcing the driver to halt the carriage well away from the door. Mrs. Lambart mentioned the late hour and the need to rest her horses, but my father ignored her as she sat, stunned by his rudeness.

I alighted, eager to complete the final step of my journey, but he grabbed my arm and shook me. "You have defied me again, but you have defied me for the last time. I know where you have been, trying yet again to destroy me. I denounced you to the Privy Council and I will denounce you again, do you hear me? If they had chosen to hang you today instead of Emmet I would have applauded the justice of their ruling."

"You would hand them my head on a platter if they would make you a judge," I said.

His head seemed to expand, as if it would explode with a violent rage. "Get out of my sight. Never let me see or hear of you again. You are dead to me. Do not ever come here again."

With that, he turned on his heel and strode off. He crossed his threshold and I saw Amelia still standing there like an obelisk, unmoving, enduring. Mr. Curran slammed the door shut.

TWENTY-THREE

Mercy placed a veil over my memory of the weeks that followed. Later, when I asked Caroline if I had slept for days, she assured me that I had not, although I imagined that I had lapsed into some sort of unconscious state. I have no recollection of retreating to Little Dargle, the Ponsonby country seat, where I was put into a heavy sedation due to an attack of hysteria. What had I said while I was insensible? Based on Caroline's version of events, she wove a tale of golden romance and chivalry, a touching saga of lovers exchanging letters despite the disapproval of the evil father. Skirting the very edges of propriety, but how many women of our acquaintance had not, at some time in their youth, done the same?

After one night, we left for Castle Rath in Wicklow, and it fell to Mrs. Ponsonby to carry the gossip to the neighbors. Within hours of my being turned out of my father's home, the word had been spread through the circle of liberal politicians and barristers, from Rathfarnham into Dublin and beyond. Rumors out of Dublin Castle added a certain degree of nuance and shading, and Mr. Curran was drawn into a most unflattering portrait of selfishness and absolute cruelty. The image grew sharper a few days later, when Richard was fished out of the Dodder River, the pockets of his coat filled with rocks. He was put away in an asylum, diagnosed with a debilitating melancholy.

Denied the death I desired with all my heart, I fell into the depths of sorrow where food and drink were impossible to swallow. For several weeks I wasted away, always hoping that I had seen my last sunrise, while Mr. Lambart bargained with his old friend to restore the paternal bond that should not have been broken for an incident of female weakness that was not unexpected in a girl without a mother's guidance. Nothing would move John Philpot Curran after he had made up his mind.

I wrote to my brother John, begging for financial help, but I had little hope. His pay as a midshipman was nearly insignificant, but I had no other brother to turn to. Richard was recovering in an asylum, James was completing his studies at Trinity, and Will was but a schoolboy. Mr. Lambart dismissed the possibility of John having the means to maintain me, let alone the funds to pay for my passage to America. The notion of emigrating was madness, but I was half-mad in those days.

So many of those I loved had been taken from me that I wrote to every person of my acquaintance out of fear that I would lose all friends. To Anne Wilmot and the Penrose sisters I poured out my heart along with my terrors, and begged for their advice. The notion of leaving Ireland took hold of my imagination and I saw it as the solution to my ills. There was nothing to hold me in Ireland, no family ties or tender bonds. I would have to make my way in the world alone, a vessel to hold a cherished memory of a fallen martyr. Why else had I been denied the death I planned so carefully? What purpose did I serve if not to mourn Robert Emmet?

The reply from Anne Penrose came, not in a letter, but in her father's carriage. She arrived at Mr. Lambart's door with Bessey and their dear mother, under the order of Mr. Penrose to fetch me home. Like Mary Pike all those years ago, I was an orphan in need of assistance and he would not shirk in his Christian duty to provide for those in need. "A father may discipline the child, but your father went too far," Mrs. Penrose said. "You have suffered too much for a minor transgression. But I fear he has done much damage to himself as well, and that will be his punishment."

Four weeks after Robert's death, I became a resident of Wood Hill in Cork, almost a third daughter to the kindest man who ever walked the earth. I wish that I had returned generosity with generosity of spirit, but I was too broken. Instead of taking my meals with gratitude at being fed at all, I toyed with my food and gave the impression that something was wrong with the soup or the meat or the wine. New gowns were provided but I showed no enthusiasm for pretty clothes, and Bessey thought that I did not like the fabrics she had selected. Her brother William tried to engage me in conversation but I could not speak, his gentle tone reminding me too much of Robert and Richard and John, all of whom I had lost so abruptly.

Mr. Penrose was fond of entertaining and it was common for him to welcome strangers into his home. Anyone who came to view his magnificent art collection was, as a matter of course, invited to stay for dinner. More often than not, I would sit in silence and hurry from the room at the first opportunity. My behavior was quite eccentric, but I could not explain it when I feared that a word taken the wrong way could see me put on the road. I lived in constant fear of losing my new home, which in turn made me a rather difficult guest when I intended to be agreeable.

After one such incident in early December, Anne left the drawing room to chase after me when I fled to my bedroom after Mr. Penrose praised my musical ability.

"Did you not hear them?" I asked. "Whispering to each other, but I heard well enough. That is Sarah Curran who was betrothed to Robert Emmet, and they come here to gawk at me. I am not an exotic beast in captivity, to be stared at. Please, my apologies to your father, but it is unendurable."

"I can assure you that Captain and Mrs. Edwards are in complete sympathy with Mr. Emmet's cause," Anne said. "Although the Captain does not condone his methods."

"So much the worse," I said. "They wish to see what remains, I suppose. To pick over the bones of this carcass or collect souvenirs."

"Do you think my father would countenance such inexcusable conduct?"

"How would he know? They come under false pretenses, and take advantage of Mr. Penrose's storied generosity."

Anne took my hands in hers and I fell under the spell of her voice. "He is your guardian and your protector. Your champion, upholding your right to be respected. But you must place your trust in him. In my father and my brother as well. Can you try? Can you surrender yourself enough to allow us to look after you?"

"I will bring you all bad luck," I said. "Love has brought me nothing but sorrow, and woe to those who loved me."

"From what I learned of Mr. Emmet during his time in Paris, he was far from sorrow."

"He came to it soon enough."

"Because he loved you? How is that?"

"He would have escaped if he did not love me. I would not elope."

"Of course you would not. To do so would have harmed your father and you would never seek to harm him."

I grimaced as I realized the irony. "He seems to have harmed himself by his actions. Perhaps the sting would have been less if I had done something improper."

"Such an unpleasant lesson you have learned," Anne said. "We ladies can but suggest, or encourage, or perhaps badger if we dare to risk becoming fishwives. But we cannot compel. It is the man who takes action while we may only advise. If that advice goes unheard, we have not failed."

My failing was too painful to mention to Anne, even though I felt that I could confide in her. She would find me reprehensible, I was certain, if she knew that I was the traitor who exposed Robert Emmet. My inability to keep silent was the root cause of his death. As long as he could remain hidden he had a chance, and in time he might have worn down my resistance. When I replayed events in my head, I saw my mind gradually turn towards the unthinkable, my heart ruling my head, or Eliza all but pushing me to go. Do not hesitate on my account, I imagined her saying as she helped me to pack a change of clothes. Society could forgive a lady who ran off as long as she lived discreetly, and the far-away wilderness of America would have swallowed up our memory soon enough. Mr. Curran would have gone on with his work, unharmed by his own cruelty towards me, and Robert would be alive. I would be alive, rather than a dead woman walking the earth.

My sleep was often disturbed by nightmares and I rose early, to find peace in Mr. Penrose's quiet gardens. I was surprised to find Mrs. Edwards joining me at sunrise, an unwelcome disturbance that set my teeth on edge. She might ask questions I did not wish to answer, and I was easily trapped by the confines of the boxwood hedges. How to escape became the center of my thoughts, making it difficult to listen to what was actually being said.

"I am a creature of habit," she said. "Accustomed to rising early to look after my children, even though my dear girls are at home."

"Are you a native of Ireland?" I asked.

"In a way," she said with a spark of good humor. "My late mother was Irish-born. My father was an Englishman. After they married, eloped in all honesty, they emigrated to France and set up a porcelain factory in Rouen. We were, I suppose, part of the evil bourgeoisie and so we fled back to Ireland. All but my sister, who had married a Frenchman and chose to remain. You can imagine our joy when we were reunited during that too brief moment of peace. Most of Ireland must have gone to Paris, so many of our fellow countrymen did we meet."

"You have seen the portrait of Mr. Penrose that was painted by David?" I asked.

"An impressive likeness, yet not one of Mr. David's best efforts. I hope that you might visit the art museums in Paris some day."

I would have, if I had gone with Robert when he asked. The museums, the gardens, the palaces and the parks would have been ours to explore. If only.

"Mr. Penrose tells me that you play the harp."

"But poorly."

"How unfair is our lot," she said. "Trained to be modest when a man equally skilled could crow of his ability without fear of censure. Therefore if you claim to be a poor player, you must be brilliant. Will you favor me with a song this afternoon, so that I can judge the truth in my statement?"

"You will be proved wrong, I am afraid. I practice but little, and seem to have no head for it."

"Until you have recovered from your losses, and they are deep losses, Miss Curran, you will find it difficult. After my mother died unexpectedly, I lapsed into a deep melancholy. One might think that marriage would lift my spirits, but it did not. No, it was not until I held my firstborn in my arms that I understood the power of love."

"Love is quite powerful," I said. It could destroy as easily as it could heal. I was finished with love. It was too dangerous an emotion. "And we are powerless."

"And there is something else I discovered after becoming a mother," she said. "We are the first teachers of all our children, and that is a very powerful position indeed."

"Children belong to their father. A mother is powerless in the face of the law."

"Who forms a child's mind, in those early years, in the nursery? Who instructs in the most elemental ideas of fairness, of cooperation? Who instills in her children a love of liberty? You have not lost Mr. Emmet completely. His ideas will live on through you, through your children."

"Someone else's children, perhaps."

"Are you considering seeking a position as governess? That is the typical route we must take when we are made to fend for ourselves."

"My notoriety precludes it," I said. "Mr. Penrose was kind enough to make inquiries, in a very general sense. In his opinion, it is unlikely I could land a position. And then too I must consider public opinion. What would people say about my father if I were employed?"

"He has a good many enemies, as does any man in public life who rises above the rest. You are most thoughtful towards one who has mistreated you," she said.

"I brought it on myself," I said. "He told me to have nothing to do with Mr. Emmet but I persisted."

"The madness of love. So too did my grandfather advise my mother, and like you she did not listen. My parents were fortunate in that my grandfather recognized how impossible his demand was. In the end, he welcomed my father and provided the financial support that was needed for the porcelain factory."

"My father is not one to forgive," I said.

O nce before I had conquered my emotions and put on a brave face. Day by day, I forced myself to do what others asked of me no matter how painful the experience was. If Mr. Penrose asked me to play the harp for dinner guests, I played and never let on that I had last performed a particular tune for Robert when he was welcomed at The Priory. I sang and acted as if I did not associate the lyrics with a summer evening at home with my sisters when the tenants gathered near the open windows to enjoy our impromptu concert. Former pleasures gave me pain that some might have treated with laudanum or liquor. I consumed the misery as if it gave me sustenance, as I found food unpalatable. Even there I learned how to appear to enjoy a meal that sickened me. I became an accomplished actress.

The holiday season was one of great joy in the Penrose home, and I found that I could lose myself in the swirl of guests who populated the rooms. The conversations often turned to politics, with the recent rebellion still quite fresh in everyone's mind, but to my relief I was not an object of scorn. To be sure, there were those who canted their heads towards me and repeated the phrase "betrothed of Robert Emmet", but they spoke those words without malice. It was during the ball held on the first day of 1804 that I was told that Mr. Penrose had helped to hide Lord Fitzgerald after the uprising of 1798 failed. The kind gentleman would have sheltered Robert, I was certain, and my heart melted at the realization that he was doing Robert a service by sheltering me. I was among friends. My effort to act like a normal young lady was redoubled.

The rhythms of Wood Hill were quite different from those I knew at The Priory, just as the rhythms of a family are unique to each house. Fitting in to the Penrose way of life meant I had to forget what it was to be a Curran, no easy task but one that I battled with determination. I had to find my place in their world, more than a guest but not quite a sister. My desires were suppressed and I lived to do what others wanted to do. If Bessey requested company to make calls, I was at her side. If Anne wished to read, I picked up a book. The Penrose ladies called on the poor or the sick in Cork and I joined them with a smile. I was constantly on edge, never sure if I was being too accommodating or not agreeable enough. The strain wore away at me and by the summer I was as thin as a sapling, so tightly strung that I feared I would snap.

I could not control the nightmares that plagued me. Robert appeared in my dreams, the heat of his body warming me so that I woke up dripping with sweat. Some nights I woke up crying, the vivid images of Robert waiting for me at Gertrude's grave dissolving into confusion when I found myself in a strange room before realizing where I was. Somehow Anne knew when I had passed a difficult night, and she would walk with me in the gallery where we were surrounded by beautiful works of art that helped to calm my nerves. She encouraged me to be frank, to be honest, to share my most intimate thoughts and perhaps exorcise the demons that hounded my every step. By baring my soul, I found relief.

Like a doting mother, Mrs. Penrose fussed over me. She prescribed drives into the country to take the air, which often led to calls on friends who were delighted to introduce their sons to me. Her attempt to draw me out into society were considerate, but I found that the company of flirtatious men dredged up powerful emotions. Some words could evoke a strong recollection of a meeting at Gertrude's grave, with Robert's words of love echoing in my head, and it took all my willpower to carry on a conversation.

A yachting expedition in early July helped to restore my spirits, in large part because the change of scenery was so drastic that I was disarmed. Confined to a sailing ship, I was in close company with my dear friends and far from the constant interruptions of everyday life. No one came to call and disrupt a train of thought. For a few weeks it was possible to really think.

Since my arrival at Wood Hill, I had wanted to fade into the background, to not be a nuisance. Indeed, I might have shrunken down to a pile of dead bones if not for the persistence of my new sisters who badgered me to take some sustenance. During the pleasure cruise, Anne discussed the turbulence that had rocked me. In her mind I was a sculpture in the making, all rough edges in need of smoothing. Such work took time and dedication to complete, a daily application of tools to polish the marble. As we are the artists of ourselves, it was my duty to chip away at the parts that were not me, to leave those scraps behind on the studio floor. Her advice was sound and I tried to follow it, but how was I to chip off the base that held me up? I was responsible for Robert Emmet's death and that was an unpardonable offense, the most unforgivable of sins.

TWENTY-FOUR

The friends of Anne and Bessey became my friends and I was welcomed into a society of unmarried ladies, drawn from the landed gentry of Cork. Without husbands or children to intrude, we had ample time to engage in spirited debates over current events or a dissection of the newest novel. What should have brought me great joy resulted in a deepening of the malaise that festered in my soul. My father's home had been one of melancholy, where I was shaped into a creature of sorrow and tears. To be suddenly awash in love and concern was overwhelming to me, and I often looked to the past with bitterness. Set free, I thrashed about, searching for the familiar confines of the cage.

I was brought out of my constant introspection after a year of deep mourning by an ordinary activity. Mr. Penrose practiced his Christian faith to an uncommon extent, funding various road improvement schemes and developing a woolen industry to provide work for the disenfranchised Catholics whose ancestral lands had been confiscated by the Crown centuries ago. The level of poverty in Cork was so severe, however, that he could not reach everyone, and the Penrose ladies played an important role in bringing aid to the desperate. Bessey and Anne formed their own charitable society that Kate Wilmot termed the Lady Bachelors.

On an appointed day, we called on neighbors who had amassed a collection of useful items that we would then distribute to the needy. From the first, I discovered what true poverty was, the poverty that existed on the other side of the demesne wall. Women and children were half-naked, dressed in rags that provided scant coverage. Robert's passion for Irish liberty was made clear and I understood what drove him without regard for his personal safety. These people had nothing due to centuries of British abuse, nothing but their Catholic faith that harsh laws had failed to eradicate. The opposition to Catholic emancipation arose from the determination of the colonial overlords to keep all they had taken. My father did not stand a chance of altering such convictions, with only words as a weapon in a battle against greed. Greed was too powerful to be overcome with anything other than blood. The realization was startling.

Having given away our treasures, we crowded into the carriage to deliver the Lady Bachelors to their homes. Anne Latham and Anne Penrose were bunched up against the sides with Anna Chetwood wedged between them. I rode with my back to the horses, taking the inferior position with Bessey who did not mind the unpleasant sensation of riding in reverse. She thought first of the comforts of others. "There are too many in this district who ignore the poor at their doorstep," Anne Penrose said. "How can we entice them to help?"

"They are not interested because they believe the poor are lazy and have only themselves to blame," I said. "Could we educate them to show their prejudice is unfounded?"

"Then there are those who will not help unless the Catholics convert to the Church of Ireland," Anne Latham said. "Nothing we say or do would change that."

"What if we could trick them into donating to charity?" Bessey asked. We all knew that if Bessey concocted a clever scheme, we would have great fun in realizing it. "We have attended subscription balls but never asked for an accounting of the fees. And why not?"

"Because we are only concerned with the ball, of course," Anna Chetwood said.

"Precisely. What if we were to stage a musical event. A grand evening of entertainment. In this group alone I see ladies of great ability. We could organize ourselves into a small orchestra and perform a few select pieces. Sarah could sing. Yes, Sarah, you could sing and we would ask for additional donations after each song to entice you to sing another."

"My small voice would not command much enthusiasm," I said. To appear on such a public stage was to expose myself to ridicule and I could not do it.

"We must have costumes," Bessey said. "Exotic costumes."

"Let us dress like Turkish ladies," Kate Wilmot said. "Perhaps not even proper frocks, but exotic veils and turbans and feathers."

"So that the gentlemen will be so preoccupied with keeping our figures on display that they will pay generously for the privilege?" Anne Penrose asked. "Really, Bessey, do you think that our mother would approve? To say nothing of our father."

"We will not be nude," Bessey said. "Did you not notice the ball gown that Miss Dwyer wore at the subscription ball last February? She came close enough to nudity in my opinion and no one rushed at her with a shawl to cover herself."

I burst into tears, my mind filled with images of the tatters worn by the women in the miserable hovels, the hungry eyes of their children, the shame of their men in not being able to provide the most basic needs. For months I had thought only of myself and my own sorrows that paled in comparison. After Robert was taken from me, I had retreated into my private thoughts, put my insignificant concerns first. How many of the downtrodden had lost their homes, as I had, but had no place to go but out on the road? I had never gone hungry, never been cold, but I had cared only about my suffering and my heartache. In the process, I had been unkind and cruel to the Penrose family that sheltered me, never considering how hard I made their daily existence with my pettiness.

"I am so sorry," I said. "I have been selfish and there is no excuse for my behavior."

"Not selfish," Kate Wilmot said. "You are naturally retiring. It is your nature to shrink back from acclaim."

"From the day I arrived I have thought only of myself," I said. I had heard Bessey's brother William describe me as excitable. Yes, I was excitable, because I distorted everything into a calamity that harmed me. And while I wallowed in misery, I was blind to the many blessings that had befallen me since Mr. Penrose took me in. "While I am uncomfortable in being the center of attention, I cannot beg off from an event that will do so much good to those most in need. I will sing, Bessey, as many songs as you like."

"And accompany yourself on the harp," Kate said. "The Irish airs are wildly popular, and your voice is so sweet. We shall lift all of Cork out of poverty in a single evening."

"To accomplish that, we may need to sell army commissions," Anne Penrose said. By changing the subject she provided me an opportunity to compose myself. "Have you read of the scandal? The mistress of the Duke of York has been turning a tidy profit in the sale of officers' commissions. And to make matters worse for our poor blighted land, her assistant in the scheme is an Irishman. William Fitzgerald, of Ennis. He was quick to turn on her and provide all the evidence requested to save his own skin."

"His father has been agitating for a peerage, has he not?" Anne Latham asked.

"Do you think the son sold out the Duke's paramour for a baronetcy?" Anna Chetwood asked.

"He courted me," I said in a soft voice. The man who could not make up his own mind had been manipulated by a skilled courtesan. It would have been his father's doing that William cooperated with an investigation, but I would not speak of him. He was part of my past that I had to leave far, far behind.

The conversation shifted, as it typically did, between gossip and political matters. War was a common topic, with England battling most of the known world it seemed. My brother James had decided that a career in the army was preferable to reading the law. He was commissioned a cadet early in the year, and had written me from his post in India where the unrest reminded him very much of the tumult we had known in Ireland. The Indians were taking advantage of England's distraction in Europe to wage their own uprising, thinking they could defeat their colonial overlords but finding it as impossible as our friends had discovered a year earlier. He was not quite certain which side he favored in the conflict.

Kate Wilmot shared her thoughts on France, and Bessey remarked on the drastic shift that the country had undergone. There had been a time when the liberal politicians had trumpeted the glories of the French revolution, but they were tripping over one another in a mad dash to decry the current state of French governance, as if they could erase all the words they had uttered less than ten years ago. It came to me at that moment that the time for rebellion had come and gone. There was no new Robert Emmet waiting in the wings to enter the stage. The best that I could do would be to take action against the result of British rule, as I could not overturn it. If the poor could be fed and clothed, it would ease the pressure applied to them to convert. I could support Catholicism as a way to undermine the

Crown. Aid to the Catholics, without strings attached, would be my small act of rebellion.

A rehearsal schedule was organized after we rifled through all the sheet music we could find. The Lady Bachelors could boast of three pianists, a violinist, and a harpist. William Penrose agreed to join our orchestra so that we had a viola di gamba to add the necessary lower range. For two months I sat with Bessey and taught her how to play several Irish airs, instructing her as Tom Moore had once trained me. The memory drew me back to the past, back inside my own mind where guilt enjoyed a resurgence for several days. Like a weed in Mr. Curran's garden I plucked it out but it kept sprouting in another corner, a fresh crop awaiting me every morning. I could not eradicate it. At best, I could only control it.

We could not have had a better promoter than Mr. Penrose, whose influence reached well beyond the Quaker community. He invited friends and invited them to invite their friends. Those who were entertaining guests were free to include their visitors, and soon the list of attendees grew until Mrs. Penrose did not know where she could put them all. There was some talk of erecting a marquee on the lawn, until William Penrose noted that a steady breeze could carry sound away. Those who came to hear the music would be disappointed, and our fundraising drive could suffer. We had to perform indoors, perhaps on a small stage in the gallery. His management of the Penrose business interests declined while he gave his full attention to the setting. Bessey encouraged him to decorate our stage in an appropriate manner, although we had no idea what an Arabian tent might look like.

In all the excitement, Anne overlooked one of her long-time friends, another unmarried lady who did not play any instrument well. Miss Elliston was very bookish, the daughter of a clergyman, and she saw me as an interloper. Since I appeared, Anne showed a preference for music and Miss Elliston felt slighted. That she did not like me was quite obvious. Never once since meeting her did she ask me to call her by her first name.

She was stiff and formal, always Miss Elliston, a cold fish who found ways to come between me and Anne.

"I should try to find some role for her," Anne said.

"Why not ask her to circulate through the room soliciting donations?" Bessey suggested. "You were not thinking of asking her to sing, were you? No, Anne, her voice is dreadful. She is utterly tone deaf."

"William, could you perhaps distract Miss Elliston?" Anne asked. "When you are not playing in our little orchestra, that is."

"While Miss Curran is singing, you mean to say but dare not," William said. "You wish to drag me into the middle of this contretemps, which will grow more heated after Miss Curran sings and every unattached gentleman is hovering around her like a swarm of bees feasting on the sweetest flower."

"Mr. Penrose, you tease me mercilessly," I said. My face burned with embarrassment at his effusive praise.

"What are brothers for, if not to bring a blush to a sister's cheek?" he replied. "And you will be swarmed, I have no doubt. Reverend Bullen has informed our father that he will bring the officers of the Royal Staff Corps who are constructing the coastal defenses nearby. Perhaps some of them have poor eyesight and will buzz about Miss Elliston, thereby relieving me of the onerous chore."

Let them all hover like a cloud over Miss Elliston and I would be content. My heart was not fully healed. And yet. I could not remain under Mr. Penrose's roof for the rest of my days. The charity of the father would not necessarily be secured in the son. Under a veneer of hospitality was a level of annoyance that William held for me. I disrupted routines, and snatched away a large portion of the consideration he received from mother and sisters. He never once asked how long I intended to stay, but I saw the question in his eyes.

TWENTY-FIVE

The fancy dress party was held in September, one year after my heart was broken into irreparable bits. Music kept me from dwelling on my losses, the repetition of rehearsal providing enough distraction during the day. I mourned privately, in the dark of my bedroom after the house had gone to sleep, the grief given its hour upon the stage before dawn brought down the curtain on my sadness. My enthusiasm for my costume was subdued because of a lingering malaise, although Mrs. Penrose assumed that my natural modesty was the cause. The Lady Bachelors were to be dressed in Turkish trousers, which shocked the dear lady's Quaker sensibilities.

The day of the event approached, responses arrived in the post, but I did not hear the names I longed to hear when Mr. Penrose notified us of the latest addition to the party. I did not expect Richard to come, not after his letter written last March. His three month rest in the asylum had not cured him completely, and he continued to battle melancholy. A festive gathering would possibly make him worse. I wanted my sisters to attend, to enjoy the pleasures of society that were lacking in Rathfarnham, but they could only come if Richard brought them under some ruse, and he was unable to travel. He did not even extend the invitation to them, he said, knowing how disappointed they would be. It was tragic enough that they could not correspond with me, nor I with them, unless our brother acted as messenger. We did not wish to add to their misery with talk of parties that I would enjoy while they sat at home.

Life had changed at The Priory since my exile, as if a pall of mourning had descended. With James gone and William at school, Mr. Curran took to inviting young gentlemen to his discourses, plucking his acolytes from among the rabble of legal scholars who drifted through the Four Courts. The barristers who once frequented the drawing room were no longer appearing, and so Eliza was no longer provided with new hearts to win. As for Amelia, she completed the trio of sorrowing siblings. Her request to study painting in Italy had again been denied. I was lucky to have escaped, Richard assured me, but I did not feel lucky at all.

The Lady Bachelors gathered in Anne's room to complete toilettes and adjust costumes as needed. Even though Miss Elliston had been invited to match our attire, she found the Turkish style to be far too revealing. As if she had to play up a contrast, she draped herself in heavy velvets, her frock inspired by the court dress of Charles II. I paid her a compliment, but her response was one of restrained jealousy. Anyone could see why she envied me. The flowing silks of the Arabian lady were far more enticing to the male eye than her dowdy apparel, and I would shine the brighter for it. The greatest act of kindness I could perform that night was to keep my distance from her, to avoid others making the unflattering comparison.

A platform had been erected in the art gallery to serve as our stage. Screens were placed to mask the doorway for our entrance, with the set draped in yards of fabric to suggest the interior of a tent. William supervised the construction, based on sketches he had received from an acquaintance who had fought in the Alexandria expedition. Miss Elliston was given her duties, which she accepted with a haughty upward tilt of her nose to indicate her displeasure, and the Lady Bachelors gathered their instruments.

Applause greeted our arrival, along with cheers from the gentlemen who heartily approved of our masquerade. There was laughter at William's garb, a robe with a bright scarlet sash and a headdress tied with red cord to keep it from falling over his eyes. During a solo piano piece performed by Bessey, I sat on my fabric-draped stool and stole a few glances at the audience. I caught a glimpse of Charlotte Edwards, whose husband had returned to his regiment and left her alone to manage the impending birth of their fourth child. Miss Elliston wove through the crowd in her wide gown, sidling along like a crab, although she did play the role of beggar with good grace.

My heart beat its way up into my throat when my turn came. I swallowed down my nerves, although I was not able to fully suppress the fear that my skill was lacking and I would play poorly. Beads of sweat sprouted at my temples. I rested the Irish harp against my shoulder and imagined that I was playing for Robert, just the two of us together. One of his favorite songs was *The Coulin*, an air that Tom Moore had taught me when I was first learning to play. As if I were that child again, I sang of exile and longing for Erin. Why had I not listened to the lyrics, the vow of the maiden promising to fly away with her long-haired rebel lover? "In exile thy bosom shall still be my home," and I felt the pain of my foolish pride that cost Robert his life. He had known he was doomed, that I had the power to save him, and he thought I heard the song as he had, but I was deaf.

The ladies were weeping when I finished, and several gentlemen appeared touched as well. William jumped up and asked if there might be another song, to which Kate Wilmot replied, "He who pays the piper call the tune."

Amid much laughter, a bid was made, followed by another, until it was apparent that my voice was up for auction. Reverend Bullen won the contest, and requested any tune of my choosing, as long as I sang in Irish. Again I played for Robert, a song I had sung for him at his last visit to The Priory. *Is mian liorn labhairt ar an oig-mhni* was a lover's tale told by the young man who wished to talk about the young woman with whom he was smitten. In keeping with the traditional style, I used inflection and vocal ornamentation to convey the emotions expressed in the words. Coupled with the soft strains of the harp, the selection took on a magical quality, an ethereal beauty so captivating that my listeners stood in stunned silence as the last note vibrated.

"*Ned of the Hills*," a lady's voice called out. It was Charlotte Edwards, for whom I would gladly have sung without payment as an act of love. A man in regimentals appeared at her side and took her arm. Dark eyes, thick black brows, full lips; his face was oddly familiar.

"*Sile ni Chonnallain*," came the counter-request.

A Cork barrister who had called on me several times had thrown down the challenge. He named his price, and Mrs. Edwards' companion raised the bid. The friendly banter took on a heated edge, to a degree that alarmed me. Mrs. Edwards perceived my distress and laid a gentle hand on her escort's arm, silencing him at once. With grace, the combatant withdrew and I sang the third song. To avoid a repetition I put a hand to my throat to indicate weariness, and William directed everyone's attention to an opening bid for any tune in which he might be the featured player. "There's a money-losing venture," Reverend Bullen quipped. "You would have to pay us to listen to you scrape that bow across those poor maligned strings."

A lady in masquerade became a woman of mystery, no longer Miss Curran but an exotic Turkish flower. I moved through the assembly with the ease of one who had acquired a new identity by donning a costume. For an evening I felt free of my past, a great burden removed. I enjoyed the company and the accolades that fell on my ears, although I felt a bit guilty to receive what my poor sisters were denied. I searched out Mrs. Edwards, to thank her for her help in snuffing a potentially unpleasant display.

"My brother can forget himself. Daily he is in the company of soldiers and the manners of the battlefield linger," Charlotte said. "I wanted to introduce you to him but he said you had already met. And that he did not know if he could acknowledge you without causing offense. Do you know what he meant by that?"

A painful memory exploded behind my eyes, pulsed like a fierce headache and shot fire through my veins. Robert delayed his trip to see his brother in prison for my sake, but I had not realized the depth of his dedication. Why had I not told him that night, at my debut, to devote himself to the cause of liberty and not concern himself with my happiness? So many lost opportunities to save his life and I failed to notice even one of them. "We were introduced at the Lambart home, in Wicklow, I believe," I said. "I do not know why he thinks he would offend me if we were to speak. If I seemed abrupt towards him that evening, I meant no offense. It was the night of my debut, you see, and I was pulled from pillar to post."

"Our time is not our own when we first come out into society," Mrs. Edwards said. "You are pale, Miss Curran."

"The rooms are quite crowded," I said. "I need some air and I shall be fine."

I had to get away from the clamor, to find some corner where I could be alone with the sorrow that pressed down heavy on my heart. I hurried to the front door, the nearest exit, intending to hide myself in the shadows of the demesne wall. The autumn air was refreshing and I breathed in deep gulps of it, pulling the chill down to my toes. My Turkish costume proved inadequate to the temperature, however, and I was torn between warmth and solace.

"An escapee from the Sultan's harem," a man called out. "Let us capture her and demand a reward."

Men under the influence of drink could be unpredictable and I could not know if those stomping through the bushes were friend or foe. I could not guess which direction they came from or which way I should go. The house, with every window glowing brightly, was a beacon and I charged straight ahead, only to crash headlong into an army officer. He toppled backwards, calling out an alarm about the wily vixen. Thinking I had made my escape, I adjusted my turban while I continued across the lawn, to re-enter the house with my dignity intact.

"Your plume, I believe," a gentleman behind me said. I turned to find Mr. Sturgeon looking extremely sheepish. "Please excuse Lt. Long. And Mr. Napier as well. Both prone to excessive exuberance."

"Your uniform is not the one I recall," I said.

"That you remember such a minor detail," he said. He tugged at his coat with pride. "I was a lieutenant when we met, in the artillery. The Duke of York undertook a complete overhaul of the army and I was most fortunate to be selected for service in the Royal Staff Corps. A captain on merit, Miss Curran, unlike other units of the army where ranks are sold to the highest bidder. I have no doubt that the changes are the result of public outrage. When the mistress of the Commander in Chief is found to be feathering her nest with the profits from her despicable business, how could the matter be ignored?"

"I heard of the scandal." His boasting of merit rankled. I was familiar enough with British army traditions to know that commissions for artillery officers were never sold, not when the post required genuine intelligence. Commanding a gun was far too complicated for the average British gentleman.

"A pity, I believe, that the lady at the heart of the incident did not have better legal representation when she sued for libel. She might not have lost her case. Although her assistant Mr. Fitzgerald was not particularly helpful to her, either. The little toad."

"He was often welcomed at my father's home," I said by way of warning to watch his words. The past had been resurrected more than enough that evening.

"While you are not. Nor was I, Miss Curran, when I made overtures, although your father has quite forgotten me."

"How can you know that?"

"I have often been a guest of the Reverend Bullen since I was posted to Ireland, and your father was present at dinner last night. We spoke at length about my noble service and the general state of the war. He paid me the highest compliments, which he would not have if he had recalled our earlier correspondence."

The floor beneath me swayed. My father was in the vicinity of Wood Hill and had not come to see me. My disgrace was reinforced, strengthened like the walls of a fortress designed to keep me out. The finality of it struck me with the force of a cannon ball. "Mr. Penrose has been a father to me this past year," I said.

"He is the most decent man I have ever met," Capt. Sturgeon said. "My sister and her husband came here to view his art collection and he invited them to spend the night. A most rare individual."

The Captain escorted me to the dining room, insisting that I take some nourishment before I fainted. We found Mrs. Edwards there, in company with some old friends she was staying with nearby at Hayfield. The group managed to keep a conversation going without me, and I retreated into my own thoughts. Had it really been a full year since Robert was torn from me? How had I survived all those days without him, knowing that I would never see him again until merciful death would reunite us? Cruel fate had brought me to the Penrose home where I was wrapped in a warm blanket of love and tenderness, to demonstrate with absolute clarity the contrast between my former life and my tenuous present existence. I should have been happy, having found happiness, but like wisps of smoke I could not grasp it.

My mind wandered, bringing me back to The Priory and the naïve group that gathered there to discuss rebellion. From Tom Moore came the overture to our theatricals, with his trove of traditional songs that he was collecting to preserve them in the face of British attempts to eradicate Irish culture. All those songs of failed rebels, all those romantic lyrics that celebrated heroic doom. "Ce he sin amuigh a bhfuil faobhar a ghuth ag reabadh mo dhorais duinta," the lyrics of *Eamonn an Chnoic, Ned of the Hills*, sprang forth from the depth of memory, and it felt as if Mr. Moore was standing over my shoulder while I practiced, his hand sweeping through the air as he kept time. None of us knew that our little world was already crumbling even then. The tune was as short as our shining hours, and like those heady days it came to a close. To my surprise, Mrs. Edwards embraced me with tears in her eyes.

"I must find Mr. Penrose," she said. "You gave me the song I requested and now I must make the donation promised."

A lapse on my part, to allow myself to descend once again into self-introspection. I had to bring my thoughts under control. I had to master emotions or be ruled by them, a heartless tyranny that almost cost me my life.

TWENTY-SIX

Captain Sturgeon was not the first gentleman to call on me at Wood Hill, but he was the most persistent. The nephew of the late Marquis of Rockingham, whose education had been provided by his esteemed uncle, would have been welcomed in any respectable drawing room. I had no doubt that Henry Sturgeon would have been granted permission to call on me if my father had known of the family connection, instead of assuming that the gentleman was merely another soldier who would fall in battle and leave behind an impoverished widow who would return to her father's home and cost that father further expense. Perhaps it was the knowledge that Mr. Curran had denied Henry, as he had denied Robert, that influenced my attitude when Henry came to Wood Hill to drink tea with the Penrose family. I did not turn him away or claim ill health to avoid his company, as I had done with others before him.

On fine days he took me driving in the country with Anne as our chaperone. Miss Elliston joined us on more than a few occasions, although her presence had a great deal to do with winning Anne's attention, rather than concern for my reputation. That Miss Elliston encouraged me to pursue the Captain was an indication of her desire that I exit the stage. She encouraged me to pursue every gentleman who had shown the slightest interest in me, no matter how unsuitable the man might be, or how unsuitable I was.

For the sake of novelty we traveled to the military camp and observed the soldiers drill, their evolutions precise and crisp. I thought of Robert and his motley band of untrained laborers, walking along Thomas Street in complete disarray. They had been playing at soldier, a group of dreamers lacking the discipline required of a military unit. Of course the uprising had failed. A leader required actual experience, not a conceptual understanding gained from reading treatises on warfare. Silly children had gone out to meet hardened men on that July night, children who thought they were fully grown adults. Was it any wonder that high-placed gentlemen kept to the shadows? They had anticipated disaster and failed to give Robert the slightest warning. He would not have heeded it, in any event, a fact that I was coming to realize a year too late.

"Do the men engage in artillery practice?" I asked. "Naval gun crews shoot at barrels, I understand."

"We do exercise the men, but my interests are in experimentation," Capt. Sturgeon said. "To improve accuracy, for instance, by calculating the best gun placements. To an extent, a warship will seek the most propitious angle of attack, but on land my cannons are far more flexible. Much of my work here in Cork has involved determining optimum locations for shore batteries."

"You were commended for your performance at Ferrol, I believe," Bessey said. She had investigated the officer with utmost diligence. I knew everything there was to know about my suitor, whose high-born mother eloped with her footman. Captain Sturgeon was not impoverished, nor was he well-off. He had hoped to come into a respectable sum upon the death of his grandfather, but heavy spending on political campaigns had eaten into the fund. One hundred pounds per annum supplemented his army pay, enough to start a family. Advancements in rank, with accompanying rises in salary, would allow for growth. He intended to have several children, like so many gentlemen who were the youngest in their families.

In those moments when I could study him, I compared him to my ideal. Where Robert had been thin and wiry, Henry was taller and thicker, a reflection of their very different careers. Their features could not have been less similar, except for a slight likeness in their aquiline noses, but they were equals in intelligence. Like Robert, Henry was comfortable in discussing philosophy or politics with me, treating me as his equal. All well and good in courtship, but how was I to know if this behavior would carry on for the next five or ten or thirty years? I accepted the sad fact that I could not devote the rest of my days to mourning Robert Emmet, lacking any means to support myself, but that was no reason to rush into marriage either. A mistake could prove fatal. I had only to look to my mother to find the embodiment of the wrong choice.

Mr. Wilmot invited us to dinner, with Kate using the pretext to interrogate Capt. Sturgeon. I trusted her analysis, confident that she could locate the same qualities in Henry that I loved about Robert, if he indeed possessed them. If she found Henry lacking, Kate would be honest with me, and I very much wanted honesty. Or so I told myself. Not one of my doubts was dissolved by her glowing recommendation. No matter how alike the two gentlemen might have been, I was not so sure that I could love again. Had I not given my heart away? How, then, could I reclaim it and hand it to another, tattered and torn? Yet if I did not do so, I was consigning myself to a life of dependency, made worse by my orphaned state. What right had I to become a burden to my brothers? I was miserable throughout the holiday season, finding solace in music.

The pressure built up over the weeks as Captain Sturgeon become a fixture at the dinner table, almost a member of the family. My guardians were quite fond of him, and Mrs. Penrose was often heard to boast of the most propitious marriage that was sure to be announced soon. Henry did not have wealth, but he had connections and a ready supply of ambition. It was reason enough for Anne or Bessey to encourage the match, but their reasons for promoting the Captain had nothing to do with pedigree. He was a far more interesting person than any other gentleman of my acquaintance, capable of intelligent debate or witty banter. I enjoyed his company and looked forward to every occasion that brought us together. What more would any lady need in her life's companion?

"He absolutely adores you," Bessey said. We were driving along the Lee on a gloomy March afternoon, returning from the milliner's, a new bonnet on my head. "You both are so well suited. Do not let him slip away, Sarah. You would come to regret it."

"We are anticipating a proposal that has not been made," I said. "I may be worrying about something that will never happen."

"It will be made, and soon," Anne said. "Father received a letter just this morning from Capt. Sturgeon. That can only mean one thing."

"It could mean that he wishes to extricate himself from a situation that he did not intend," I said. "The result of gossip carried too far."

"Miss Wilmot is exceedingly fond of him," Anne said. "I hope I may speak frankly. Your thoughts have been turned from sorrow and I would not wish to be the cause of a relapse, but."

"A fondness that is based on the observations of one who was acquainted with Mr. Emmet," Bessey said. The nagging pain in my heart intensified. "Beyond Kate's enquiries is the fact that Mrs. Edwards has become a sister to you. Your life has changed a great deal in a few short months. What you loved about one may no longer be of importance. Indeed, some traits may no longer be appealing going forward. Other considerations should be made, as if you were starting fresh. Because you are, do you see?"

"I cannot replace him. I accept that," I said.

"Of course not," Anne said.

"You will not find a better man if you searched the length and breadth of Ireland," Bessey said. "He is a good man in his own way, an individual to be judged on his merits."

The best man in Ireland had been executed, but I kept my thoughts to myself. The passage of time was supposed to have aided my recovery, and out of consideration to my hosts I would play the expected role. It was all just another masquerade, a life in costume. "What should a lady seek in marriage? Is it nothing more than the acquiring of a home, or a protector?"

"Can we manage without either?" Bessey asked. She was being hotly pursued by a Mr. Jeffries, who we suspected was more interested in her fortune than her charm. Thanks to her father's wealth, she had a home, and her two brothers were ready-made protectors. A husband had to offer more to Bessey Penrose than worldly goods.

"You are blessed, or cursed, with an open and loving heart," Anne said. "Cursed because it has led you to the abyss, but blessed because you can find happiness if you take the first few steps."

The Penrose sisters were happy because they were shielded by their father's wealth and prestige. They had access to books, music and travel, the company of lifelong friends, and the good fortune to be able to remain single by choice. Would I be content to gain some of those pleasures, and would those pleasures sustain me if we were all very mistaken as to Captain Sturgeon's true nature? My mother had lived in a comfortable house, with a pianoforte and a library. She did not hesitate to abandon her children, however, when those comforts were not adequate. All that I had witnessed as the daughter of John Philpot Curran had left me wary of others. Neither did I trust my judgment.

Well-meaning friends put me in Captain Sturgeon's company with such frequency that everyone assumed my days as an unmarried young lady were coming to a close. At balls he was my first and last partner of the evening. At dinners I was seated at his right hand. During a musical performance when I accompanied myself on harp, I had only to lift my eyes from the sheet music and find him in the front row, an enraptured gaze affixed to his face. Sweet agony, to recall how Robert was once equally captivated. How different their faces were, Robert and Henry. One was youthful, almost boyish, with a serious demeanor that reflected the depth of his dedication to our country. Never could anyone label Henry's features as boyish. He had seen war, and the rigors of combat had sculpted the sharp line of his jaw. His was a man's face, although there was little difference in age between Robert and Henry. It was the difference between experience and theory, between action and philosophical study. My interest in theory had faded. Perhaps it was time to consider experience and action.

On warm evenings, guests of Mr. Penrose were entertained in the garden, to capture the last nights of the season before winter held us indoors. The gatherings were intimate affairs that were celebrations of music, featuring performances by anyone who cared to take up one of the many fine instruments in the Penrose collection. A few days before the last such soiree of 1805, I was busy teaching Bessey an Irish tune so that she could play as a surprise for her father, who was uncommonly fond of the harp. I was not expecting Captain Sturgeon in the middle of the afternoon and his arrival came as a surprise. No sooner had Bessey greeted him than she was off to see about refreshments. The trap was sprung and I was caught, with no hope of escape. My knees quaked with such violence that I had to put down the harp before I dropped it into the flower bed.

"What news of the war?" I asked like a ninny. "I heard from my brother John recently. There are rumors of a new offensive to be launched before winter."

"Credible rumors, yes," Henry said. "The threat of a French invasion seems to have waned in recent months and I expect to be called back to headquarters quite soon, to prepare for a new expedition. It seems that we are to open another front, to attack Bonaparte from the south."

My powers of conversation were limited, more so when I was too preoccupied with what might be said to consider what should be said. I sat mute and Henry proceeded along his plan of attack, assaulting my defenses with a display of his own vulnerability. Soon he would leave for England and the military exercises needed to prepare for battle. "Would you go with me?" he asked.

"I cannot give you my heart," I said. An offer of marriage was expected but when it was presented I realized how foolish I had been to consider any match. A husband deserved his wife's love but I could never love another. "You must know that it was broken and will never mend."

"I cannot agree," he said. "Scars will remain. I understand how deeply you were wounded. You have only to allow yourself to heal, and put your heart in my hands for safekeeping so it can never be broken again."

"Have you considered the damage to your career that would ensue? My reputation was savaged and that is all that I would bring to you. Scandal and ruin. The end of your future prospects, you cannot deny it, with an alliance to one who was betrothed to a traitor. I must say no, Captain Sturgeon, for your sake."

"Miss Curran, I would gladly stare poverty in the face if you were at my side. My future happiness depends on you, and is happiness not worth more than a higher rank? Others might rejoice to be commissioned a major, but to me the honor is hollow if I could not share it with you. Can you deny that your feelings for me are of the highest esteem and, dare I add, utmost consideration? Do you not look kindly upon me?"

"When your career has been blighted because of me you will not feel as you do now," I said.

"Do you care at all for me?"

"It is because I care for you that I deny you," I said. Those who dared to love me were doomed. Gertrude was dead. Robert was dead. My mother was essentially dead. I could not allow another to perish.

"It is because I love you that I ask again if you will marry me."

"You will come to despise me."

"I will not ever despise you. I admire you. Your resilience. Your fortitude. You have overcome obstacles that would destroy a lesser being. Be my wife, dearest Sarah."

"I can offer nothing," I said. "I am all but an orphan."

"It does not signify."

"You will have my highest regard, to be sure. It cannot be enough for you."

"It will be the foundation of our love. If you will but say yes, and make me the happiest man in Ireland."

"Would you grant me two weeks to consider carefully? You, too, must consider my objections carefully."

"Your objections are duly considered, my dearest, and duly dismissed. Think long and hard, and you will come to recognize what you feel for me is love. Not infatuation, but love."

"I should write to my father. Even though he will not acknowledge me, or respond, I must give him the opportunity."

"If you like. Give him the chance to make a bigger fool of himself in the court of public opinion," Henry said.

If the world saw my father in the wrong, perhaps there was some hope that I would not damage Henry's career. I cared too much for him to take advantage of his offer for the sake of escaping my difficult situation, but if I caused no harm, I could be restored to my rightful place in the world. Never would I forget Robert, however. He would remain always in a quiet corner that I would reserve for his memory.

In my mind, I felt that we had traveled but a short distance together, and had reached a fork in the road. It was time for us to go our separate ways. As I continued on life's journey I would carry with me the principles for which Robert Emmet fought and died, and instill them in my children. Through me, Robert's legacy would be passed on to the next generation. His epitaph might yet be written by one of my sons.

Henry, however, was not the radical that Robert was. Doubt burrowed in deeper and I thought I might postpone my decision a little longer. I was a citizen of a country at war, however, and events beyond my control forced my hand. Within days of Henry's proposal the world learned of the greatest naval battle ever fought. Admiral Nelson had defeated the combined fleets of France and Spain. The tide of war was shifting. The time to hesitate was lost.

TWENTY-SEVEN

The banns were read in the Glanmire church and my friends showered me with well wishes and gifts. Even though Mr. Penrose had provided me with a complete wardrobe upon my arrival two years earlier, he insisted on sending me off with the same largesse he would have shown Bessey or Anne. If I was not being fitted for a walking gown I was calling at the shops in Cork town, frequent excursions that were the result of Mrs. Penrose thinking of some other item I needed to outfit my new home. I had no time to think about what I was actually doing, or how final the vow.

The night before my wedding, Mr. Penrose threw a party and invited all the ladies of my acquaintance. My last hours as Miss Curran were spent with great cheer, particularly in the case of Miss Elliston who was eager to return to her former position in Anne's social circle. A note of sadness stole into my heart when I considered the changes that marriage would bring.

While I would remain a friend of the Penrose sisters, our relationship would be different because my husband would take precedence over the ladies. Such was the belief of Caroline Lambart, who felt that she was all but abandoned by old friends once they became wives. The chain of correspondence was a weak one, and that would be all that would remain of a loving friendship. Who would I turn to when I needed advice? How would I cope with my fears and anxieties without Anne nearby to offer her wise counsel?

I did not sleep that night, and rose the next morning to a gloomy, wet and cold Sunday. After I dressed, the maid packed up my nightclothes, as if to demonstrate the finality of the events that would soon follow. She pinned up my hair and tucked the hairbrush into the trunk that stood open at the foot of the bed, its gaping mouth devouring my possessions until the room I had occupied for two years was empty of me. A great fuss was made over my appearance when I arrived in the foyer where everyone was waiting for me, my friends who would take me to my husband and then leave me with him, like a lost lamb returned to the shepherd. Bessey and then Anne adjusted the bow of my bonnet while Mr. Penrose fretted at the time, proclaiming that we would be late and Captain Sturgeon would think he had been jilted.

Anne and Bessey sat on either side of me in the carriage, with Anne Lapham and Kate Wilmot the bookends to Mr. Penrose. I had no family to see me off, no blood relations to witness my triumph. Such misery had been visited upon me but I had survived. I had lost so much but I was about to regain my respectability and take my proper place in society. Where were my sisters, who should have been riding with me? A familiar pain cut through my middle, the agony of my father's rejection, the wound of Robert's death reopened, and I could not stop the tears from falling.

Poor Henry was left to wait in the church while the ladies mopped up the tears and pinched the roses back into my cheeks. If he noticed my red-rimmed eyes he never said, but I believed he was, like most men, blind to a lady's overwrought state. The warm glow on his face did not dim when the excitability that I thought I had conquered was resurrected. A few words gave it new life, 'Who giveth this woman', and my heart sank as Mr. Penrose announced that the honor was his. My father had thrown me away like so much refuse, and I could not shake the depressing thought. My imagination played cruel tricks, creating lovely pictures of Robert Emmet standing with me in the church in Rathfarnham, the dreams of a long-gone time. My hands shook, my knees quaked, and I wanted the spectacle to end so that I could sit down and compose myself. Henry held my hands in his, felt the trembling, and squeezed just enough to tell me that he was my pillar of strength, to be leaned on whenever needed.

What was served at the wedding breakfast? I paid no heed to the food while my stomach tumbled and churned with emotion. Our guests ate and drank, there were toasts and wishes for great happiness, and suddenly it was all over. I was rushed out to a carriage by a mob of crying women and boisterous gentlemen, embraced and kissed until my bonnet was almost falling off my head. Mr. Penrose handed me up and William Penrose clapped Henry on the back as my husband climbed in. A chorus of good-byes rang out like a choir of discordant angels. I leaned out of the window to get a last look at Wood Hill, my beloved sanctuary that would never appear to me in the same way again. The carriage rolled away while I waved my handkerchief at those I had to leave behind, those I would have left behind no matter who I married because such was a woman's lot.

Twice I had kissed Robert Emmet with what I thought was passion. In the church, Henry planted a rather chaste peck on my lips, a coolness that I blamed on myself. If I worshipped Henry, I thought, I might have felt something more. Alone in the closed carriage, I discovered how mistaken I was. Everything about Henry's kiss was so unlike the sum of my prior experience that I was stunned. "Have I told you how beautiful you are?" he asked, and I could not move my mouth to speak. A powerful force flowed through my veins, an indescribable sensation that frightened me. All my childhood dreams were gone, the hazy visions of my future painted over with the vivid hues of regimental scarlet. I had betrayed Robert once before when I exposed his hiding place. Was I betraying him again?

The journey from Wood Hill to Carrigtwohill was made over roads turned to muck in the autumn rain. I was worn out by the time we reached our lodging, a somewhat run-down inn that was popular with the military. Fatigued, in a daze, I sat and watched Henry's reflection in the glass as he took down my hair. He helped me out of my traveling dress, a confection of rose pink silk trimmed with a Greek key design, and tossed it carelessly over the open lid of the trunk. I stared at the scar on his leg, his souvenir of the Alexandria expedition, to avoid staring at the rest of his body after he pulled his shirt over his head.

Our intimacy was slow and patient under his guidance; his offers to stop at any time were never accepted. Yes, I had given my body to him, but I wanted to yield. He had chosen me for myself. Despite my flaws, he wanted me.

Overwhelmed by a barrage of sensations never before experienced, I could only stare wide-eyed at the ceiling as Henry's breathing grew deeper and I knew he was asleep. When I did close my eyes I was plagued with frightening nightmares of my brother John. While I had heard that his ship was unable to sail with Nelson's fleet and he had not fought at Trafalgar, I could not stop wondering where he was, or if he was safe. In a vivid dream, I was standing on the deck of a ship of the line with him, but we were surrounded by African faces, dark and treacherous. Startled awake, I did not know where I was for a moment, my alarm increased when I felt the heat of a body next to me. I tumbled to the floor as quietly as I could, where the chill of the room brought me back to my senses. A fog of regret enveloped me, a melancholy that I attributed to the first pinch of homesickness.

Wrapped in a robe de chambre, I stood at the window and looked out at the small town in the back of beyond. Isolated, like Newmarket, and memories of my childhood flooded back to ease the ache in my heart. I could picture Gertrude at my side, holding my hand as we walked to services with Grandmother Curran. For a moment, I felt the warmth of the sun on my face and the tug on my arm when I slowed to look at a bird circling over a field. "You'll be left behind if you do not walk faster," Gertrude said, and to show her up I broke into a run. Grandmother snapped at both of us for our unladylike behavior, for acting like farm girls with no sense of themselves. We smiled, my sister and I, smiled at each other and then ran even faster until we reached the church door, where we stood with the priest and waited for our grandmother to arrive. She could not upbraid us in front of the minister, not after he commended us for our haste to reach God's house.

"Did I wake you?" Henry asked. "How beautiful you looked just now. Your smile. Come back to bed, my love, and I will keep you warm."

A woman's life changes so abruptly after she marries that it is no wonder a new bride appears stunned. From the comfort of Wood Hill I found myself in two small rooms, a temporary residence while Henry reconnoitered locations for a series of defensive towers to protect Cork Harbor. While he was gone from dawn until dusk I was left alone, with nothing to do. It was too wet to go walking, too confining to remain indoors, and my mood sank for want of female companionship. My friends would have come to visit me if we had remained in place for more than a fortnight, but Henry's duties saw us on the road.

Instead of a colorful caravan I traveled in a carriage, but I lived like the tinkers, never staying in place. I had no home, no place to settle into and set up housekeeping. I saw all there was to see of West Cork and Bantry Bay, heard all I cared to hear about gun emplacements and enfilading fire. Henry showed me his maps at night to explain what he had been doing all day, meeting with contractors and adjusting plans for arming the gun emplacements that would ring the harbor. The work was going slowly, said to be complete at one place but not finished at all. He arrived to train a gun crew and found that the guns had not been mounted, the second level of the structure little more than an architect's drawing and not likely to be completed before summer. As he spoke I thought longingly of my embroidery, marred as it was by a memory of how I once thought to use the stitched map of Ireland. I had not included the tiny islands that were of such great importance to defend against an enemy invasion. Little French knots of green, a small piece of satin stitch for Bere Island, and I wished that I could go back and retrieve my work, to add all that I failed to notice before.

With December's arrival came images of holiday seasons past, which did nothing to alleviate my melancholy. I had given up the happiness of Wood Hill for a peripatetic wandering, to open 1806 without friends or the smallest festivity. Henry proved himself a man of surprises, and my shock was quite evident when he brought me to our next lodging, where we would spend a week as the guest of a gentleman who could match, or likely surpass, the fortune of Mr. Cooper Penrose. Seafield House was the most magnificent residence I had ever seen, situated on the hills overlooking Bantry Bay. Our host was Viscount Berehaven, a name unfamiliar to me. If Henry had told me he was Richard White, I would not have come.

We were ushered into a splendid drawing room already crowded with other guests, almost all of whom knew Henry. I was thrown into the situation I most disliked, forced to be agreeable to strangers and make conversation when I lacked the talent. It did not help that I was subject to inspection by the other ladies who were assessing the quality of my frock and the attractiveness of my face as I stood near the door, thanking my hosts for their kindness. Lady Margaret-Anne took me by the arm, to make introductions, and left Henry to continue an ongoing discussion about erecting a Martello tower on Whiddy Island.

"Your drawing room is beautifully appointed," I said.

"The nursery is, in my mind, the most beautifully appointed. You are married but two months, I believe? Too soon to understand what I mean. I shall show you later, and brag of the beauty of my three delightful ornaments. My daughter is my delight, after two boys," she said.

"I am the fifth child of eight," I said. "A large family would be my ideal."

"You are not a native of Cork."

"I was born in Rathfarnham," I said. "Although my grandparents long resided in Cork, in a small rural town. My parents and eldest siblings were born there."

"This house has a history that you, in particular, will find fascinating. But let us save the lesson for a later time."

Three days later, when I took advantage of a brief moment of solitude to play the pianoforte, I counted my blessings as a way to stop counting my regrets. I missed the musical instruments of Wood Hill, but in time if I was patient Henry might be in a position to provide me with a home. We would need no furnishings, not even a bed, for I would sleep on a pile of straw if I had to choose between a bed and music. Did I not have the use of the viscount's instrument? It was better than nothing at all, even if the time was short. My fingers found the notes and my voice followed eagerly, as if it had been lost but found the way. *Ridente la calma* was a favorite of Anne Wilmot and I thought of her as I sang to myself.

"It is true, Mrs. Sturgeon," the viscount said as he crossed the music room. How long had he been listening, and failing to make his presence known? "You have a very pretty voice."

"I hope I did not disturb anyone," I said.

"Not at all. I very much enjoyed it, so I did nothing to make you stop."
He stood near a window and looked out over the water where a few ships
bobbed at anchor. "A commanding view, would you say?"

"It is indeed," I said.

"There is, perhaps, no part of Bantry Bay that I cannot see from here.
I watched Wolfe Tone's invasion force founder. It was in December of 1796.
A terrible blow for days, scattered the ships. You would have been but a
child in those days," he said.

"Fourteen," I said.

"We lived in such fear of the French invading, bringing their brand
of rebellion to our shores. Well, I was having none of it. No guillotine for
my old neck. The cellar of this house was packed with armaments. Powder,
shot, muskets, all the tools of destruction needed to repel an army. I had
my own army, every man loyal to our king, trained for combat. I was sure
the French would land here, to take advantage of an excellent harbor, and I
was proved correct," he said.

"I never heard of a landing," I said. The attempted invasion was but a
hazy memory, another link in the chain of misadventures that characterized
the revolutionary movement.

"Because God intervened before I could," he said with a laugh. "A
tremendous storm, and there was no invasion. What was left of the French
fleet turned tail and made for home. Although one ship was scuttled, just
across the bay. Too badly damaged to sail. And for having the foresight to
predict that which was obvious, Richard White was elevated to the peerage."

"I did not know that your home figured so prominently in the affair,"
was all I could think to say.

"Your father, I know, defended the rebels. Yes, yes, every man entitled
to legal representation, I have heard it said often," he said. "While I do not
trade in gossip, one cannot live in Cork and not be aware of your flight to the
Penrose home. Here you are, married to an officer of excellent reputation, a

gentleman who has been dogged in his determination to see these Martello towers constructed to avoid a repetition of '96 with less favorable results."

"Such has been his assigned duty," I said.

"It speaks to character, Mrs. Sturgeon, character and the inner workings of the mind. You need not say anything. Your actions have spoken."

"My actions, sir?"

"You married a man who has sworn an oath of loyalty to the king. Yes, his family has long favored Catholic emancipation which I find ridiculous, but the papists are more free today than they were ten years ago without armed insurrection. Might I add, at some point during our many conversations, Captain Sturgeon did mention that his initial overtures were rebuffed. You see, one takes all the pieces and forms the complete picture," he said.

All that Lord Berehaven stood for was all that I found repulsive in the closed-minded bigots who championed Catholic suppression. I wanted to leave his home at once, but my desires were second to Henry's and he was enjoying a respite from the road. "I continue to believe in equality for people of all faiths," I said.

"Because you are a lady, therefore blessed with a kind and generous heart," he said. "Mercifully ignorant of the chaos that would ensue if we were to recognize every religion under the sun. It is our faith that unites us to our king, and it is the papists who seek to rupture that sacred bond."

"Thank you for your hospitality, Lord Berehaven," I said. "It has been my greatest joy to play such a fine musical instrument after a long absence."

"I know that ladies do not like to perform before large throngs, but would you perhaps consent to a small concert for our female guests? My wife would be particularly delighted. She has so little time to play these days."

My confidence was shaken by His Lordship's nonsense. Nonsense, perhaps, but he opened my eyes to the public perception of my marriage, which was a very public thing given my father's prominence. Those whom

I did not respect had created an imaginary scenario that was far from the truth, as if they would resurrect my disobedience as another means of attack against my father's principles. As I saw it, I chose Henry when I could have waited for another, but after listening to Lord Berehaven I wondered if I had indeed accepted Henry for what he represented, rather than for himself. Who else might think that I married an army officer as a way to escape my father's liberal politics and seditious beliefs, and was I the one blind to obvious facts? I worried the notion to death, and came away from Bantry with serious doubts about my ability to love my husband.

My heart ached anew for Robert Emmet and The Priory, as if I had to go back to show men like Lord Berehaven, to show myself, how very wrong we all were. I examined my political beliefs and felt that they had not changed. In looking back at my flight to Wood Hill I could find misery at being forced to leave my father's house in shame, but if I probed deeper I could identify some joy in making an escape. I needed to talk with Anne Penrose, to help me find the way to resolve this crisis, but she was miles away. A letter would not suffice. I had to hold it in, all the worry, all the distress, and I fretted myself into a miscarriage in March. For Henry's sake I had to contain that sorrow as well, so distraught was he at our loss. He cared for me with such gentleness. With room for but one broken heart, I yielded every square inch to him. I thought it gave me strength, but it was an illusion.

Events beyond our control shifted the landscape, with the Third Coalition coming apart after Austria made peace with Napoleon. Henry received new orders and we left Cork in June, bound for Dublin. He had to settle his affairs before a possible deployment, and with a new wife to look after, he was granted a short leave to put all in order. We found lodging in town and I went about my usual activities of settling in, seeing to a more thorough cleaning of our quarters. The maid arrived, and my mind played such cruel tricks on me.

I could think of nothing but Anne Devlin, brave and fearless, loyal to Robert with unfailing constancy. Where was she, over two years gone by since that dreadful day? In prison, perhaps, forgotten and left to rot. For all I knew she could be dead. There was no way to find her, no way to discover her fate. At last I was in a position to help her but I could not. Troubled thoughts plagued me as I sat at the writing table with paper and pen. Someone could make inquiries on my behalf, but I was an outcast unsure of where I stood in the Curran sphere. I wrote to Richard and invited him to call at his earliest convenience. Then I wrote more letters, seeking companionship from any old friend who was in Dublin at the end of the season. Caroline Lambart arrived the next morning.

The past pulled me back down to the abyss. A chance comment over tea was enough to trigger a memory that resurrected more recollections. Seeing Caroline was to see the night of my debut play out in my dreams, but I had no refuge, no garden or hidden grove where I could share my dark thoughts with Gertrude. My nerves were frazzled with an effort to exude cheer in Henry's presence, and my eyes ached from holding in tears that I dare not shed. My spirits low, I found it took all my willpower to get out of bed in the morning. Each day represented another opportunity to make mistakes that Henry would correct, another day in which I secretly compared him to Robert and compiled a long list of deficiencies. The only productive activity I found was to alter my gowns, taking in the seams as I shrank to a shadow.

Henry's leave was coming to an end and he had to decide if I should remain in Ireland or join him at Royal Staff Corps headquarters in Hythe, near Portsmouth. Several of Henry's fellow officers were Irish and had homes in Ireland, and their families would stay in place. We, however, had no home, and my husband wanted me with him. The prospect of leaving Ireland was another dagger in my already shattered heart, and I inflicted even more pain when I accepted Caroline's suggestion that I say a final goodbye to Robert. No one knew where his body had been buried so there was no grave to visit. She thought it would serve if I called on the artist who had sketched my poor darling during his trial and had recently completed a portrait that I could use as a substitute for a headstone.

Mr. Petrie said nothing to me as he escorted me to his studio. The viewing was private and I was left alone with a canvas mounted on an easel and covered by a canvas drape. I stood before it for a long time, afraid that I was being disloyal to Henry. Just a look, I decided, a brief glance to see the artist's impression of Robert Emmet undergoing a horrible ordeal. I lifted the heavy veil covering my face and paused for a moment, a last chance to escape that I chose not to take. With a careful tug I removed the drape and there was my beloved, his long nose and sharp cheekbones, the depth of his dark eyes that saw death but did not blink. I absorbed every shadow and highlight, the curve of his ear, the straight hair that fell on his forehead no matter how often he pushed it to the side. I stared and stared until the agony of remembrance overwhelmed me. He was gone. I had to accept the fact that he was gone and our dreams executed. The privilege of mourning him was denied me by my father who disowned me and left me homeless. Bitter tears fell as I leaned against a wall to keep from falling to my knees.

Wrung out, exhausted, I replaced the veil and somehow found my way back to the front door. I collapsed in the carriage, as I had collapsed in that same carriage on the twentieth of September in 1803. Caroline put me to bed and sent for a physician, but what use was a doctor when we could not tell him the source of my malady? I could not even tell my husband why I appeared to suffer from nervous prostration when the only reason he could see for my state was his pending return to the battlefield.

"Dublin has made her ill," Caroline said. "It is for the better that she leaves here."

"The doctor recommended a change of climate," Henry said. "And you shall have that change, my dearest. You should bathe in the sea at Hythe. That may be just the thing for you."

"You would not leave me there, would you?" I asked.

"We are going to Sicily as I promised you last week," he said. A victory over the Bonapartists in Calabria had given England an inroad into the French empire from the southern front, the first defeat of Bonaparte's forces. Henry and his men were being rushed to Messina to garrison the island and organize the supply depots that would be critical to the next phase of the war.

"The climate in Sicily is said to be salubrious," Caroline said. "Warmth and fresh sea air, different scenery. All must be changed to bring you back to health, dear friend, and nothing will change if you remain here."

A complete and total change might shake out the darkness that lingered. Were the recollections rooted in Irish soil? I had to tear myself away to fully pluck them out. "I must go. No, I cannot remain here," I said. A tiny flicker, a fleeting thought, crossed my mind. I would go, but I would never see Ireland again.

TWENTY-EIGHT

Richard joined us on the packet to Holyhead, his journey the result of the long-anticipated ascension of the liberals in government. He entertained us on the voyage with a detailed description of the political contortions that marked Irish governance after the Act of Union, a chaotic series of blunders that saw the Tories go down to defeat, heralding better days for the Whigs. Better days for the politicians only. The Catholics of Ireland were in the same place they ever had been, their faith a potent barrier to equal rights under the law. The new administration was a boon to Richard, who was heading to London for further study on the vagaries of chancery law. After acquiring sufficient knowledge, he would return to Dublin as our father's deputy. At last he had a place where he might excel and begin his life's work, if he could but put his heart into it.

And what of the estimable Mr. John Philpot Curran? For more years than we cared to count, he had awaited a liberal victory. As one would expect, Mr. Charles Fox had a long list of supporters to reward after such a prolonged siege. For those who stood steadfast by his side in Commons through the bitterest days, the Whig leader bestowed coveted government positions, with those who showed the strongest support expecting the largest plums. Friends in high places, as Richard described them, had told Mr. Curran that he was certain to be the next Attorney General for Ireland, while other friends in high places were assuring the sitting Attorney General that his position was secure. It came down to a contest between those who had ushered in the Act of Union, with their plunder secured, and the newcomers like Mr. Curran who were given the remaining scraps. His was the consolation prize. John Philpot Curran was named Master of the Rolls and given a seat on the Privy Council. His outrage was heard throughout the kingdom.

"When we were young, he liked to rake Earl Clare over the coals for denying him a place in Chancery," Richard said. "Now he is the chief judge of the chancery court and one would think he had been seriously insulted. It appears as if I was given a job, he said to me in a most disgusted manner."

"You must admit that the higher, and more prestigious post, is that of Attorney General," Henry said.

"It is, very much so. But he demonstrated a complete lack of the basic human quality of mercy, and he showed his true face to Standish O'Grady when that gentleman was Attorney General. Mr. O'Grady, in turn, pulled off the mask before the Privy Council," Richard said. "Too many know him for what he is and no one would defend that which is indefensible."

"It is my fault," I said. "If I had obeyed him this never would have happened."

"If he had shown the slightest hint of paternal compassion, my dear, he would not have brought such damage to his reputation," Henry said. "I look to my grandfather's conduct towards my mother and see an example of a father's love. As I was blessed by Mr. Curran's ill temper, however, I will say nothing more on the matter, other than I thank God every day for my great good fortune."

"All has come right for Sarah," Richard said. "When she was cast out, I despaired, but now I realize that she would not have met you if our father had not disowned her."

"Do you believe in fate, Richard?" I asked. "That our lives are pre-ordained?"

"Ah yes, the Fates. Measuring the thread of our lives and snipping where they please. Some short, some long. Some tangled, perhaps," Richard said. His was a tangled skein, to be sure. His aversion to the laws he was supposed to uphold made him a failed barrister, dependent on his father to procure employment. He was made Mr. Curran's deputy in the hope that he might find his way somewhere, but he was so clearly lost. Richard was not the same man I knew at The Priory, before melancholy wrapped him in its unhappy embrace.

From Holyhead we took another boat to Portsmouth so that Henry could introduce me to his favorite aunt. His mother's older sister had never married, and became a second mother to my husband after he lost his mother at a tender age. She received me warmly, and showed me all kindness, but I could not wait to get out from under her roof and into my own household. Lady Charlotte Wentworth was an ancient relic of a bygone era, as were her few surviving friends. To be in their company was to sink into boredom. After a week in Hythe, however, I was longing to return to Portsmouth.

For the first time in my life I was on my own, a complete stranger who did not know another living soul. Henry's duties took him from home from early morning to late night, while I had no one to talk to for those long hours. He opened accounts in several of the local shops but I did not know my way around and was afraid of getting lost if I dared to venture out. The bathing season was over and the town was little more than a military camp, with all the associated unpleasantness. There were some who knew I had once been betrothed to Robert Emmet, the consort of a traitor, and few calling cards were left for me. Never before had I been without friends, and the isolation wore me down. A summer cold escalated into a deep cough that rattled my lungs and left me gasping for air.

"Soon we shall be in Sicily, my love, and you will bask in the healing warmth of the sun," Henry said as he sponged my face with cool water. "Good company, and others who share our love of music. I have a gift for you. I wanted to surprise you when we arrived at our destination but you need something to cheer you."

The Irish harp was an exquisite piece of workmanship, the frame a marvel of the woodcarver's art. Shamrocks and ivy twined along the neck and column, the maple wood polished to a high sheen. I plucked at the strings and found that the instrument was in tune. I burst into tears. "Go with your men and leave me here," I said. "I am worthless to you, nothing more than a burden."

"My life is meaningless without you," he said.

He climbed into bed and held me while I cried myself into exhaustion, a commanding officer consoling a green recruit seeing combat for the first time. Something gave way inside me and words spilled out, a confusion of unformed thoughts and disjointed sentences. I heard voices and I was transported back to The Priory, to the drawing room when we gathered to debate politics, the young generation who would liberate a nation so that we could inherit a free country. Where did those idealists go, I asked Henry, but he only shushed me softly and pressed my head to his shoulder.

"How can you possibly love me, Henry?" I asked.

"No one who meets you can help but love you," he said. "Do you love me, Sarah?"

"I do not know what love is," I said. "Not any more."

"My sensitive little flower. You have shown me with thousands of little signs that you love me," he said. I wanted to remain forever with my head resting on his chest, listening to the thump of his heart. "You feel too deeply and bruise with such ease. I would shield you from the world's pain if I could."

O ur household goods were sent ahead to the troop ship at Plymouth and I was never so glad to leave a place as I was to put England behind me. That I was putting distance between myself and my dearest friends at Wood Hill was a counterbalance to any joy I might otherwise have felt. Added to that was an oppressive weight of memory. It had been three years since I lost Robert, three years of seeking forgiveness for my role in his death. I had no one to share my sorrows with, and I dare not speak for fear of expressing thoughts that Henry was not to know about. He took my silence for fear of the unknown, as I had never been on so large a vessel before.

"We could not be safer," he said, bowing like an obsequious footman as he opened the door to our quarters. The room was no larger than a stall for a horse, and might have served that same purpose on another voyage. "The *Royal George* is sailing with us for protection. Do you think your brother John would stand idly by and allow his captain to abandon us to the French?"

John had recently been frocked, as he described his elevation in rank. He had passed the lieutenant's examination with ease, and was put under Sir John Duckworth, one of the most well-regarded captains in the Royal Navy. My brother was nearby but unreachable. I had only Henry, who watched over me like a guardian angel, unaware of the turmoil in my heart and in my head.

The turmoil soon settled into my stomach, a queasiness that grew steadily worse when we reached the open ocean. On a small ship, I had nothing to do, and found that reading only made me more wretched. Homesickness struck me down as I longed for the company of my friends at Wood Hill, the idle chatter, the music, the long walks and the solid ground under my feet. I was plagued by regrets, for not doing more for Robert, for not obeying my father, for marrying Henry and letting him drag me half way around the world. My tears fell after Henry left me to attend to his duties, my eyes dried by the time he returned. It was my duty as a wife to be cheerful, and I was determined to be a good wife. Never would anyone say that I gave Henry Sturgeon a reason to stray.

October was not the best time for sailing, and the delay in leaving port due to bad weather was the proof. We sailed into a storm within a week, a howling wind roaring through the rigging and tearing at the sails. I was certain that the ship was going to be battered into pieces and we would all be thrown into the middle of the ocean, our cries for help carried away on the waves. My dreams were filled with images of death and drowning, so vivid that Henry had to wake me before I could alarm our fellow passengers with my crying,

"You cannot give in to these baseless fears," he said. "The men see you as an extension of myself, and if you continue to appear terrified during this gale you will reinforce their concerns."

"Then I will keep to our room," I said.

"You will not hide. You will exhibit the demeanor that is expected of a lady, and you will be calm. Because, my dear, you are a tiny slip of a thing and if you are not frightened by wind and waves, the men will believe that there is nothing to be afraid of."

"A mask to be donned."

"No, not a mask. Feel cheerful. Feel confident in our captain and his crew. You are as much a member of the Royal Staff Corps as I am, Sarah. Do not forget who you are and what that means to the fifty souls below deck."

It is one thing to be told how to behave. It is quite another to see that behavior and experience the benefit of it. The storm battered the ship and I imagined the little vessel would be turned keel-side up at any moment, but I did as my husband ordered and stumbled through a corridor to reach the captain's cabin where we took our meals. Instead of a table, which was useless, and chairs that we had been thrown out of at breakfast, the cabin steward set the cloth on the floor and handed us our plate and cutlery. Henry, Lt. Willermine, and Ensign Wright roared merrily like little boys on a summer's holiday in the country. The scene was charming, recalling the picnics I enjoyed when I resided with the Crawford family in Lismore. Those meals had been great fun, and why should this not be an even greater lark?

We took our seats, so to speak, and were thrown into each other by every wave that crashed over our heads. The gentlemen offered apologies like comic actors, overdone and very silly, and I understood what was meant by the phrase 'laughing in the face of death' for they were in raucous good humor despite the danger. "And now the storm-blast came, and he was tyrannous and strong," Lt. Willermine said with theatrical excess, quoting from Mr. Coleridge's new poem about an ancient mariner. The ship tilted heavily to larboard and the lieutenant rolled against me, knocking me over and sending my fork clattering across the planks. He begged my forgiveness, but there was no stopping the tumbling. The ship rode up a wave and for a moment I was suspended, weightless, only to crash back down and nearly land in Henry's lap. He grasped me around the waist to hold me in place but another wave knocked me from my perch.

"The lady's stays are insufficient," our captain said. "Backstays are in order, Captain Sturgeon. Make fast Mrs. Sturgeon, sir, lash her to the leg of the map table."

Henry made a show of removing his uniform sash, which he used to tie me up to one of the few things in the cabin that was fixed in place. I rested my plate on a napkin I draped over my lap, and held my fork in one hand and a glass of wine in the other. Dinner was served, but dinner did not sit still. The platter holding a roasted goose slid from side to side, and soon the goose itself rolled off and tumbled towards the captain. "Not cooked through it would appear," the captain declared. He picked up the carving knife and stabbed the runaway, pinning it to the deck.

"And I had done a hellish thing, and it would work 'em woe: For all averred, I had killed the bird," Mr. Willermine continued his recitation, "that made the breeze to blow."

"Ah wretch! Said they, the bird to slay," Henry added.

"The breeze has not abated, gentlemen," I said. "Did you perhaps slay the wrong bird?"

Never before had I laughed as I laughed that night, tears of merriment running down my cheeks. The joy that I lost when Gertrude died and my mother eloped had returned to my bruised soul, in an altered form to be sure, but I felt it with every beat of my heart. My second chance had arrived when I was not looking for it, but there it was and I had only to grasp it firmly. All that had gone before was behind me and I saw nothing but sunshine ahead.

TWENTY-NINE

"**W**as that possibly an albatross that was served last week?" Henry asked. From a pounding gale the weather switched completely around and left our ship becalmed. We could see the mountain peak of Gibraltar, but could not reach it.

"The weather is so extreme on the ocean," I said. "My respect for the Navy has increased tenfold."

We took the air on deck, glad to escape the musty confines of our quarters. I shared an encounter with Henry, an anecdote I hoped would amuse him. One of the soldiers' wives had asked me to remember her to Miss Penrose, and I had to ask how she came to know my dear friend. Her story brought back sweet memories of Wood Hill and the little school that Mr. Penrose had started to teach useful skills to the poor children. I had often visited the school with Anne, who was a doting patroness, and considered for a time asking for a teaching position so that I could support myself. However, the impoverished of Cork had no use for music lessons. Neither did Mr. Penrose think it suitable for the daughter of an esteemed gentleman to be employed in a salaried position.

As soon as the wind blew, the sails were unfurled and so too did our enemy set sail. We were near Gibraltar when a convoy of French ships was sighted. I fretted, alone, below the water line until Henry determined that our adversaries would not attack. I was back below deck when a large group of gunboats appeared, where I remained until our ship had outrun the danger. We reached the port and sat there riding at anchor for days, waiting for the damaged ships of our convoy to be repaired. I amused myself by reading, and when loneliness threatened to get the better of me I made a sketch of Bessey in her Turkish costume. A dollop of remorse crept in to my heart as we waited for an order to weigh anchor. If only I had made sketches when I was at Wood Hill, I would have something of my dear friends with me. I often gazed with longing at that image, wondering if I would ever see my friends again. I was, as Henry stated, as much a part of his military unit as he was, and I went where I was ordered. That place might never be Ireland.

I wanted desperately to see the town of Gibraltar, to see anything different after weeks of staring at the same faces and uniforms, but Sir John Duckworth did not wish to undergo the required fourteen days of quarantine that landing would require. Instead I was blessed with the appearance of an old familiar face. Sir John allowed my brother to pay us a call, and his arrival was a moment of absolute joy. John had grown a little taller and broader, his face tanned, and his smile more bright than I recalled. He took to Henry at once, and I was soon forgotten as the military men exchanged intelligence on events of importance to their mission. "Sir John Stuart evacuated Calabria," John said. "A surprising turn of events, in my opinion. No new expeditions are planned."

"What does it mean for us?" I asked.

"I suspect that Sir John intends to concentrate his efforts on maintaining a garrison in Sicily while keeping a close eye on our French friends," Henry said. "We have to establish a base of supply and Sicily is the most easily defended. With the assistance of the Royal Navy, of course."

"Please God let us settle in for a peaceful stay," I said. Henry gave me such a look that I did not say more. I was delighted that he would not be going into combat, and why should I deny it? I did not want him to die, no matter how noble the cause.

"The mail has caught up to me at last," John said. "Richard tells me that our illustrious father is likely to be elected for Westminster."

"He is miserable in his present position," I said. "I do hope he wins."

"A rather idle occupation in Chancery," Henry said. "For one accustomed to the slashing repartee of Parliamentary debate. I wish him well."

"Have you been back home?" I asked.

"After seeing combat, The Priory would be too dull," John said. "And it would serve as a reminder of other battles I do not care to revisit."

An off-hand remark, a short phrase; John's words festered in my mind and came alive when I slept that night. My dreams were again filled with images of the past that I thought were left behind. Robert walked in the grove and sat in the drawing room with Tom Moore, and we sang of Irish rebels until my father appeared with a buggy whip in his hand. I heard Anne and Bessey calling to me as if they were in distress, begging for help, but I could not find them. So vivid were those pictures, so clear and troubling, that they lingered into the next day. I could not share my burden with Henry. Instead I forced myself to remain sunny, to recall the days when I wished that I could have toured France like my father and many of my Cork friends. The opportunity to explore a foreign land was mine at last, thanks to my loving husband. I owed him my smile, at the least.

From the moment the sails were unfurled at Gibraltar, I threw myself into preparing for life in Sicily. I had purchased a book of basic Italian grammar before we left England, and I studied the language for several hours every day. Being able to sing in Italian was not at all the same as being able to converse. Coupled with the tongue's resemblance to French, which I spoke fluently, my head was soon spinning and I imagined I would arrive at our destination with an inability to converse in any language.

We came to Tetuan, on the coast of Africa, and disembarked for the last leg of our journey, which would be completed on a merchant ship. My mind was a canvas on which I painted an impression of the whitewashed town glowing in the sun. Natives swarmed around us, babbling in their local patois interspersed with bastardized French, an incomprehensible garble. I clung to John and Henry, terrified by the press of humanity and the rude stares directed at me. We had to walk through the mob on the wharf, an act made all the more difficult by the whirlwind that roared from the interior of Africa and blasted us with dust and sand. So strong was the wind that I was almost lifted off my feet, and I would have toppled if not for two strong men to hold on to.

"How very strange," I said. "I had a dream not long ago, where I was with you, John, and we were surrounded by black faces."

"My own included," John said, although Henry had acquired some color since we left Gibraltar.

"How did it end?" Henry asked. "With a reunion in Messina? Should you find yourself in Sicily, John, you will be welcomed, although I cannot vouch for the quality of the accommodations I will provide."

"Very kind of you," John said. "However, I expect that Sir John has designs on the Dardanelles. The Russians have been active in the eastern Mediterranean and there are rumblings about a peace treaty that would put them into Bonaparte's camp."

Dust coated regimental scarlet and navy blue, transforming my escorts into sculptures made of sand. I turned my head away from a strong gust and a shower of sand fell from the brim of my hat, reminding Henry of an earlier expedition to Egypt where he had seen incredible statues almost entirely submerged in a sea of shifting sand. His curiosity about the buried objects led him to Mr. Penrose, who had purchased a large quantity of such antiquities for the new wing of his house. As it turned out, the ship carrying the items sank, and so Henry found no artifacts when he called at Wood Hill. "I discovered a far greater treasure," he said, placing his hand on mine. "And now she is about to be entombed by the same sands. We must board the ship or it will leave without us, and I have no desire to remain in Africa."

A small boat was waiting for us at the wharf, manned by a most motley crew of local sailors. "In naval parlance, you will refer to that vessel as a jolly boat," John said.

The small craft bobbed on the waves, offering a rough crossing to the ship riding at anchor in the harbor. We would be drenched by salt spray, knocked about like unsecured cargo, and I saw nothing jolly about the boat at all. "It is a little miserable boat, in the parlance of this poor bogtrotter," I said.

Henry boarded first and John all but lifted me in, setting me on the bench so that I did not topple into the water. My husband saw me seated with a gentleness that expressed his concern for my health. One glimmer of hope for a baby in over a year of marriage troubled me, especially because I expected to be as fertile as my mother. For Henry, the stumbling block was nothing more than the hardship of constant travel, and the sooner we reached Messina, the sooner I would conceive. It was a goal I longed to achieve, but to do so required a departure from my dear brother, and I was in no hurry to leave him. It grieved me to say goodbye, not knowing when we would meet again.

The jolly boat shoved off and ran parallel to the beach, where John followed along until we headed out to sea. He waved his hat, and kept waving it until we were out of sight. If I had known it was the last time I would set eyes on him, I would have given him a lock of my hair as a keepsake, but one cannot predict the future. Would I have accepted Robert's proposal of marriage if I had known what would befall him because of me? An ocean of regret washed over me and I took Henry's hand to keep from sinking.

The *Peace* was a small merchant vessel hired by the army to transport the men and materiel that would supply much of the military forces in the Mediterranean. As Henry explained to me, Sicily was centrally located, close enough to France to make for a short supply train, and easily defended by the Navy. Just what the army intended to do with the Sicilian base was a matter of conjecture in the lower ranks, and a subject of intense infighting among the commanders. Sir John Stuart had resigned his post over the disagreement, and Lt. Gen. Fox who replaced him was being undermined by his deputy Sir John Moore. All in all it did not appear to be an easy posting for Henry, who would have to dance to an ever changing tune.

With another three weeks of sailing expected, I went about settling into our quarters, but before we were under weigh we were hit with a fierce storm. The ship was riding at anchor, but that anchor was no match for the hurricane. There was nothing for us to do but pray, and pray we did, while the crew fought the wind. We watched through the stern windows as the ship was pushed closer to the rocks, ever closer to being broken to bits. Be brave for the men, I recalled my earlier lesson, and I was brave even though I saw the truth in Henry's eyes.

To escape the dangers of the shore, the ship's master ordered the anchor cable cut, taking his chances with the open sea. The Royal Navy vessels that were to sail with us for protection were battling the same storm, and the convoy was quickly disrupted and scattered. After the wind died down, we found ourselves alone in hostile waters, prey to pirates or an easy target for the enemy. What could I do but call upon Providence to spare us? For four days I watched the horizon, as alert as any sailor, and I cheered with them when a portion of the British fleet was spotted. We were sailing into war, I realized, but it was hard to accept that we were heading towards such ugliness when surrounded by great beauty.

Words could not express my amazement and wonder when we approached the port at Messina. The town spread out before me like an ancient Roman amphitheater, rising up from the water. Beyond the houses perched on the side of the mountains were fields of green and red, lush orange groves and vineyards going to sleep until Spring, set against a backdrop of verdant trees. "Oh, Henry, if I had oils and canvas to capture this," I said. "Our friends would say that we were well compensated for the arduous journey if they could see what we see at this moment."

"It is magnificent," he said. "And the climate, not as hot as I expected. More like Cork at the end of autumn. Quite pleasant."

A Sicilian pilot came on board to guide the *Peace* into the docks. He was swarmed by a cloud of British officers who peppered him with questions, all in English. "Cricket pitch," Lt. Willermine said, enunciating every syllable as if a clear voice would make all the difference. "Is there a good place for cricket here?"

"Mt. Etna, just there, do you see it smoldering?" Henry called my attention to a distant peak enshrouded in a cloud. "They say that when it erupts it causes earthquakes. I wonder when they last felt the earth tremble."

One of the army officers overheard Henry and decided to try his hand at interrogating the pilot. "Earthquake?" he asked, but the Sicilian could only shrug in confusion.

"Terremoto," I said.

The sailor was so delighted to hear a word of his own language that he proceeded to explain to me in a comical blend of Italian and English that they had experienced an earthquake but six weeks earlier, and several people had lost their lives after being struck by falling debris. It was death at God's hands, however, and so the people were resigned to the tragedy of a natural disaster. The beauty of Messina faded as I imagined our billet shaken to rubble while we slept, to be entombed under the wreckage.

"I cannot tell you how anxious I am to hear you play again," Henry said. "When I thought of your harp just under our feet in the hold, yet unreachable, when I needed musical diversion."

"We must have a musical evening as soon as we can," I said.

The broad walkway along the waterfront was crowded with the most diverse throng I had ever before seen. Turks and Greeks, Sicilians in threadbare finery, and Catholic clergymen in their many drab colors mingled freely. Before me was Messina. Behind me the hills of Calabria rose up from the sea. The beauty was breathtaking.

"We shall be happy here," I said. Ireland was far away, too distant to make itself felt, and the bouts of melancholy that I had hidden from Henry would fade as well when I could insert myself into local society as Mrs. Henry Sturgeon. Society, however, had other plans. Ireland and my past had joined me in Sicily.

THIRTY

In the chaos of settling into our home and hiring capable servants, I had no time to pay calls, let alone receive callers. Only after I had put hours into training the maid, whose standard of cleanliness was far, far below mine, did I peruse the cards that had been left. With the holiday season approaching, we were swamped with invitations to parties as well, and my head was swimming with all the details that needed attending if Captain and Mrs. Sturgeon were to show themselves in public. We carved out a few hours to send around our calling cards, in keeping with protocol, and I entertained my first guests less than a week after arriving in Messina.

"General Fox was made to pay the price for the lack of vigilance in regard to Mr. Emmet's rebellion," Mrs. Fox said as she sat in my Sicilian parlour with her two daughters at her side, sipping tea. Her husband had been the military commander in Dublin in 1803, the general who would have surrendered to Robert if the plan had succeeded. By rights, she should have despised me, knowing as so many did that I was previously engaged to Robert Emmet. She could not have been more welcoming.

Irish politics had much to do with it. Her husband was also the brother of Charles Fox, the leader of the Whigs and the man to whom my father gave his total allegiance. The Fox family being indebted to Mr. Curran for his lifelong and continued support of the liberal cause meant that Mrs. Fox was returning loyalty with loyalty. As General Fox was the Minister Plenipotentiary in Sicily, she was the leading lady of local British society and I was tucked under her wing without a second thought. The man I was to marry had caused her husband to be shipped off in shame to a distant island, but none of that signified. To Mrs. Fox, I was the daughter of John Philpot Curran, unjustly treated but fully recovered thanks to perseverance and pluck. I was too stunned to argue against it.

"In truth, Mrs. Sturgeon, our father secretly wished that Mr. Emmet had captured Dublin Castle," Caroline Fox said. At the age of eighteen, she was as excitable as I had once been, and equally rash in her choice of words.

"Philosophically, you mean," I said.

"Mrs. Sturgeon is thoroughly acquainted with the principles that the Whigs fought for," her sister Louisa said. Turning to me, she added, "You cannot imagine what a delight it is to be able to speak one's mind freely, among others who share the same thoughts. We are in the minority here, as we were in Dublin."

"I did not mean that Papa would have opened the door to the rebels," Caroline said.

"Of course not," I said. "General Fox recognized the need for a violent upheaval to force Parliament to notice the distress of the Irish people."

How different our lives would have been, but I did not wish to dwell on fantasies that had long since expired. Robert was dead because of me, a fact carved in marble, and it did no good to ruminate on what might have been because it never could be. I had somehow come out the other side of an ordeal, granted a second chance, and like the ladies Fox I would do the best that I could given the circumstances into which I landed. They, too, had been essentially exiled, as I had been cast out. The common thread bound me to them, and so the Fox clan became my anchor in Messina. The Misses Fox were delightful company, and they formed the heart of my new circle of friends. For the first time since leaving Wood Hill I had the pleasure of female companionship, and my mood began to improve. People who knew my history were charitable enough to keep silent, and my episodes of melancholy became more infrequent.

Not all were so amenable to an interloper in the settled order of things. Mrs. Warrington had to have known who I was, as she was the type to closely monitor every marriage announcement posted in the London papers. My wedding had been dutifully noted, with Captain Henry Sturgeon marrying Sarah Curran, daughter of John Philpot Curran, and by implication the former betrothed of Robert Emmet. The vulgar woman thought that her wealth gave her a certain cachet that I lacked, and it irked her that I became an intimate friend of the Misses Fox while her own daughter was largely ignored. How could such a notorious individual be so closely connected to the offspring of a man shamed by Emmet, I imagined her asking her equally vulgar husband. She could not hope to understand the complexities of Irish politics and undying loyalty. Indeed, it was a wonder that she could understand anything at all. She had nothing good to say about my dear friend Kate Wilmot, whom the Warringtons had met when Kate traveled through Naples during the peace, and so she stoked my distaste for the entire family. I wanted nothing to do with them if possible, but I realized that our social circle was small in Messina. That I would be forced into their company set my teeth on edge.

We were the honored guests at a party hosted by General Fox, who wished to welcome the new arrivals from Ireland. To make things particularly special, Mrs. Fox engaged an opera company and full orchestra, said to be the finest in Sicily, but I did not care for the style of singing.

The soprano seemed to be screaming at the top of her lungs, her melodies projected with unaccustomed force. "I find that I much prefer Mozart," I said. "Somewhat lighter in flavor."

"I have never heard of him," a gentleman said.

"Surely the great Cimarosa is far superior to this Mozart fellow," Mrs. Warrington said. Her pomposity was infuriating but I would not lower myself to her level. "When we resided in Naples, his operas were highly in demand. I cannot say that anyone ever requested the work of any other composer. Indeed, Mr. Cimarosa was the pride of Naples, a true genius. Very popular."

"You have never heard Mozart's work?" I asked.

"No, I cannot say that I have. If it were any good I would recall, as I recall perfectly the lovely arias of Cimarosa," she said. "You do not seem to have a grasp of Neapolitan music, Mrs. Sturgeon. I must invite you to my next musical evening, to introduce you to the work of a great artist. And do bring your harp. I have heard that you accompany yourself. Perhaps some Irish tunes would be amusing."

"I have been battling a terrible cough that I acquired in London, and the stone floors seem to have made it worse," I said. I often felt as if I were living in a sunny mausoleum, encased in slabs of marble broken by large windows. The view from every room was magnificent, but the interiors were quite vault-like.

"You will be grateful for those stone floors when July greets us with heat such as you have never before felt," Miss Warrington said. Her smothering concern for our welfare irked Henry to no end.

"I insist," Mrs. Warrington said. Clearly she wanted to put me on display when I would be at my worst, so that she might enjoy a sense of superiority.

That old demon, jealousy, was at play and I could not help but recall Miss Elliston's envy when Anne Penrose added me to her roster of friends.

My presence in Messina meant there was less room for Mrs. Warrington in the Fox sphere, the most prestigious social milieu, and she was determined to push me aside, using her wealth as a wedge. How it rankled, but I was powerless against her. My tongue was no rapier and I lacked the quick wit of John Philpot Curran. At any rate, it was Henry's choice to accept or deny the invitation, and he was a great lover of music. Even the most unpleasant company would not dissuade him from a performance.

Henry packed up the harp and off we went, only to find that we were not attending an informal gathering. Instead, we were brought into the drawing room where a circle of chairs was arranged around a small stage, not unlike a theater. I had always been frightened by public appearances before large groups, but my husband promised to sit where I could look up and see him. "Sing to me, as you sang at Wood Hill when you thought no one was listening," he said. "Imagine that we are alone at home, and let all the other guests fade away."

"I should like to make Mrs. Warrington fade away permanently," I said. "What an odious individual she is. To think that she is better than me because her husband is wealthy."

"She thinks herself better than you, my dear, because she is British and you are Irish. It is as simple as that."

"People like her are the reason that Robert Emmet fomented rebellion," I said.

"You are quite right, I am afraid." He shifted the cumbersome box that held the harp. "Emmet in his way, your father in his, my grandfather and uncle in their fashion. It is appalling to be in the company of such people, but we are outnumbered."

"Yet you joined the army to defend a government comprised of bigots."

"No, not to defend them. To protect everyone from foreign invasion, from falling into French hands. You cannot imagine the misery that is left in the wake of the French army after it strips the land bare and leaves the people to starve. I believe that we can improve our existing government, and so it must be protected from destruction."

"What would you have done if Dublin Castle had fallen?"

"I would most likely have been sent back to the Continent," he said. "What need of defensive batteries on the Cork coast if Cork is not part of England? Consider as well, our friend General Fox would have been present to open negotiations for peace. Would events not have proceeded in a favorable way for the liberals?"

"Or the King might have sent you to conquer Ireland," I said.

"Perhaps. Or the French might have landed their forces to take advantage of the chaos, and the Irish would beg His Majesty to send troops to stop Bonaparte's march."

"Some would have welcomed Bonaparte."

"For freeing the Catholics, yes. Which is a point that many have made in Parliament, spoken to deaf ears."

"To people like Mr. Warrington and his ilk."

"When one agrees to defend a nation, one cannot select the citizens one wishes to protect."

The guests took their seats and Henry had to hurry to claim the spot in my line of sight. General Fox pushed ahead to sit at his right, while Mrs. Warrington sought the honor of the chair next to the general. I was nervous and felt that I started rather badly, but I followed Henry's advice and pretended that I was performing for him. Even so, I was not entirely pleased with my voice which was still a bit ragged from a nagging cough. Miss Warrington was quick to step in after my first song concluded, rather too quick in my opinion, but I was glad to be spared from singing again.

Perhaps I had fallen in love with Henry long before, my head refusing to accept the ability of my broken heart to heal and place itself in another man's hands. I knew at that moment that I loved him, in a deeper way than I had ever loved Robert. Miss Warrington screeched out of tune, her voice shrill, and Henry smiled a little smirk of victory. Just when I looked his way, his mouth curled up and it was all I could do to not laugh out loud.

"Mrs. Sturgeon, another, if you please," General Fox said the very second that Miss Warrington concluded.

I selected a light air, a Robert Burns poem set to the tune of *Robert Adair*, but again my voice was not at its best and I hoped to be finished with the night's performance. The last note was just dying away when Mrs. Warrington, in a rather loud voice, asked her daughter to sing again. "You have a Scotch song, my dear. Do sing it. I sometimes like these little, easy things."

General Fox rolled his eyes and leaned towards Henry, to whisper in his ear. Henry caught my eye and smiled again in a conspiratorial way. Miss Warrington proceeded to torture the ears of all present, while the other guests shifted in their seats in a way that expressed their discomfort at what was a most unflattering comparison. The applause was polite, almost non-existent, and the young lady returned to her seat with her nose in the air. A third guest came forth to sing an English ditty, and I overheard General Fox tell Henry that Captain Sturgeon was the luckiest man alive, with such a songbird perched on his arm. Only a deaf man would take Miss Warrington as a wife, and to date he had not noticed any so afflicted in Sicily, hence the lack of suitors for her hand.

I had triumphed, without cross words or cattiness. By being myself, I had proved my voice and musicianship to be superior, and Mrs. Warrington's sour expression was clear evidence of my conquest. My husband proved himself to be my firm ally, and my victory was that much sweeter because I shared it with him, and him alone. We exchanged glances during the remainder of the concert, the communication of lovers who did not need words because our minds were one, as were our hearts.

The evening's entertainment came to an end and Henry looked about for a place to set the harp until he could send someone to fetch it the following day. "If it is not inconvenient, Mrs. Warrington," he said.

"Oh, no, indeed not, sir. Please, leave it here. Mrs. Sturgeon, do come and practice with my daughter," she said. I could envision my beautiful harp becoming part of her household, where I would have to ask for permission to enter and play my instrument.

"My dear Mrs. Warrington," Henry said. His tone was effusive in an artificial way, masking his outrage. The harp had been a gift from husband to wife, a very expensive gift, and he was furious at the audacity of the woman. Too polite to say what we both were thinking, he occupied himself with packing up the instrument. "I could no more part with this harp than with my life. I eat my music. I drink my music. To be deprived of my music for even one night would be too great a burden to endure, and I cannot sacrifice a single moment of enjoyment. In less than a week I shall be in Milazzo and I must have my music before I depart. A stockpile of music to nourish me during the coming nights."

Our hostess could not get a word in, although she tried. Her mouth hung open like a startled fish as Henry picked up the case and made our good-byes, leaving Mrs. Warrington to discover that her money did not signify to a man whose family connections were more powerful than her husband's wealth. He maintained a pleasant facade until we turned a corner and were out of sight of the Warrington home.

"Leave the harp here, oh yes, and Mrs. Sturgeon can become Arabella's music tutor," he said. "She would have you providing free instruction, I guarantee it, as if you possess some secret that no other music master knows. God forgive me for laughing at that girl. How can she know how badly she sings if her mother does nothing but shower her with praise and push her forward when she should pull her back."

"It was quite dreadful," I said. "So few people here really appreciate music. If not for you, Henry, I would go mad. You are so precious to me."

"I wish I could take you to Milazzo with me," he said. My monthly was late, and he thought it best that I not be subjected to the rough, rocky roads.

"But I shall be perfectly fine," I said. "Mrs. Fox is like a mother to me, and my calendar is quite full."

"So full that you will not notice my absence?" he asked.

"I shall miss you terribly," I said. "When you return, I will have a new song for you. I am sure that Mrs. Warrington can give me the loan of some music for one of Mr. Cimarosa's famous arias. Perhaps a duet with dear Arabella?"

"Do not let this harp leave the house," Henry said. We both burst out laughing.

THIRTY-ONE

While Henry was in Milazzo, I hungered for him. Still, when he returned to Messina, we had our first quarrel, and I understood how painful it was to hurt and be hurt by a person one loves. Yet what I did was done for love. The wound was not quick to heal.

During his absence, I attended a dinner where I was introduced to the Duchessa di Milano, the first Italian I befriended. We shared a mutual connection in Anne Wilmot, who had met the duchess while traveling through Naples, and so found a topic on which our conversation began in a most comfortable way. My husband was part of the British military upon which her family depended for protection, which added to her consideration of me, but her lack of regard for rank was remarkable. She spoke with me as she might have spoken with a peer, even though I was the daughter of an ordinary gentleman and my husband bore no title. I found her to be a most fascinating creature, and did not mind if she seemed to monopolize my time. The duchess was also acquainted with the Warrington family, long-time residents of Naples, and I should have known that Mrs. Warrington would very much resent a further intrusion into her sphere of influence.

The duchess invited me to call on her, and I arrived a few days after my hope of being pregnant had been proven false. A faint glimmer of sorrow might have been noted, but it was also true that women of my acquaintance were routinely concerned with my childless state. Even though the duchess was an educated woman, she found a core of God's grace in local folklore and customs related to fertility, and as a kindness she shared with me the beliefs of Calabrian and Sicilian wives who swore by the efficacy of the treatments. As she suggested, I made inquiries.

My household staff was made up of the Agostinelli family, a widowed mother and her two children. Maria was our maid of all work, and Gian Franco came in to perform whatever heavy tasks needed a strong arm to complete. Because I made an effort to learn their language so that we could communicate, they held me in rather high esteem, and Mrs. Agostinelli doted on me. She became concerned when I did not conceive in my first month in Messina, a distress that expanded after she learned that I had been married over a year. After two months, she changed the menus so that Henry was eating more artichokes, figs, and sauces made with pine nuts. While my husband was in Milazzo she stuffed me with noodles and vegetables, thinking that my slim build was part of the problem. When I asked about other methods known to ladies such as herself, she clapped her hands with joy and assured me she knew of a method said to be nearly foolproof. I wanted a child. I would try anything.

Gian Franco arrived one morning with a little cart that was pulled by a mule, a popular form of transportation on the island. The Agostinelli women climbed up next to me and off we went to the local cathedral, a splendid work of art that I had visited for its frescoes. Under Mrs. Agostinelli's direction I lit a candle, asked St. Anne to intercede on my behalf, and left a small donation for the poor at the church. From there, we drove to the beach where Gian Franco took his place near the road in company with rough-looking men who acted like guards, to keep all males away. I joined three other women with their retinues, following where I was led, and soon I was up to my knees in the cold water of the Mediterranean Sea. My cook dunked me under the waves and held me down until I thought she was trying to drown me. Soaked through, shivering, I was brought back to the cart where Maria wrapped me in blankets. Anyone on the street who saw me ride by must have wondered at my appearance, looking like a survivor of a sunken ship. Someone did see me, and told Henry that I had not behaved properly in his absence.

"Were you baptized?" he asked, not even removing his hat in his urgency to interrogate me as soon as he arrived. "I was told you went to the Catholic church and came home dripping wet. Dear God, Sarah, what is happening? Are you seeking some sort of revenge on the British by changing faiths?"

"What are you talking about?" I asked. "That is absolute and utter nonsense. Who is telling such lies about me?"

"Did you or did you not go to the church?"

"I did nothing wrong," I said.

"Sarah, what have you done? And without asking me, how could you go behind my back and do something foolish?"

"Prayer is foolish? Then I am a fool indeed, for praying for your safety every day when you were gone."

"Do not put words in my mouth," he said, his anger rising. "What prayers? Did you speak to a Catholic priest?"

"Have I not spoken to Catholic priests since we arrived? Do you think that we are so far from civilization that they do not know how my father champions their faith in Ireland? Why would they not express their admiration and appreciation?"

"This has nothing to do with your father," Henry said. "It has to do with you, and it is quite apparent that you do not wish to tell me what you did, which means you did something you know to be wrong. My enemies will not hesitate to use it against me, do you understand that? Any future advancement could be jeopardized if you do not conduct yourself in a proper manner."

"What is that proper manner, Henry? Should I join the others in mocking the Sicilians? They move their arms and hands with such vehemence when they speak, why can they not be like us? Their expressions are far too exuberant, why can they not regulate their speech? Excess emotion, why can they not be calm? What else shall I denigrate, to be like the others?"

"Stop it. I will not have this petulance."

"Petulance? Is that what you call it? Seeking the help of Providence to give me a child is petulance? Do you not want children?"

"Children come in the normal way if you are patient," Henry said. His voice was so loud I was sure that he was heard at the top of Mt. Etna. "Your health was poor for months after I married you, but did I complain? Did I criticize your elevated mood or fail to comfort you when your hope was crushed?"

"Then do not criticize me now for bathing in the sea, which I believe is a very popular pastime in Hythe during the season," I said.

"I should have left you in Hythe," he said. "At least I would have avoided the distress of being informed by my superiors that my wife, whose father continues to promote Catholic emancipation in direct contradiction to the King's wishes, appears to be turning towards Catholicism."

My mother had rejected me and my father had rejected me and even my husband wished that he had rejected me as well. "I told you not to marry me," I said. "It will ruin your prospects, did I not say that? Now that

I have fallen in love with you, you would put me aside. Have you found another you prefer?"

Henry sighed with a husband's exasperation. "Forgive me, my dear, I spoke in anger. I would never wish to be without you. Just tell me what you did."

"I prayed, Henry. I prayed to a Catholic saint. I bathed in the sea at a place where women who wish to conceive go to bath. I did nothing unseemly."

"You could have taken a chill," he said. "You could have fallen ill and died, do you realize that?"

"I was assured that women have been bathing there in all weather and none have suffered ill health because of it," I said.

"And they have all become miraculously fertile, I presume."

"Yes. So I was told."

"I am disappointed in you."

A chill nestled in our bed and our intimate moments became rather routine, just another bodily function to be seen to on a regular basis. Henry gloated when my religious treatment failed, while I descended into a bleak melancholy such as I had not experienced in over a year. To add to my despair, I received a letter from my brother Richard, who had become embroiled in a criminal conversation suit brought on by the cuckolded husband of his lover. He was about to flee Ireland, but London might not prove a safe haven for a barrister who was hardly a stranger to the British authorities. Sanctuary might be needed, and he expected me to help him hide in Sicily if necessary. How was I to ask Henry for such a great favor when he was still angry with me? Yet how could I deny my brother, who was so in need of help from all quarters. His mental state had never recovered and he was incapable of practicing law. I feared that he would try yet again to take his own life.

I muddled through the remainder of February, distracted at times by Louisa Fox's upcoming marriage. It was all we ladies spoke of at our social gatherings, and all I cared to discuss. For as much as Mrs. Warrington tried to sound me out, I would not say a word about my strained marriage. A mention of churches would be turned into a travelogue on the sights I had seen nearby, of Roman and Greek ruins, the indescribable wonder of Caravaggio's works. At a party hosted by Mr. Drummond, England's envoy to the Court of Naples, I was engaged in a discussion of the power of chiaroscuro to add depth, thus avoiding Mrs. Warrington's query about sea bathing in winter, and would have merrily rattled on all evening if I was not interrupted by Sir John Moore.

The officer was second in command to General Fox, undermining him all the while, but I still found him intriguing. I enjoyed listening to his tales of military prowess and bravery during the conquest of Maida, and had often imagined him meeting my dear Bessey. She would love him, to be sure, and if he would open his heart he could not help but love her as well. Reports of my matchmaking intrigues had reached his ears, I had heard, and I was ready to be teased.

"I wish to commend you on your command of the Italian language," he said.

"Merely adequate, sir, and scarcely enough to manage my servants," I said.

"That you would make such an effort is a testament to your domestic prowess. I see now why Sturgeon was miserable at Milazzo." He bowed as if to take his leave. "You have immersed yourself in the local culture, which is also commendable. If we are to parlay with these people, we should know their habits and customs. How else are we to force reforms on the Court of Naples if we cannot approach them from their level?"

"Consider, Sir John, the degree of corruption that is the hallmark of British governance in Ireland. You are in a weak position, through no fault of your own, when you seek concessions. Rather like casting a stone when you are not without sin," I said.

"The Duchess of Milan is a friend of yours?"

"I am so honored, yes. We speak openly on all sorts of topics. She is a woman of great faith. A firm Catholic."

"Not everyone can appreciate the intelligence to be gathered by the fairer sex, Mrs. Sturgeon, and I wish to express my sincere thanks for sharing another's opinion with me. In keeping with the traditions of espionage, I will never reveal my source, on pain of death."

The following day, Sir John made me the loan of Plutarch's *Life of Pompey*. His gesture of friendship was an indication of esteem, a sign that spiteful gossip had no place in his corps of officers. When Lord Tweedale, the aide de camp, asked me to accompany his party on a tour of the island, I knew that the request had come from Sir John, who granted Henry a month's leave so that we could enjoy a rather belated honeymoon trip.

It takes a great deal for a man to admit he was wrong, and to my credit I was gracious when Henry apologized for heeding rumors without first hearing my side of the matter. We spoke in an honest way, such as we had not spoken before, sharing our deepest emotions. Rather than turn my husband away from me, my dissection of my unhappy childhood brought him closer, as if he could compensate for all that I had been denied. My bouts of melancholy were non-existent during the month of March as we became starry-eyed curiosity seekers gazing in awe at sights I had only read about in books. My husband was voracious in bed, while my desire was unquenchable. I gave myself to my husband without hesitation or fear, as if he had set me free. We were, after so many months of marriage, truly married.

Words cannot do justice to the sensation of standing in a temple in Agrigento or sitting in the seats of an amphitheater in Taormina, knowing that others had been in that same place two thousand years earlier. Would England one day be in ruins, I wondered, a mighty empire fallen into the dust of history? I wrote to my friends, but when I reviewed my prose I saw how impossible it was to share my impressions. The beauty was indescribable, it was palpable, all sensation as it spread out before me. The tumbled down stones, broken pillars entangled with sweet peas, Mt. Etna framed by stone columns, and even the fragments of pottery that local boys dug up to sell to the tourists, were exquisite. We visited museums and gaped at statues of gods, marveling at the ability of an ancient sculptor to capture emotion in a piece of marble.

Our little house in Messina was decorated with souvenirs of our trip, my most prized possession a pair of jugs in the Etruscan style. I wished that I had the financial means to pack up even half of what was available on the market and send it to Mr. Penrose, who would prize such treasures. If I had two hundred pounds, I wrote to Anne, I would send such wonders as would amaze everyone at Wood Hill. Two hundred pounds, however, was a great deal of money. A woman could live comfortably with that sort of annual income, and I could not help but think of my sister Amelia, who would cherish such a stipend if it allowed her to study in Rome. Even Eliza's prospects would be much improved if she had two hundred pounds per year as an enticement.

The weather in Sicily was a delight, the days warm and sunny, with less rain than I experienced in Ireland. Henry and I fell into the local custom of walking at early evening, strolling along the wide road that followed the coastline. Our lives were comfortable, the atmosphere remarkably peaceful, and we fell into a somewhat indolent existence. I took to joining my maid when she ran to the window upon hearing the funeral bell, dropping whatever I was doing so that I might offer up my Protestant prayers for the soul of the recently departed as the cortege passed below us. As if that were not bad enough, I slid into the Sicilian habit of passing two languid hours after dinner, a time that should have been put to practicing the harp rather than reading novels. I could have lived like that forever, with my beloved, sweet husband whom I adored above all else.

By the end of May, the climate changed slightly and I found that I did, indeed, appreciate the chill of the marble floors. I was violently ill every day, often unable to keep down so much as a sip of water. Mrs. Agostinelli served me cups of mint tea and rubbed my hands with cut lemons, to suffuse my nose with the scent. Henry observed the procedure with a puzzled expression, and when I met his gaze, his mouth fell open in surprise. "A gift to the nuns is in order, it would seem," he said.

"To thank St. Anne for granting the request," Mrs. Agostinelli said.

Should we all be mistaken, I waited to tell anyone else. May became June, and the heat became debilitating. With the approach of July, I took to dressing for breakfast and then disrobing the moment my husband left for headquarters, spending as much time as possible in a thin muslin chemise. All the British ladies took to wearing the lightest muslin that was decent, and remaining indoors in the middle of the day, making our rounds of calls either very early or very late. With so little fabric to cover my middle, it soon became obvious that I was going to have a baby, and my circle of friends was wildly happy for me.

Just when everything was falling into place so perfectly, the Russians made peace with the French and yet another coalition fell to pieces. I learned what it was to be a military wife that summer, with the uncertainty of our situation requiring constant reassessment. General Fox had sent a small contingent to Egypt, to the detriment of our Sicilian garrison, and had taken Alexandria with ease. With the Russians leaving the battlefield, it was feared that the Turks would seek the help of their French allies to retake Alexandria, and more men would have to be sent from Sicily to reinforce the British position. Henry would be ordered into combat, and if that were to happen, he wanted me safe in England, far from a war zone, and in the company of people who would love me as he did. He contacted his dear friends, Mr. and Mrs. Rushwood, but the tide turned once again before their reply could reach us.

There were not enough men in Sicily to protect the strategic island and also reinforce Alexandria. The troops evacuated their toe hold in Africa, the Turks reclaimed Egypt, and Sir John Moore managed to get what he had long been coveting. General Fox lost his strongest patron when his poor brother died, so soon after finally realizing his political dreams. Thus weakened, the general was vulnerable to the machinations of Sir John who managed to get his superior officer recalled to England. My heart broke, to know that I would lose such dear friends. With a change in commanders, Henry saw a potential change in strategy, although no one could predict which direction that change might take. Austria had fallen to Bonaparte, he had crushed the Russians, and Henry could only hope that England would stand fast against the tyrant.

For myself, I wanted to remain where we were until our child was born. I had great confidence in the midwife, a woman of vast experience who relied as much on God as she did on the ancient spirits. I was in the best of hands, cared for by a woman who dangled a sewing needle over my belly and declared that the child was a boy. Neither did Henry want to be parted from me at such a time. As soon as he was told that the troops were evacuating Alexandria and returning to Sicily, he guessed that Sir John meant to hold the island and the neighboring Calabrian territories. We saw logic in maintaining the garrison as it was, to build up forces until a new expedition could be mounted to attack Bonaparte from the south, where he had already been proven vulnerable. A garrison on Sicily would be critical to supplying that expedition, and so we might remain as we were. Surrounded by Rome's former glory, we failed to see the deeper truths in the ruins.

THIRTY-TWO

A lliances changed and so the British military reacted to setbacks. The expedition to Egypt was one such failure, a mission that was poorly planned and undermanned. Six thousand men came back to Sicily in September, and Henry was ordered back to Milazzo. Given the treacherous nature of the Straits of Messina, Sir John believed that a potential French invasion of the island would strike at Milazzo, arriving from the port of Naples. Once our mercenary forces on the island of Capri were routed, he was certain that Sicily was Bonaparte's next target.

The territory that Sir John Stuart had taken in Calabria was attacked by Bonaparte loyalists, and the mood in Sicily shifted from one of confidence to one of insecurity. My husband brought me to Milazzo with him, rather than run the risk of my being alone in the event of some catastrophe. This was no pleasurable sojourn, however, and the atmosphere was tense.

I kept busy with sewing for the new baby, my expanding size making it uncomfortable to take long walks. A letter from my brother Richard provided me with a much-needed respite.

His legal troubles were somewhat alleviated when the British court found that he could not be prosecuted in England for running from justice in Ireland, but the damage to Mr. Curran's name was already done. The scandal would die down, of course, as scandals always did. While the slow demise proceeded, Richard thought it was a propitious time to call on his sister and brother-in-law and nephew, or niece if the soothsayer was mistaken. How I longed to see his face, to hear his voice, and chatter away knowing that I did not have to watch my words as we gossiped about one and all. From Sicily he thought to travel up to Vienna, and although he did not say it, I understood his intent. The leading doctors in the treatment of the mind were to be found in Vienna, and Richard was desperate to find a cure for his crippling melancholia.

All such dreams of the future were lost to the vagaries of war. Rather than return to Messina in November, Henry was ordered to Gibraltar. It was an evacuation, and a hasty one at that. Indecision ruled from London, with only our departure certain. From Gibraltar the soldiers might be sent to Portugal as reinforcements, based on intelligence reports that pointed to a French invasion of our last remaining ally against Bonaparte. At the same time we heard rumors of a planned invasion of Sweden, to open another front and weaken French strength on the Continent. The situation was fluid, uncertain, and moving too quickly for Henry to arrange for my passage to England. My beautiful harp that I had ignored during the hottest summer months remained in Messina and my heart broke at the thought of leaving it behind, but eight thousand men were departing Sicily in haste and one woman's trinket did not signify.

We set sail as we had before, in the stormiest weather imaginable. Seasickness struck as I knew it would, my misery compounded by advanced pregnancy. When I should have been preparing for my confinement I was tossed about in a ship, the mood on board radically different than my previous voyage. One year earlier, we were on our way to garrison a peaceful town. This time the travelers were heading towards combat, and they were a somber group, speaking largely of tactics and past battles in serious discussions that excluded me.

A few days out of Gibraltar, I felt something was not right. Henry asked for permission to remain there with me so that I could recover, but every soldier was needed and the request could not be granted. The best he could do was to ask among the soldiers' wives if any were experienced in childbirth, and all three women on board came forward in a display of sisterhood that cheered me. The baby was not due until January and Henry was confident that we would reach Portsmouth well before that time, but still a nagging concern kept me awake at night.

My tongue revolted at the wretched food and my throat joined in the protest. After a year of Mrs. Agostinelli's delicious creations I could not swallow the colorless assortment on my plate. I had no appetite, with my stomach compressed by the little boy who delighted in kicking me until I was certain my ribs were bruised. The only relief from distress came when Henry joined me in our berth and we reminisced about our year in Sicily. "Do you remember when Miss Wilmot's brother, the lieutenant on the *Thetis*, called on us to deliver my shoes from Dublin?" I asked. "And how happy I was to find the box was filled with letters from my friends?"

"Will we ever forget those musical evenings with the Warrington menagerie?" Henry asked. "One would have thought it was the banshee howling."

"Truly that was the happiest year of my life," I said.

"And the year to come will be better," he said, caressing my belly as he would soon caress our child.

"Can it really have been a year since we sat in General Fox's drawing room? The style of the singing, it was so different to my ear, and all those people who never heard of Mozart."

"Last year at this time, what were we doing?" Henry asked, his prod to goad me out of morose reflection.

"We were rushing hither and yon in an attempt to furnish our house," I said. "To be ready to receive callers. And now I shall have my first Christmas at sea. Will we enjoy Twelfth Night on land, do you think?"

"A fair wind will blow us home," Henry said. "I will have to leave you in my aunt's care. We land at Portsmouth and I can hurry you there to begin your confinement. No one better to watch over you during your lying-in."

"Will she mind the disruption?" I asked. "She never had children, after all, and we shall be such a burden."

"Of course she will not mind. If my deployment can be delayed I hope to bring you to Canterbury. If not, you will be comfortable with Lady Charlotte until I am granted leave."

Despite Henry's careful analysis, he failed to consider one important element over which we had no control. The ship sailed into another storm that tossed us about unmercifully, and on the day after Christmas I woke with sharp pains shooting across my belly. Thinking that rest would alleviate some premature spasms, I had Henry make a bed for me on the floor of our cabin where I could lie down without fear of being pitched out of a bunk. There was no rest on rough seas, and the pains grew in intensity and frequency.

"There is a doctor on another ship in the convoy," Henry reported back after making enquiries. "It is too rough to lower a boat to send him here. Can you manage, darling?"

"Will you call for the soldiers' wives, please?" I asked.

The terror I experienced upon losing my childhood home was nothing compared to the dread I felt when I realized that I was in labor. No fire could be built in the cabin, nor was there a private compartment where a fire could be set to heat the room. There was no midwife to fill me with confidence that all was well. My attendants were three women who may or may not have had children of their own, but that was the extent of their knowledge. I was chilled to the bone, frightened half out of my wits, and in grave danger.

Matters were beyond Henry's control and he grew more frantic as he realized that he could do nothing to alleviate my distress. His task was to wait and pray, no easy chore for a man of action. Neither was it easy for him to leave me in that cold cabin, knowing the risks I faced. We were both relieved, or at least pretended to be relieved, when the ladies rummaged in my trunk and found the small clothes I had sewn in Milazzo. They set things out on the bunk with an efficiency that suggested a wealth of experience, the oldest of the trio ordering Henry about before asking him to leave.

December's cold winds penetrated every crevice of the damp, musty compartment. The proxy midwives propped me up against the bulkhead in a seated position, my chemise pulled up to my waist. In shifts they sat with me, rubbing my back or sponging my face to bring a bit of comfort. Their kindness brought me to tears that I choked down when I grew aware of my neighbors in the compartment behind me. I could not lose my composure within hearing of two Army officers.

"Go on, Missus, let it out," the older woman said. "Scream and let the pain go. This is no time to be brave."

In the middle of the afternoon I took a few sips of tea to fortify my strength and warm me when the cold became nearly unbearable. Any sense of modesty was gone by that time and I cared not that my private parts were fully exposed. Giving birth, reaching the end when the pain would cease, was all that mattered. The hours dragged on until I feared I was going to die with the baby stuck inside me. My attendants sponged my dripping face and cooed in a discordant chorus of assurances that all was proceeding in a normal fashion. The first baby took the longest. By the time I was dropping my fifth, they said, the wee little ones would slide right out without trouble.

"Not just yet, love, not just yet," they told me when my body wanted me to push. "Not just yet."

The ship's bell rang but time at sea had no meaning to me. Below deck it was always the same gloom, the same dim lantern light. "There's the head," someone said, followed by an order to push, push, push but I was too exhausted. Push, push, push, the women insisted, encouraged, cajoled. Push to make the pain stop. Push to bring the baby into the world, the baby I wanted.

"A boy," three women crowed. The strangest sound ever heard on a troop ship announced the arrival of Henry Sturgeon's heir, a great wailing as my son entered an icy cold world. I could not believe my eyes when I looked down between my upright knees and saw the tiny, red, squalling mite. The cord was tied with sewing thread and then cut.

"A little thin but that's how it is when they come a bit early," the soldier's wife said. She wiped him clean and rubbed the blood into his limbs before wrapping him in a piece of flannel, hardly enough thickness to hold in his body's heat. "Put him to the breast, now, Missus. The milk's not in yet, but the suckling will bring it in a day or two."

How he protested the miserable chill, even when pressed to my skin. I was cold myself, shivering so intensely that I held my son that much tighter to keep from dropping him. His poor little head was distorted and the cap was perhaps a little too big, but he was the prettiest baby I had ever before seen.

"Is this all there should be?" the senior midwife asked.

"I don't know," said her companion. "Is there not more to the afterbirth than this little bit?"

"The babe's come early," the third said.

"Is he suckling, Missus? That should shake out the rest."

"No, push on her belly I seen it done that way once."

I was too weak to protest, too weak to do more than murmur about the pain they inflicted with their prodding and poking. All I wanted was rest, a cup of hot tea and rest. And advice, about what to do with the protesting bundle in my arms. "A doctor's needed," they all said in unison.

A numbness took hold of my middle but I could feel a warmth like running water, as if I was sitting in a puddle. I became aware of the rags the women had tied to the belt around my waist, changed and changed again, and noticed the cotton fabric soaked with blood. My life was trickling away between my legs and I gasped with shock.

"It's a bloody business," I was told. "Let the baby suck as much as he likes, now, and it helps to stop the bleeding."

The child cried himself into an exhausted sleep and only then did one of the ladies bring the boy to meet his father. I dozed off myself as well, only to wake with a shock when the rags were changed and a damp bundle slapped against my sore bottom. There was not enough time to dry things, so rapidly did I need changing. All I could do was pray for God's mercy, and He answered me the following day. The sea calmed long enough for a doctor to be rowed over from another ship in the convoy.

Like staunching an open wound, the doctor said, and he packed me inside with muslin bandages, a procedure I endured with the same grace I exhibited in childbirth. The concept of modesty was consigned to the scrapheap. All the manipulating left me queasy, however, and I was terrified that I might drop the baby in my weakened state. My poor, cold baby. I held him close to me, wrapped in the only shawl I had, and together we waited for my milk to come in. My nipples were sore, cracked and bleeding from those two little toothless gums, the child sucking with vigor to no effect. How he fussed, his hunger becoming my obsession, while I cried out my frustration. Every time I changed him he wailed anew, the small clothes damp from washing and no place to dry them properly.

Within minutes of the doctor reaching me the storm resumed, and so he was forced to remain on board. For those four days I waited for my breasts to fill, waited for my body to nourish the child, but for four days I had nothing but a doctor's assurance that the milk would come in time. He left just as a slight fever took me, what the soldiers' wives claimed was the milk fever.

At some point, my mind grew addled and I thought I was in the nursery of The Priory, a book in my lap. I read to Gertrude who did not want to listen, spoke the words in a loud and clear voice to make her hear the beauty of Milton. "'Therefore since he permits within himself unworthy powers to reign over free reason," I said, "God in judgement just subjects him from without to violent Lords; Who oft as undeservedly enthrall his outward freedom: Tyranny must be.' Do you not understand, Gertrude? It is what Papa speaks of in Commons. 'There was a nymph, who long had loved, but dared not tell the world how well; the shades, where she at evening roved, Alone could know, alone could tell.' Tommy Moore wrote a poem about me, Gertrude, about me and Robert and you, you are the shades who knew."

My sister tried to steal the book away, to run and make me chase her to snatch the book back but I would not let it go. I clutched it to my chest, held tight, but it was Anne Devlin come to put the book away and then Henry was holding my hand, tears running down his face. "The women have taken the baby down below decks to care for him until you are better. You have been reciting poetry, my dear. How strange our minds are in the grip of fever. I have settled on a name. What do you think of John? More to honor your brother than your father, but he does not need to know that."

Would I have fought against illness if I was not fighting for my Johnny at the same time? I was so weary that the idea of giving up was tempting, but I had an infant who needed me. My milk was driven back by the fever and I existed in a world of constant torment, plagued by anxiety that the boy would starve to death before we reached land. Time was the great healer, time and the sight of land. We arrived at Portsmouth ten days later, my fever broken and my milk flowing at last. I was too weak to walk off the ship. Johnny was weak as well, having nothing for nourishment during his first days of life but a bit of pap that gave him dreadful gripings.

Henry found lodging but he was not capable of nursing a sick wife. He set off to inquire at his aunt's home while I sat down before a blazing fire and wrote a letter to my beloved Anne Penrose. The last note I received from Anne Wilmot had mentioned Miss Penrose's plan to visit Miss Elliston, who was residing at her father's home in Lincoln. Of all my friends, only Anne Penrose was in England, within reasonable proximity to my sickbed. If I could just make her understand how very much I needed her, how very ill I was, then I was sure she would abandon Miss Elliston and come to me. Poor Henry was nearly out of his mind with worry, not knowing what to do in a situation normally relegated to females. Even if Anne would not come for my sake, she had to come to relieve Henry. While Miss Elliston might balk at first, I had faith in her sense of Christian charity. She was, after all, the daughter of the archdeacon.

My poor, dear Henry. He thought he could rely on his aunt, but Lady Charlotte had gone up to London and we were very, very much on our own in a strange city, without friends. How it grieved me to see him in such distress, and I was unable to comfort him. I added to his worry, no doubt, with my own fretting about John. What did I know about babies, and there I was with a newborn and no one to give me advice. I felt so utterly alone, unable to ease even a small part of my husband's burden, but I had to give all my attention to the baby, who grew more limp and listless by the hour.

Two days later, Johnny died in my arms.

THIRTY-THREE

Such regrets, an ocean of regrets, filled my heart to bursting. I thought with longing of the poison I had hidden away and wished with all my heart that I had taken it instead of waiting to see Robert one last time. I wrote again to Anne, to plead with her and demonstrate my great distress, my anguish. Henry needed her as much as I did, the grief-stricken father who had to buy a coffin and shroud for his first born son without anyone to console him. I was beyond consolation. I wanted Anne to come to look after my husband, who so desperately needed help.

Henry made all the arrangements while I lay in bed, too sick to attend the burial. "He was so very pretty, Sarah, after he was laid out. It was nicely done," he said. We both sobbed for days, and I tried once again to contact Anne but there was no answer. In my darkest thoughts I cursed Miss Elliston, who must have seen the letters from me and kept them from Anne. She had read the first one, I believed, and it was jealousy that guided her hand as she put the epistle to the flame. Anne would come to me and fall in love with Johnny, and Miss Elliston would fade into the background, the attraction of a weak baby too strong to be overcome by petulant demands from a cloying spinster. Lincoln for all its beauty would not enthrall our mutual friend like the soft skin and rosebud mouth of my beautiful little boy. Now my beautiful boy was dead, and I could write and write to Anne and get no response while Miss Elliston sorted the mail for her own benefit.

We reached London at the end of January, with Henry planning to leave me in his aunt's care while he returned to duty. My condition had only grown worse in Portsmouth, and he trusted in the wisdom of the city doctors to diagnose my ailments and find a cure, which Lady Charlotte would administer. Bad luck continued to follow us. His aunt was away, calling on friends, and could not return home before Henry had to report to headquarters. Again we found lodging at a decent inn, where I was seen by a doctor who was certain that I was suffering from nothing more than melancholy, a state to be expected in a lady who had lost her first child. I was burning up with fever, but Henry took such comfort in the doctor's determination that I could not help but accept the potential for recovery. I was bled, but the heat did not abate.

After a few more weeks in London, waiting for my promised recovery to take hold, Henry was called to Hythe and we had no choice but to leave. He was at his wits' end, not knowing who he could find to nurse me during the day. Anxiety wore on him as he anticipated his deployment, not sure if he could delay long enough for his aunt to reach us before he had to leave. It was desperation that drove him to contact Mr. Curran before quitting London.

"He can send your sisters to you," Henry said.

"He will not. I am dead to him, as I have been all these years," I said.

His head dropped into his hands and his shoulders were racked by sobs. "What else can I do? God help me, I do not know what else to do."

When I did not hear from Anne, I wrote to Mrs. Wilmot and asked her if I had done or said something to turn Anne against me. Her reply put everything in a different light, and I cursed Miss Elliston as a demon from hell, an evil being devoted to cruelty. It was Mrs. Wilmot's opinion that Miss Elliston was talking Anne out of coming, no doubt by suggesting that my claims of ill health were exaggerated in a ploy to draw sympathy. It was not unlike Miss Elliston to play on Anne's kindness by implying that she was unwell and more in need of Anne's nursing. What help Anne might need in arranging transportation for such a long distance could easily have been stymied by Miss Elliston's entreaties to her father, who would take his daughter's side and postpone matters.

By some miracle, I received a letter from my friend and my spirits climbed. Poor Anne had been ill for a time and had been unable to travel, but she wanted to know the latest news regarding my health. She would come, I was certain, if I could make it clear how very low I had sunk. A quick response was best, to convince her to come to London before I would be forced back to Hythe.

"You are too weak to write," Henry said when I asked for paper and pen. I made an effort to rise from bed, but I could not take two steps without stopping to catch my breathe. A deep cough settled into my lungs and rattled my insides. Another physician was called, and I was bled again, to treat the excess of fluid in my lungs. Pneumonia was stalking London, we learned, and the army camp at Hythe was in the grip of an epidemic.

"All the dampness on the ship," I said. It was well known that dampness caused pneumonia. How wet we had been on that miserable ship, when I was helpless to provide dry garments for my poor little boy or myself. It was the dampness that took Johnny and the dampness was going to take me.

"Rest and nutritious food will help you recover," Henry said. "Pneumonia can be beaten."

"If I put my mind to it," I said.

"Let me write to Miss Penrose, to ask her to come to you. If I send a letter by special messenger she will receive it, and have an opportunity to respond, before I must leave for Hythe."

"Wait until tomorrow," I said. "I would rather write the letter myself."

The next day I was worse, and the day after and the day after. As my body grew weaker I regretted not asking Henry to pen just a few lines asking Anne to come at once, but I knew that I had to make amends for my earlier letters in which I all but accused her of abandoning me in my moment of greatest need. Then, too, I had to show her that Miss Elliston was exerting a dangerous influence that had led me to think my dear Anne no longer loved me. A man could never put such sentiments into words, and the task was mine to complete. By the time I could manage, I was returned to the most miserable corner of England, far from the land of my birth, far from all my friends.

"I have been sent here to die," I cried, and at once I regretted an outburst that arose from fear. I begged Henry to forgive me for hurting him with my cruel words, pleaded and sobbed while he held me and tried to convince me that what was true was not, in fact, true.

Fever burned me, the tips of my fingers radiated heat, and my belly was a cauldron. Fluid gurgled in my lungs, while my hands and feet swelled. When did I know that I was dying? We know not the hour, but we can hear the clock ticking.

With the last of my strength I wrote letters of farewell to my friends. Such was the end of an orphan girl, with no family around her as she breathed her last. I had nothing but pieces of paper to attend me. I ached for Henry, more than for myself. He was so attentive, at my side doing his best to nurse me to health but I knew his efforts were futile. Like so many other women, I entered my confinement and entered the tomb. The sin of Eve, a clergyman might say, but I had so many other faults in need of atonement.

"Have you heard? Napier?" I asked Henry. I lacked the air to speak to my husband, a man defeated by that which he could not conquer.

"You are awake. Will you take some broth, my love?"

"Will Napier? Come?" His dearest friend was an army captain who had been wounded in Spain, and was convalescing in England. At such a time, Henry needed male companions to see him through what we both knew was coming.

"Within the next ten days he hopes to ride down to see us. He says he has recovered from the wound he received at Corunna. Well, you shall have our war stories to amuse you, my dear."

"So glad. A friend. With you."

"Your brother Richard sent a few lines," Henry said. His face was a mask of bravery but his eyes gave him away. I could see the truth, clear and bright. "He is settling a few business affairs that must be attended to, but he will be leaving London at the first opportunity."

I fell asleep again, my body worn out from the fight against an infection that began in my womb and spread throughout my body. I was tired and I wanted to be with Johnny, tired of being blown from one place to another, without a home. I was ready to go, even though I did not wish to go. Leaving Henry behind, alone, was as unbearable as the pain I felt when our baby died. Love held me to earth like a tether that I did not want to cast off. I woke up and saw Robert standing at the foot of my bed, holding a baby.

"He is so very pretty, Sarah," Robert said.

"My father denied me," I said to him. Henry was consumed by grief, it seemed, as he did not seem to hear me, or notice Robert for that matter. "I asked to be buried next to Gertrude but he informed me, through his associate Mr. McNally, that he would not turn his garden into a graveyard."

"The name of John Philpot Curran means next to nothing these days," Robert said. "He is as insignificant as any other governmental official. A glorified clerk. All his ambition come to naught, because he cast you out for the sin of falling in love. He showed himself incapable of mercy. A judge must be merciful."

"I love Henry," I said to Robert. "What was it I had for you? It is so different, the emotion."

"Love's first glimmer," Robert said. "Had we been allowed to court in the accepted manner you would have grown tired of my passions and we would have parted as friends. You had other suitors who intrigued you for a time, and I would have joined their ranks."

"I rose up," I said.

My love for Robert was fueled by rebellion against my father's tyranny. That sort of infatuation was weak, lacking the structure that a good marriage was built on. My love for Henry had been allowed to grow and blossom because the seed was sown in Wood Hill instead of The Priory, a true and lasting love. What I felt for Robert was a child's attraction to a new toy. In time, we would have broken up on the rocky shoals.

"You have known great happiness at last," Robert said. "For all your sins, you paid a price, but you also reaped a reward."

"The happiest moments of my life," I said to him. The days in Messina, with the warm sun shining and the first stirrings of life inside me. Henry's caress, the light in his eyes when he looked at me. How many others walked the earth without a moment's happiness? My father never knew what it was to be happy. I felt such sympathy for him. He would go to his grave without experiencing a minute of absolute joy, too busy accusing others for the lack of pleasure in his life. That he blamed me for all the disappointments he found after 1803 suggested a touch of envy at my good fortune, and his complete blindness. One could not experience true happiness without giving of one's self to others freely, unconcerned with gaining any reward. All he did was take. "My poor, sad father. Such a small, small man. 'The mind is its own place, and in itself Can make a heaven of hell, a hell of heaven.' You see why I was always so fond of Milton. So much truth to be found in *Paradise Lost*."

I called for Henry, to share with him my observations and show him that we had nothing to fear. After I was gone he would be free of any entanglements and could marry again, perhaps name his firstborn daughter after me. One last request remained. He must not fail me.

"Swear to me," I said to my husband. "Bury me. In Ireland."

"I will take you to Ireland, my love. I promise you. Do not fret. You have been so restless this afternoon."

A spark of knowledge flared in my feverish brain. I had won. In the end, I would triumph. "He cannot keep Gertrude from me. He wishes to separate us, but he cannot, it is out of his hands," I said to Robert. My father had disowned me. He had separated me from my sisters, forbidding them from communicating with me in any way and denying them permission to be with me at my deathbed. I laughed. For all his power as a father and a man, he could not keep me from joining Gertrude. My beloved sister and I would be together for all eternity and there was nothing he could do or say, nothing at all.

"'This having learned, thou hast attained the sum of wisdom.'" I quoted Milton, not sure if Robert was as familiar with the poem as I was. "'Hope no higher, though all the stars thou knewest by name, and all the ethereal powers, all secrets of the deep, all Nature's works, or works of God. Add faith. Add virtue, add love, the soul of all the rest; then wilt thou not be loath to leave this Paradise, but shalt possess a Paradise within thee, happier far.' Yes, there is the truth of it."

"Sarah, my love, my dearest," Henry said. "Did I make you happy? Please tell me. We were happy, were we not?"

"Paradise," I said.

Epilogue

Richard Curran reached Hythe too late. Sarah was already gone, dying on the fifth of May, 1808. He accompanied Henry Sturgeon to Newmarket, in County Cork, where Sarah was buried in the Curran family vault.

Two years later, Eliza was married by special license to Reverend James Taylor of Clifton, an indication of the haste with which she was wed. Amelia remained with her father and traveled through England with him. After his death she went to Rome to study painting and renewed an acquaintance with the poet Percy Byshe Shelley and his wife Mary. Her portrait of Shelley hangs in London's National Gallery.

James reached the rank of lieutenant in the Bengal Native Infantry and died in the East Indies in 1815. William, the youngest of the Curran clan, became a barrister like his father, looking after his mother in England where the disgraced Mrs. Curran resided quietly in Marylebone. John never married. He retired from the Navy, and died in Edinburgh.

Richard's life was marked by mental illness that was described as a 'settled melancholy'. He retired from the law prior to 1817.

The last years of John Philpot Curran's life were marked by melancholy. He died in England in 1817, surrounded by his estranged wife, Eliza and her husband, Amelia, Richard, and William. To Amelia and Mrs. Curran he left small annuities. The remainder of his estate, including The Priory, was given to his illegitimate sons Philpot Fitzgerald and Henry Grattan Fitzgerald. His remaining children received nothing.

After Leonard McNally died, it was found that he had been on England's payroll as a spy since 1798, his place in Curran's world ensuring a ready supply of information on rebel activities, and Curran's defense strategies.

Sturgeon's friend Charles Napier wrote to his mother upon Sarah's death and noted that Henry "...bears his sorrow too well to forget it easily... The endeavour to get killed, even if not successful, would save him much anguish..." Henry Sturgeon went on to a distinguished career during the Peninsular War, only to stumble at the Battle of Orthez. Following a severe rebuke by Wellington, in the presence of his fellow officers, he set off on a reckless reconnaissance mission and was killed by an enemy sniper at Vic en Bigorre, France, in March of 1814.

Also by Katie Hanrahan

The Leaven of the Pharisees

A Terrible Beauty

The Liberty Flower

The Second War Of Rebellion

Katie Hanrahan invites you to visit her
website:
www.katiehanrahan.com

CPSIA information can be obtained
at www.ICGtesting.com
Printed in the USA
LVOW01s0920020417

529320LV00025B/210/P